NOBODY DOESN'T HATE RATS!

The rescue squad had come and gone, and Cesar was standing talking to the bearded man when Stella came in from the alley.

"Nick!" she said. "Somebody said Chips is dead! Who killed him? What happened?"

"Nobody killed him, Stell. He had an accident when the air conditioner he was trying to put in backward fell on him."

"Maybe Sandy pushed it on him."

The two men turned to look at her.

"Well." She stuck her chin out. "Don't look at me like I'm crazy, Nick. She's such a bitch. Even if she didn't, anybody else could have."

"Why would anybody want to?" asked Cesar.

"You didn't know Chips," said Stella. "If you did, you'd understand. Everybody hated his guts. Even me. . . ."

SIGNET MYSTERY

MURDER MOVES IN

by A. M. Pyle

A SIGNET BOOK

NEW AMERICAN LIBRARY

PUBLISHER'S NOTE

This book is a work of fiction. Names, characters, places, and incidents either are the product of the author's imagination or are used fictitiously, and any resemblance to actual persons, living or dead, events, or locales is entirely coincidental.

This is an authorized reprint of a hardcover edition published by Walker and Company. The hardcover edition was published simultaneously in Canada by John Wiley & Sons Canada, Limited, Rexdale, Ontario

SIGNET TRADEMARK REG. U.S. PAT. OFF. AND FOREIGN COUNTRIES
REGISTERED TRADEMARK—MARCA REGISTRADA
HECHO EN CHICAGO, U.S.A.

SIGNET, SIGNET CLASSIC, MENTOR, ONYX, PLUME, MERIDIAN and NAL BOOKS are published by NAL PENGUIN INC., 1633 Broadway, New York, New York 10019

First Signet Printing, July, 1987

1 2 3 4 5 6 7 8 9

PRINTED IN THE UNITED STATES OF AMERICA

1

IT WAS MAY and it was hot in Cincinnati. For that matter it was hot all over the Midwest, but a lot of people in Cincinnati had decided they were having a worse time than anyplace else in the country. You could understand why. Two weeks ago a big fat slug of hot, heavy, wet air had heaved itself up the Mississippi and Ohio Valleys and stopped in the Queen City to pick up a load of automobile exhaust and other visible and smelly ingredients and the slug never left, so now the air looked like lemonade to the eye and felt like embalming fluid to the lung.

And the heat was having its effect. Cincinnatians, people who took pride in being better behaved than people in other cities, were whining, complaining, and murdering their relatives, just like New Yorkers or Clevelanders. Even the swells in Hyde Park and Indian Hill were having a tough time, since it was too early to pack up for Michigan or Cape Cod.

It was worse for anyone who lived or worked downtown at river level. The little designer trees in the business district, chosen for their ease of maintenance, cast only a thin and useless shade. The mulberries and stink trees in the older, undesigned neighborhoods bordering the business district were too few and too mean to beat back the waves of heat billowing from the orange bricks and granite cobbles that were the fabric of the old city.

5

The cops and firemen were caught off guard by a lot of early summer activity and it made them nearly as cranky as their knife-wielding, hydrant-violating clients. People who didn't have air conditioning had moved down into the streets to get away from the foul air in their apartments. So it was impossible for the police in their cruisers to tell a bunch of crap shooters from a bunch of harmless breeze shooters. Except when they were white, of course.

And in the middle of the afternoon of the first Saturday in May, there was a bunch of white breeze shooters hanging out on Abigail Street in the neighborhood called Dutchtown, five blocks from City Hall.

The topic was the heat, naturally. Greta Grimes was doing the complaining. Tall and thin, with long hair that used to be blond, Greta was usually considered the most attractive woman in her set. Greta's set was comprised of the white, middle-class couples who were reclaiming the old houses in Dutchtown.

Complaining didn't become Greta. Her hair was coming loose from its bun, and her smallish face had gone red under a layer of sweat.

"It's terrible. No one's going to come. I wouldn't come. I wouldn't go anywhere when it's this hot. It's ridiculous. Crazy." She stopped to blow her nose. She had countless allergies. "And the mess. You know what's going to happen tonight. It's Saturday, right? And who's going to have time to clean up what *they*"—and she waved her long arm in a jerky circle meant to include many, many people—"what *they* are guaranteed to throw out tonight? It's always ten times worse when it's hot like this." She paused to blow her nose again.

The forum was the sidewalk in front of Greta's house on Abigail Street. The people surrounding Greta were all friends, or at least friendly. They were all in their late twenties or thirties, all attractive, some only moderately or intelligently good-looking, but no one looked less than well-fed middle-class. Their clothes, smudged with dirt from the basements and backyards they had been cleaning, were nearly uniform. Shorts and T-shirts, and the occasional halter top. It was too hot for anything else.

The group stared glumly at different stretches of the street. They all knew who Greta meant by "they", and they all knew what "they" did on Saturday nights. If Greta and her friends, shock troops in the battle to reclaim Dutchtown from near-total decay, were "we," "they" were the enemy, the more numerous but less enlightened hundreds of poor blacks, poor hillbillies, destitute alcoholics, pimps, prostitutes, small-time pushers, ex-cons, storefront preachers, fences, and mental patients who populated the rest of Dutchtown and its parent neighborhood, Over-the-Rhine. "They" spent their Saturday nights drinking and making a mess.

"It's going to be worse than usual, too," said Greta's husband, Nicholas. Nick, leaning on his own fence and picking sawdust from his dark beard, looked very little like the prospering architect he was. What he looked like today was one of "them". As both the strongest and the most helpful man on the block, he had been in everyone's basement at one time or another that day, and he was far and away the grubbiest body on the sidewalk. "It's the first of the month," he said. The statement brought groans from most of the crowd.

"What's wrong with the first of the month?" asked Theresa McDowell. Theresa missed a lot. She was usually concentrating on her husband when they were out together. He demanded her attention.

"Welfare checks." Nicholas rolled his eyes and shook his head. "Party Night!"

Paul McDowell cleared his throat. Since he planned on a run for city council sometime in the not-too-distant future and considered himself a neoliberal, he wasn't comfortable with negative generalities about potential voters. Not in public. "Well, you know, it's not just welfare recipients who throw trash, dear." He addressed himself to his wife, his only sure support. Theresa looked up at her husband and smiled to indicate understanding. Actually, she was wondering if her husband needed a haircut.

"Right. We have to be fair," said Greta. "The symphony crowd is really trashy. Especially the May Festival people. They're always pitching wine bottles when they roll through."

"And White Castle wrappers," added Nick.

"I just mean that—" McDowell started.

"We know what you mean, Paul." Bill Sharp spoke from his seat on the Grimeses' sidewalk step. He was sketching with a stone on concrete, failing to remember how fussy Nicholas Grimes was about things like that. "But don't worry. We're not being racist. White winos do their share too." He had drawn a horse in a hammock and now he was adding a bottle of Chablis.

Theresa McDowell smiled another vague smile. "Is it always this hot here?" she asked.

"Where were you this winter?" asked Greta, who had no use for Theresa when Theresa was being southern.

"I mean in the spring and summer, Greta. I thought it was supposed to be cooler up north. This is terrible."

"Damn," snapped Emma Howard's husband, Alan. "I can't believe we're starting heat-bitching already. It's only May and it's not that hot." Emma glared at him. Emma, just ever so plump, *could not bear* heat. Alan Howard, her small, wiry lawyer husband, lived for summer. It was, otherwise, a fine marriage.

"Uh-oh," said Greta. "The great air conditioning debate. You're supposed to be worried about the house tour. Forget the air conditioning. I want to know what's going to happen tomorrow. Do you think we should call it off?"

"Call it off? But we've sold tickets already," said Theresa. "And besides, they only give a rain date. Not a heat date."

"Well, *I* wouldn't go on a house tour in weather like this," said Emma. "And I think anyone in her right mind will stay home, but Theresa's right. We can't call it off."

"So what are we going to do about all the fried-chicken wrappers that are absolutely *sure* to be all over the place in the morning? I don't suppose we could get any help from the city?" Greta looked at Alan Howard, who worked part-time for the city. He shook his head no.

"We'll just have to get up early and pick up trash. I'll be up at six," said Paul.

"Speaking of trash . . ." said Nicholas, and he rolled his eyes in the direction of an approaching figure.

"Oh, shit," said Greta. "I don't need this."

The new arrival was a tanned, well-built man dressed like the others except for a tiny gold ear stud, which glowed through his blond curls. This very hip Adonis was Herman "Chips" Reber, Greta's first husband and the father of her only child.

If the group of friends had been cranky before Chips Reber's arrival, it was justified. Everyone had put in several hours cleaning up inside and out to have the town houses and yards looking their absolute best for the next day's house tour. There was some nervousness too, as this was to be the first such event and everyone was eager to have Dutchtown show well. But the mood of good-natured crankiness was replaced by one of sullen irritation when Chips joined.

Nicholas, as the husband of Chips's ex-wife, had perhaps more reason than any, save Greta, to dislike Reber. But Nicholas also had the best manners on the block, and it was he who greeted Reber.

"How's it going, Chips?"

"Great! You guys look beat."

"We've been working," snapped Greta.

"All ready for the tour?" asked Chips.

"I don't know if we'll ever be ready," sighed Theresa McDowell. "There's so much to do."

"Do what I did," said Chips. "Get the neighborhood kids to do the heavy stuff. They were done before lunch."

"You let them in your house?! I'd be . . . I mean I'd . . ." Theresa was horrified at the idea of black teenagers handling her things.

"Chips is talking about heavy cleaning," said Greta.

"Things like bricks in the dining room. Where's my check, Chips?"

"In the mail, Gret. With a letter from my attorney."

"Chips, I know who Maxine is. You don't have to call her 'my attorney.' What does she want?"

"It's in the letter."

"Damn it, Chips, if this is another of your stinking joint-custody efforts, you can sh—"

Greta's husband squeezed her arm to shush her. Reber laughed. "So that's how you shut her up, Nick. I never learned that trick."

Greta leaned over and slapped her ex-husband across the face. Reber raised his arm to slap back, but Nicholas grabbed it. For a moment there was no movement from anyone. Then Nicholas said, "You'd better apologize, Greta." Greta glared at her husband and then at her ex-husband, unable to decide who had pissed her off more. Rather than apologize, she turned and ran up the walk and into her house. Nicholas shook his head at Reber and followed his wife. Chips was left standing amid a quiet and partisan crowd.

"Boy, she's still got a temper." Reber tried making light of it. No one spoke. "She couldn't take a joke when we were married, either." Still no response, or none to his liking. "I guess that means she won't help me put in the air conditioner, ha ha ha. Any of you guys want to help? Sandy wants it in by tomorrow." Sandy was Chips's girlfriend. No one answered. "I'll catch you guys later." He threw his sexy-guy smile to the ladies, turned, and sauntered back toward his building.

"What a shit he is," said Emma.

At the west end of the block, two overweight black men had seen the little drama and were discussing it. They were sitting on identical rusty lawn chairs, perched on the generous limestone ledges flanking a limestone stoop. For all they were twenty years apart in age and dressed differently, the men looked very much alike. Both were nearly bald, and they wore the same air of timeless, judicial, and confident gravity. The older man wore a pair of limp gray cotton work trousers, a plaid shirt, and cracked leather house shoes. The younger man, who was not his son but his nephew, his sister's only child, wore a pair of yellow canvas trousers, a short-sleeved cotton shirt with epaulets, and green Italian shoes with kiltie fringes. The uncle was nursing a half pint of Grolsch beer, which he kept in a little brown paper bag. The nephew was drinking his beer from a glass.

"That boy that got his face slapped, that's the boy that's trying to buy this house off me. He's always wearing those necklaces like you got on," said the older man. "He's got a real cute girlfriend. Don't know why that there girl slapped him." He stopped for a sip of beer. "You remember Susie Berry?" His nephew nodded. "Well, she tried to slap me like that once." He took another sip and coughed out a small laugh. He was through with his story.

"How much," asked his nephew, "how much was he gonna pay?" He knew his uncle well enough to supply the end of the story about Miss Berry, one of his uncle's many admirers.

"For the house? He didn't name no price. Figured I was gonna give it to him cheap, I guess."

"Don't."

"Don't worry, boy. What I wanna sell this house for? I sure ain't gonna sell to no white boy with a necklace. Boy be snortin' coke right there in his car. Right there where your car's at." He tilted his chin in the direction of a shiny, dust-free Continental.

Both of the men took a minute to observe the splendor of the nephew's automobile. Then the nephew resumed talking about the house.

"You know, if you got enough for this place, you could get yourself something out in Roselawn. Someplace like that. Maybe you should find out how much he wants to pay you."

"I don't want to go to Roselawn."

"Then go to Florida."

"Henry, you ever been to Florida?"

"Sure."

"You either got crackers or New Yorkers."

"Okay. Don't go to Florida. Go to L.A."

"What's wrong with this house?"

"I didn't say anything was wrong with it," said the nephew. "I just said you ought to find out how much that boy wants to pay for it."

"I know how much he wants to pay," said the uncle, and he leaned back in his chair so that he looked like a Tokyo automobile magnate.

"You said he didn't make an offer."

"He didn't."

The nephew leaned back in his chair so that he looked like the nephew of a Tokyo automobile magnate and waited for his uncle to reveal the source of his wisdom. If he was irritated with his uncle's gambits, his face gave no sign. He had long admired his uncle's impassivity, adopting it as his own from the time he was five. He waited. Finally his uncle said, "Boy talked to Abernathy over there," and waved his hand toward a run-down version of his own house across the street. "Said he'd give Abernathy five thousand dollars for his place."

"Your house is worth a lot more than that, Uncle Arthur. Some of these houses are going for fifty or sixty. You better see a lawyer."

"I don't need no god-damned lawyer, Henry. You can forget that. This house is going to your mother or you, and that's it." Suddenly he pointed across the street. "See that? Did you see that?"

"What?" asked Henry.

"He's sneaking across the alley. Must be going to check up on that little thing on Franklin Street. He don't want his girlfriend to know he's over there." The two men leaned forward, peering between the two buildings directly across the street, but Chips Reber was no longer visible.

*   *   *

Stella Hineman, the little thing on Franklin Street, was sitting on her back stoop. Technically, it was Chips Reber's stoop, since Stella rented.

Stella was in her midtwenties. She was not little, except, perhaps, in comparison to someone the size of Arthur Battle, the inscrutable owner of the house Chips Reber wanted to buy. But she was slender, and only her semifamous bosom kept her from appearing thin. She had been a redhead when she was a girl, but her hair had turned light brown when she was pregnant. She had natural ringlets, which went in and out of fashion every five years. She still had the white skin of a redhead. Since her jaw was just a little too large for her face, she was thought by some to be less than beautiful. Most people, however, looked at her once, looked again, and forgot the jaw.

She had been supervising the cleanup of her backyard but the work force had disappeared. The work force was her five-year-old son, Sidney, and Greta Grimes's son, H.P. Reber.

Her yard was a mess. Stella's friends in the neighborhood enjoyed calling their outdoor spaces "gardens" or "courtyards," but not only was Stella unpretentious; she was fair. You could call Greta Grimes's elegant little courtyard a garden. Greta had cultivated and planted and pruned and potted and jardiniered and even espaliered until her yard looked as much like New Orleans as was possible in Cincinnati. But Stella could not in fairness call her own yard a garden. There were three Rose of Sharon bushes and a mulberry in the larger of two unpaved patches, but they didn't look anything like Stella's idea of landscaping. They didn't even look natural. They looked accidental.

And the yard was a mess. She had put off cleaning it until the last possible day, knowing that a too-early effort would be pointless. For one day she could pretend that conditions in her neighborhood were no worse than in her mother's. After that the winds would begin to resume the steady depositing of cheeseburger wrappings and little brown wino bags. On top of the airborne litter she could expect to find a scattering of pop bottles, wine bottles, and Pampers tossed from the tenements on either side of the yard.

And then there was Sidney's stuff. Looking at the mess, Stella admitted to herself that her son's collection of boards, bricks, and big wheels was at least as crummy-looking as the foreign garbage. She sighed and groped for the coffee cup that sat beside her on the stoop. One day she was going to have to do something about Sidney's projects. She whistled for the boys. Sidney came out by himself.

"Where's H.P.?" asked Stella.

"Went home."

"Too much like work, right?"

Sidney looked out over the small yard and sighed.

"There's so much shit out there."

Stella pursed her lips. Sidney's language was another mess she had made and left to clean up at the last minute.

"Don't say 'shit.' "

"I don't say it at Grandma's."

"Good. She'd kill you. Don't say it here anymore."

"Are *you* going to stop saying it?"

"That doesn't make any difference. Anyway, I've been trying to stop, in case you haven't noticed. Go. And get some garbage bags."

Stella pulled on a pair of old gloves, picked up a pail, and began to attack the trash. Sidney worked alongside, rounding up his construction materials and stacking them neatly in their proper niche between the cellar door and the blind wall of the house next-door. The biggest boards were on the bottom, smallest on the top, bricks filling any gaps. Stella looked at his pile and wondered how long her son would allow her to live with him. She could never be that tidy. But, thought Stella as she dropped a sodden paper diaper into her bucket, I would never *never* be as disgusting as those creeps. She looked up at the window in the tenement from which the offending diaper had been thrown.

When the yard was straight, Stella and Sidney wrestled a couple of old canvas deck chairs up from the basement where they had spent the winter and spring. They set the chairs under the mulberry tree and set themselves in the chairs to admire all the cleanliness. Stella squinted, the better to envision the yard as it could be. She had to explain to Sidney how squinting was useful and then he tried it. They were both squinting hard at the three-story blind wall next-door when someone started to rattle the chain on the back gate. They stopped squinting at once.

"Hey!" shouted Stella. "Get off!"

"Just me, Stell."

"Oh *shit!*" said Stella under her breath, but Sidney heard it. He looked sternly at his mother. "Sorry, but I don't feel like dealing with Chips this morning." Then she yelled to the gate. "Coming, Chips." But Chips Reber had already let himself in.

Chips was surprised. As both landlord and lecher, Chips dropped in fairly often, and he was used to seeing a clean and delectable Stella surrounded by disorder. Today he saw the opposite. Her light brown curls crammed under a navy watchcap, her body invisible under denim overalls and a large and badly stained smock, her face streaked with sweat and city grime, Stella was far from delectable, but the yard looked great. Today Chips was glad to see a clean yard. He had come on business.

"I didn't know you had a key to that gate. Have you always had one?" Stella had thought herself protected. At least in back.

"Just luck, kid. I've got a lot of keys. Something usually fits. The yard looks great."

"It ought to. I just wore myself out cleaning it up. You wouldn't believe the garbage I picked up. Those people next-door—"

"Whattya expect from a bunch of—"

"Watch it! I don't want Sidney hearing that."

"Sure." Chips was unflustered. "I was going to tell you

I'm glad you cleaned up. I'm going to be showing the place tomorrow. It'll look better like this."

"Show it?! To sell? Are you selling my house?"

"Don't get excited. I'm not throwing you out."

"But you are selling the house?" Stella was almost nauseated with worry.

"Maybe. Listen, it's no big deal. It's a couple of lawyers I ran into down on Second Street. They're looking for some investments and I told them about this place. They're just going to look at it."

"But you told me you'd give me first refusal if you ever sold. And besides, you said when I moved in that you weren't planning to sell for years. Why didn't you tell me?"

"So, I'm telling you now, okay? That's what I came over for."

"I'll bet."

"Do you want to buy it?"

"How much?"

"Make an offer."

"I don't want to make an offer. I want to know how much you want for it."

"Hey, Stella. If you want it, you've gotta know what it's worth. Take a stab. Maybe we can get together."

Stella glared at him. She had gone from nauseated to angry. "Ten thousand dollars."

Reber put his hand on her shoulder. Stella shook it off immediately. "Come on, Stella, this place was worth more than that when I bought it. Be realistic."

"Crap. It was a wreck. If I hadn't spent my own time and money fixing it up, it would have been condemned, and you know it. Besides, you only paid six thousand."

"Sure, but the neighborhood's come up since then."

"All right, why don't *you* tell *me* what you want for it. I took my stab."

"How about forty-five?"

"*Thousand?*"

"Yeah."

"I can't believe it."

"It's worth it."

"Bullshit." Stella ignored Sidney's shocked and accusing stare. "Is that what the lawyers are paying?"

"Hey! They'll probably pay more than that. They're lawyers."

"You know I don't have that kind of money, Chips. You knew it when I moved in and you knew it when I agreed to fix it up. Where am I supposed to get money like that? Selling coke like—"

"Look, I didn't get you in this situation, Stella, so quit complaining. I'm not the reason you haven't got any money. I told you I'd let you have a crack at the house. If you want to better these guys' offer, let me know." Chips turned to leave.

"Thanks, Chips. Thanks a whole fucking lot."

Stella waited until Reber closed the back gate before she started to cry. Her son sat up in his deck chair and wondered whether he should comfort his mother and, if so, how. He swung his foot back and forth, waiting to see what she would do. Finally he asked if they were going to have to move. His mother looked at him, sniffed, wiped her eyes with the backs of her hands. "No," she said. Then, "I'm sorry I said 'fucking' and 'bullshit.' I was pi— I was very mad."

And then, "I *am* very mad."

"See, Henry? There he goes again. Doesn't look real happy, does he?" Henry Chapman and his Uncle Arthur leaned forward to peer at Chips Reber, who was making his way between two buildings to emerge onto Abigail Street. "I don't think that little girl likes the boy." He chuckled as he and his nephew leaned back. "Looks like all his friends gone inside. Boy's got nobody to play with."

2

THE BANDK POOLROOM, The Truth and Beauty Center, and The Victorian Activity Centre were the only storefronts still occupied on the Central Avenue side of Arthur Battle's block around the corner from his house.

The customers of the BandK Poolroom had had a rough week. There had been two knifings, an eye gouging, five pistol wavings, one bottle throwing, four hot disputes over the price of sex, and too many verbal menacings to count. Most of the BandK regulars were over forty and on disability or retirement, but the heat had revived their passions. Saturday had already seen a nasty fistfight between two regulars, Stone McCullough and Roscoe Terry, a fight that left Mr. McCullough with a badly swollen left eye. Mr. Terry escaped with a mild abrasion of the chin. Following that bout, Juanita Anderson and Betty Perett, friends of Mr. McCullough and Mr. Terry, had arrived to comfort the men and had involved themselves in a less physical but no less heated confrontation, picking up where the men had left off.

Juanita Anderson was bouncing a Pepsi bottle repeatedly on the edge of a pool table in an unsuccessful effort to smash off the bottom and Betty Perett was shaking her cue and croaking her battle cry of "You a *ho!* You a *ho!* You a HO!" when the street door opened and a white man walked in. All action stopped and all eyes swung to the white man, and it was quiet for several seconds until one of the patrons, Lester Broadnax, said, "Hey! It's all right, brothers. That's Sonny."

He was right. Even in the dark of the poolroom it was easy to recognize Sonny Werk. Sonny had the longest afro of any white man in the city. At six-four and a hundred and fifty-five, he cut a distinctive figure.

"Could I have your attention for a minute, please?" said Sonny in his rather high voice.

"I'm Sonny Werk, and along with some of your brothers and sisters I operate the Truth and Beauty Feeding Program and Rap Center/Outreach Program, which we do for the many innocent victims of the current campaign against poor people and homeless and alcoholic Americans." Sonny talked very quickly all the time.

"I want to bring your attention to the latest in the attack on decent housing for low-income residents of Dutchtown."

"Broth'! Hey, broth'!" Roscoe Terry was trying to pull himself into a sitting position from his bench in the corner booth. Sonny Werk turned to look at him. "Broth', you got to slow *down*, man. Can't nobody understand what you say." Roscoe found his Hudepohl, took a hit, and dropped back under the table.

Sonny continued at the same speed. "This attack will take a new form tomorrow when the powers hiding behind the shield of so-called historic preservation which is their way of disguising the attack on low-income housing for poor people will be holding a neighborhood walking tour here in Dutchtown tomorrow and this walking tour is part of their plan to advertise this neighborhood so that other high-income and rich people will become aware of the decent housing which is yours by rights but which they'll be turning into condominiums and single-family houses which poor people won't be able to afford—"

"Ain't that a rip?" said Juanita, who had followed much of Sonny's address.

"You're exactly right. It's a shame and a ripoff," said Sonny. "That's why the outreach center is organizing a protest rally involving low-income residents of Dutchtown and other concerned and caring people who share your outrage over this latest attack on American people who have been left out of the establishment structure and condemned to live in permanent poverty . . ."

"That boy don't ever *breathe!*" said Betty Perett to Juanita Anderson. The two had laid aside their differences and were sitting together, sharing a Little Kings Cream Ale.

"This rally will take place tomorrow while the so-called historic tour is taking place and it's imperative that we have the support of all the brothers and sisters there tomorrow when we organize at the outreach center with the other concerned and caring citizens at ten o'clock in the morning and I hope I can count on you and any of your family and friends who share our outrage over this attack on poor people." He stopped and looked at his audience. It was very hard to see in the poorly lit room.

"Yeah, well I think it's *beautiful* what you're doing, Sonny. It's beautiful," said Betty. "Me and Roscoe, we'll be there for sure. Ain't that right, Roscoe?"

"Whassa?" said Roscoe from under the table.

"We'll be there," said Betty. "And my mother, too. She's coming down from Dayton tomorrow. She's *real* active."

"Dayton," said Sonny cryptically. "I really appreciate your support, sister, and what about you other sisters and brothers? I hope I can count on you to stand up to these rich people and other development forces."

There was a respectable chorus of "Right on!" and "Tell it, brother!" and "For real!" Roscoe Terry had blacked out, however, so he was silent. And since John Lindsey was angling with a developer for the sale of the building housing the BandK, he silently ducked the invitation. Sonny took another look around the poolroom, raised his fist high above his head, turned around, and left. "He's just beautiful," said Betty Perett to her good friend Juanita Anderson, who echoed, "Beautiful."

*   *   *

"Oh, *God!* There he goes! Look! No! Don't look! He's looking in here! No! Okay, you can look!"

"Who? Who *was* it?"

"Sonny Werk! Oh, *God*, I hate him!"

Alan Howard, who had seen Sonny Werk, sat back down next to Elizabeth Sackville, who had not. The two of them were alone in the Victorian Activity Centre, a branch of the Consortium for the Nineteenth Century, which occupied a storefront midway between the BandK Poolroom and the Truth and Beauty Outreach Office. They, too, had been quarreling, but they stopped for a moment to worry about Sonny.

"What do you suppose he's doing?" asked Mrs. Sackville. She had arisen as Alan sat down, and she floated over to the window to try to see Sonny.

"Something Awful. You can count on that," said Alan. He glared at Elizabeth, who was standing with one hand gracefully caught on the dull green velvet curtain. Alan had known her long and well enough to be sure that she was aware of the effect of the daylight on her lace blouse and ash-blond hair. "Get away from the window, Elizabeth."

"What? I just want to see him. Where do you suppose he's been?"

"Making trouble someplace."

"I *know* that he is going to do *something* tomorrow to wreck the walking tour. There's no way he would let an opportunity like that slip."

"What would you have me do, Elizabeth? Assail him by night?"

"Don't talk that way, Alan. It sounds ridiculous on you."

Alan sputtered. It was too much. Elizabeth talked in *the most* affected way all the time, and the last nineteenth-century novel she had read was *Vanity Fair,* at Ethel Walker's. He cast about for something equally mean to say, but gave up as Elizabeth resumed the argument they had been having before Sonny went past their window.

"You *swore* to me that we would return Yeatman's

Grove to its original state. That there would be no compromise, that for once the consortium was going to get *tough!*"

"I don't know what you're talking about, Elizabeth."

"Codswallop!"

"That's Jacobean. Maybe even Elizabethan. And stop calling it Yeatman's Grove. Nobody ever knows what you're talking about."

"You know damned well what I'm talking about."

"True," said Alan. "I do. You're pissed off because the architect had to make some changes. Well, I don't like them either, but I know and you know that these are for low-income housing, and there's no way we can hope for perfect restoration in low-income housing—"

"But I don't *want* low inc—"

"Oh, *no*. So that's what it's about. Elizabeth, we *have* to have low-income housing. We've been over and over this. God, when will you give up?"

"Never. I will never give up. This is the last, the very last chance we have to preserve a truly—"

"Oh, *Lizzy!*"

"And besides"—Elizabeth paused to examine a tiny mole on her left wrist—"I'm going to live down here. I've bought a house."

"You're kidding. Which one?"

"The Worth-Dupree house."

"*Lizzy!* How did you get it? Why didn't you tell me? Does Van Meter know?" Alan stopped gabbling and stared with amazement and jealousy at the president of the Consortium for the Nineteenth Century. The Worth-Dupree house, with its three stories, elegant limestone front, richly carved cornice, extra-wide lot, charming double-width brick carriage house, elaborate iron fence, and gorgeous molded plaster, was the dream house of every true Victorian fanatic in Cincinnati. It was also the property of Hilda Kornbrust, last of the old Germans in the neighborhood and proprietor of a rooming house for retired alcoholics. Miss Kornbrust had turned down offers for years. The offers had been many; some had been very, very generous.

Elizabeth Sackville smiled at the treasurer of the Consortium for the Nineteenth Century.

"I paid cash, Alan. Lots and lots of nice cash. And I sweetened it with a gift certificate from Lufthansa and a letter from her long-lost cousin in Munich. That answers your first question.

"I didn't tell you because I wanted it to be a little surprise. I also didn't want any of my dear friends in there outbidding me and coming up with even more cousins. That answers your second question.

"And no, Van Meter doesn't know. This," she said, laying her long cool hand on the inside of Alan's left thigh, "is *my* house."

Sonny Werk didn't miss much. He had seen that there were two people in the Victorian Activity Centre and guessed correctly who they were. But he ignored them. He strode past three boarded-up storefronts and turned in to his own command post, the Truth and Beauty Feeding Program and Rap Center/Outreach Program, where he found his troops in disarray.

"What's going on? What is this?" he snapped. The argument stopped immediately, and everyone in the room turned to face him. Many of the faces betrayed a certain fear of Sonny, a reaction Sonny noted with approval. Sonny, who lived off a trust fund, disliked anyone who made a living as a poverty worker, even those who had volunteered to work alongside him. Sonny liked poor people exclusively.

"Well," he said, "what happened? Why aren't you getting ready for tomorrow? There's a lot to do."

"We were, Sonny. We were working real hard, but that Chips Reevers came in," Louella Dwyer wheezed. Louella suffered from advanced obesity and incipient emphysema. "And Reevers, he—"

Sister Clare, a nun in mufti, interrupted Ms. Dwyer. "It's *Reber*, Louella. Sonny, he came in here to see if the computer was working okay and he saw the signs because nobody had the sense to put them away. I mean, I *tried*, but I was the only one who understood how important it was—"

"You know, Sonny, I want to know why Sister Theresa got to thinking she's the one with the answers. Well, she ain't the only one in here that knows what's going on. I ain't gonna stay here working with no Catholic that thinks she's—"

"That's enough, Louella. Ron, were you and Dick here when Reber came in?"

"Well, Sonny, I didn't actually *see* what happened 'cause I had to be back there talking to Tammy when that fella came in. I don't know what Dick was doing."

"I'll tell you what he was doing," shouted Louella. She had muttered herself to tears. "He was on the *phone*, back in *your office*. I don't know what he was talking about, 'cause he always mutters like it's some big damn important *secret!* Never lets *anybody* hear him talking on the phone. I think—"

"Now, Louella, you've got to calm yourself down." Dick Speers, the telephone mutterer, started to put one of his delicate hands on Louella's grand shoulders.

"Get your old nasty hands off me." Louella took a swipe at him.

"Sonny, if you want to know what I was talking about, I'm perfectly willing to tell you. I was talking to my wife about communion." And with that, Speers looked at Louella the way he imagined Jesus had looked at Thomas.

"All right, that's enough. I don't think you people know just how serious the situation is or you wouldn't be wasting your time and my time and the people's time blaming each other instead of concentrating on the enemy of the people. I want to know what Reber saw and what he said about it. Tammy?" Sonny turned to the far corner of the office.

"Yes, sir?"

"What happened?" Sonny relied on his secretary for a nonpartisan view of things.

"Well." Tammy Woolum straightened her desk as she recollected just what did happen. She liked to remember *everything*. "I was back here typing up the stencil for that special issue of the *True Spirit* so I can run it off tonight before I go home. I'm still missing articles from Dick and Sister Clare, by the way. Well, I was taking down Ron's article when I heard the door open and I looked up and it was Mr. Reber. I didn't think anything about it since he's on your advisory council and he gave us the Apple." Tammy nodded in the direction of a desktop computer. A thin black boy was working the keyboard, oblivious to anything going on around him. "Sometimes he comes in just to check that, so I just waved at him and went back to my typing. And then all of a sudden he says, 'What the hell are you doin'?' to Louella over there where she was making the posters and sign boards for the protest rally tomorrow. Sister Clare was trying to cover stuff up while he was looking at it, but he just sort of pushed her out of the way and looked at all the stuff they had done. I would have called you, only I knew you were out doing outreach.

"Well, after he looked at all the signs, he asked where you were and I said I didn't know and he said well I better find you 'cause you had some explaining to do. And then he came back here to call somebody on my phone and he tried to read what I was typing but I wouldn't let him. And then he didn't get whoever he was calling on the phone so he just hung up and rushed out. And that's all. Only I wrote down the number he called. It's on your desk.

"There's also a message from Donald Musselman's secretary at the foundation. You're supposed to call him, but I know what it's about. She told me he's planning to come to Cincinnati sometime next week." Tammy went back to her typing, expecting no comment from Sonny. He made none. When he had looked at all the signs, he headed for his office.

Tammy had stuck the note with the number Chips Reber had dialed on the telephone. Sonny ignored it while he took off his basketball shoes. He didn't wear socks. When he did look at the number, his eyes opened slightly. He flicked through his own phone book until he came to an entry that he compared against the note. Then he called Tammy into his office. "You gave me the wrong number. This is my lawyer's number. Where's the one Reber called?"

Tammy took the slip and looked at it. "This is what he called. I watched him. I remember."

"Son of a bitch," said Sonny, although he strictly forbade swearing in the office.

Henry Chapman and his Uncle Arthur had not moved from their seats on Arthur's stoop. The sun had dropped a little, but it was no cooler. Their steel lawn chairs sagged a little lower. The men had steadily put away several beers apiece without making any trips to the bathroom, and the great heat had relaxed any spring left in the steel. Henry, bothered by the glare off his Lincoln, had put on his mirrored sunglasses.

"You asleep, Henry?" asked Arthur. Henry gave a very slight shake to show that he was awake. His uncle had caught him just in time. "You see that goofy-looking white boy coming up the street? The one with the big afro?" Henry gave a tiny nod. "You know who that is?" Henry shook his head. "You don't know him? That's that Sonny Werk, the one that's always hanging around with all the winos." Arthur had dropped his voice as Sonny was fast nearing Arthur's gate. "Bet he's organizing something. Got that crazy look on him." They leaned forward to watch him as he loped down the street and around the corner. They were both leaning back, getting ready to relax, possibly to snooze, when a dusty, dark green Camaro turned off of Central onto Abigail. Neither man paid any attention until the car stopped alongside Henry's spotless Lincoln and then reversed, coming to a full stop even with the front end of Henry's car. The occupant stared at the car and then peered up at Arthur's stoop.

"Wake up, Henry. You got someone wants to buy your car. White boy." Henry shook himself awake and stared at the driver of the Camaro, who was staring at him.

"You can't afford it," said Henry to the driver, who had rolled his window down.

"Neither can you," said the driver. He backed his car into a space across the street and got out.

"They'll kill you in this neighborhood," said Henry to the man as he crossed the street, heading for Arthur Battle's gate.

"You know him?" asked Arthur under his breath.

"He works with me," said his nephew. "That's Cesar Franck."

3

"THIS IS CESAR FRANCK, Uncle Arthur." Arthur stuck out a thick, square hand for Cesar to shake as Henry performed the introductions. "This is my uncle, Arthur Battle, Cesar."

"Nice to meet you, sir."

"Henry, go back in the back there and get your friend a chair. Back there by the cold frame."

Henry shifted his weight slightly, but Cesar said, "That's okay, Henry. I just stopped for a second. This is fine," and he sat down on the stone ledge by Henry's feet.

"Henry, why don't you give the boy one of your beers? You like a beer, son?"

"Uh, no . . . well"- -Cesar looked at Henry's cold Groesch and changed his mind—"sure. It is hot. Really hot." Cesar could feel Henry's glare on the back of his neck, but he ignored it.

"You're gonna have to tell me your name again, son," said Arthur.

"It's Cesar, sir."

"Henry, go get Cesar one of your beers." Arthur glared at his nephew until Henry heaved himself up and went into the house. Cesar whipped his hand out from under Henry's foot just in time to avoid intentional injury. "You a detective like Henry?" asked Arthur.

"Yes, sir."

"You on the homicide squad too?"

"Yes, sir."

"How long you been knowing Henry?"

"Seven or eight years, I guess. We were in the same recruit class."

"Is that right? Well." Arthur took a hit from his brown bag.

"Are you the uncle with the Silver Star?" asked Cesar.

"What? Oh. Did Henry tell you about that?" Cesar nodded. "Silver Star. You know, Henry always used to make me get that out and show it to his friends." Arthur leaned back so far that his seat nearly bottomed out. "Take that seat there, son. Henry can get himself another one."

"No, thanks. I'm fine, Mr. Battle."

"So Henry is still going around bragging about that old medal. Henry!" Arthur yelled into the gloom of his front hall. "Henry, where's that beer for Cesar?"

"I'm coming. Tell him to hold on." Henry's voice came from all the way back in the house.

"Well, what've you boys been working on? You know, Henry, he never tells me nothing about what he's doing. Got to pry it out of him."

That's Henry all right. "Nothing much right now, Mr. Battle. Paperwork mostly."

"That's what Henry is always saying."

"Well, we've got a lot of it. Bullish—junk mostly."

"Never saw any paperwork that wasn't bullshit. You know, I . . . well, it's about time, Henry. Took you long enough."

Henry handed Cesar a bottle of Grolsch. "Yeah, well, I had to do something."

"He's been drinking beer all afternoon, Frank."

"It's Cesar, Uncle Arthur. Franck's his last name."

"Sorry, son."

"Happens all the time," said Cesar. He took a long slug of the cold Dutch beer. "Jeez! This is really good, Mr. Battle. Thanks."

Henry grunted.

"Henry is trying to tell you he bought it. But you never would of gotten any if I didn't make him share it."

"Thanks, Henry."

Henry grunted again.

The three men drank and sweated without speaking for several minutes. Then Henry said, "I thought you were off today."

"I am."

"What are you doing down here? I thought you cleaned house on Saturday."

Cesar blushed. "I—"

"Don't let him bother you, son," Arthur interrupted. "He's supposed to be helping his mama clean out her garage right now."

"Then he's in trouble," said Cesar.

"You know my sister?" asked Arthur.

Cesar nodded.

"I asked you what you were doing out of Westwood," snapped Henry.

"Hey, don't yell at *me*. I already did my work. I'm down here to pick up some tickets."

The black detective stared at the white detective.

"There's a tour here tomorrow. We've got relatives that are going to have their house open and Mom wants to see it."

"Who?" asked Henry.

"My sister's sister-in-law and her husband. They bought a place here a couple of years ago. They've been working on it."

"Which ones are they?" asked Arthur.

"The Sharps. You know them?"

"I forget most of their names."

"Oh. Well, he's an artist. Drives a van."

"Yellow one? Old van? He looks kind of like a hippie? Getting bald in the back?"

"That's him."

"Sure. I know him. Name's Bill, right?"

Cesar nodded, drinking his beer.

"Lives over there. He bought the Russian's place over

there." Arthur pointed across the street and down the block toward a three-story brick house. Like the other houses, it had a flat front and carved lintels, but Bill Sharp had painted it a soft purplish gray instead of sand-blasting, and he had picked out the trim in a purplish brown.

"Sure," Arthur went on. "I know him. He's a nice boy. Helped me haul some of that junk I had back there in the garage when Henry didn't want to get his car dirty. Boy works hard, too, for being so skinny."

"I don't know him real well," said Cesar. "He seems like a nice guy, though. Which house did you say?"

"That one that's got all the purple around the windows. Took him about a year to get that house painted. Did all the work himself. I told him I could get him someone would do it for him, but he said he wanted to do it."

"I don't think he makes too much money," said Cesar. "He hasn't sold a lot of paintings."

"Never seen the paintings," said Arthur.

"It's modern art. Or that's what my sister said."

"Modern," said Arthur. And then, "Well."

Cesar finished his beer and looked around to see where bottles were collecting. "Henry, get your friend another beer," said Arthur.

"No thanks, Mr. Battle. Really. I've got to go pick up those tickets."

"Come on, son. You got time for another. It's Saturday. Henry, go get the boy a beer."

"You want another beer, Cesar?" Henry asked without making any unnecessary moves toward the refrigerator.

"Well."

"The boy wants another beer, Henry. Move!"

"I can get it, Henry." Cesar stood up.

"Let Henry get it, Frank. I got an old dog in there that thinks she's still got a job. She got no teeth but she still goes for your leg if she don't know you."

Henry heaved himself up from his chair, clucking his tongue as he opened the screen door.

"Now, you take that chair, Frank. Henry can get himself another like I asked him to."

Cesar sat down and lost his stomach as the seat dropped nearly to the ground. He looked down at himself to see if he had gotten fat without noticing.

"So you're gonna go on that house tour," said Arthur. Cesar nodded. "You got to pay for that?"

"Yep."

"How much?"

"Three-fifty today, four tomorrow."

"Whoo!" said Arthur.

"I know," said Cesar. "I think it's crazy, but my mother wants to go."

"Got to do what the lady wants," said Arthur. And then, "Folks get to keep the money?"

"I don't think so. It's some kind of benefit. Goes for historic preservation or something."

"Too bad. I was thinking about running some folks through here. That must be what old Sonny was all worked up about." Arthur started to tell Cesar about old Sonny when Henry came back out with two more beers. Cesar pretended to start up out of the chair, but Arthur waved him back down. "Now you go get yourself a chair," he said to Henry. Henry's lower lip slid out and he leaned against the thick, carved arch that framed his uncle's entry.

"I'll stand," said Henry, and he handed Cesar a bottle without looking.

"OOOOooo! Arthur! Hey, Arthur!" The men looked out to the street, where an elderly turquoise Coupe de Ville had stopped.

"Awww, shoot!" said Arthur under his breath.

"Arthur!" The driver's door opened and a woman came out and strode around the front of the car, heading for Arthur's street gate. "Honey, I been calling you. Don't you answer your phone?"

Cesar couldn't believe it. Arthur was fatter than Henry. He was older. He was balder. But, like his nephew, he attracted the most beautiful women in the city. This one was tall, slim, and light-skinned, and everything she wore had a little polo player on it. She showed about half a mile of cleanly muscled leg as she stepped up to Arthur's front walk.

"What you want, Elsie?"

"Fights, Arthur. You were supposed to come over and watch the fights tonight. I was calling to see if you remembered." Arthur grimaced as the woman came up the steps and started fiddling with his sideburns.

"I remembered, Elsie."

"Good. How were you figuring on getting to my place?"

"I don't know. Let me worry about that."

"How you doing, Henry? Is this a friend of yours?"

"Mm-hm."

"I love these two boys because they have such excellent manners. A couple of real gentlemen. I'm Elsie McDonald," said the lady, and she held out a long cool hand.

"Cesar Franck, ma'am."

"I'm a very good friend of Mr. Battle's. Isn't that right, Arthur?"

"Mm-hm."

"Please sit down, ma'am," said Cesar, heaving himself from the droopy porch chair.

"Did you hear that, Arthur? Henry? Thank you, Mr. Franck." Elsie McDonald sat down and started digging in her handbag. The chair barely sagged at all. She pulled out a pack of Satin cigarettes and a silver lighter and lit up. "Anybody going to offer this old lady something to drink? And not what's in that old nasty bag either, Arthur. You look like something from Vine Street. Henry, I'll have whatever you and your friend are drinking."

Cesar heard a little high-pitched whine from Henry as he started another journey to the fridge.

Eighteen minutes later, his head reeling from the heat, the beer, and Elsie McDonald, Cesar staggered up from his seat on the steps. He looked around. Elsie had been running on for the last ten minutes about Aaron Pryor and how worried she was about him. Arthur looked like a zoo bear after sixteen school groups. Henry, who had brought out a hassock on his last trip to the kitchen, was propped against the archway, snoring softly. Cesar waited for a break in Elsie's analysis of the fight world.

"Well, Mr. Batt—"

"Sit down, boy. Have another beer. Sit down." He sounded like Cesar felt. Probably worse, Cesar figured, since he had been drinking longer.

"I've really got to go, Mr. Battle. No kidding. Thanks for the beer."

"Have another, Frank. Hey! Henry!" Henry stopped snoring but made no move. "I'll get you a beer. I got to go to the bathroom anyway." Arthur Battle started to work his way out of the chair. Cesar opened his mouth to protest when he was interrupted by a terrified scream coming from someplace nearby.

Dammit. Cesar couldn't get the damned gate open. He stepped over it, tearing his pants on an iron spike, and ran across the street listening for another scream. He heard Henry's footsteps behind him. "Where the hell was . . ." Cesar started to ask when they heard the scream again. They scrambled through another iron gate and chased each other down a walkway between two town houses. They heard the scream again, but they were trapped in a dead end, a yard fenced in by a concrete block wall topped with barbed wire. The two policemen were panting from their sprint, but they turned around and thudded back between the two buildings and out to the sidewalk.

"Over here," grunted Henry, and he took off down the street and turned into an alley with Cesar hot on his heels. The scream sounded again. The alley led them to another alley running parallel to Abigail, and Henry skidded around the corner and headed for the other side of the concrete wall. *"Linda! Get Back! Linda!"* The cries came from the other side of a high wooden fence across from the concrete wall. Cesar and Henry looked at the fence and looked at each other and decided in a flash that there was no getting over. Henry took off down the alley the way they had been running and turned into another alley heading north. He was starting to slow down. Cesar passed him before they hit the next street, where Cesar doubled back. He stopped. Which house? Henry huffed and pointed into a tiny yard in front of a skinny wooden house. Cesar grappled with a gate and jogged down a narrow passageway, barking his shin on a tricycle before he burst out into the backyard.

No rape.

Nobody with a gun.

Nobody with a knife.

Good thing; Cesar and Henry had both left their pistols in their cars back on Abigail Street. Henry banged into Cesar from behind. "What . . . what . . . what . . ." He was too winded to finish his question.

"Linda! Get back! Get away! Linda, stop it!" A white woman was standing with her back to the policemen. She had her arm around a little boy. They were both looking at a gray cat. The gray cat crouched, staring at the biggest, meanest rat Cesar had ever seen. The rat was backed onto its haunches, making vicious faces at the cat, who had apparently backed it into the corner formed by the alley fence and the building next-door.

"Ma'am!" said Cesar. "Ma'am?" She turned around for a second, then swung back to the cat.

"Linda! Get away! Leave it alone!" There was a rattle as some sort of projectile landed behind the rat. The rat sidestepped, and the cat countered. Cesar looked around and then up to see who was zinging rocks at the rat.

"I'll get him." Everyone looked up at a woman who was hanging out of an upstairs window in the building next-door. "Get back, honey! I got some Drano. Lemme see if that don't—"

"No! For God's sake! Don't throw Drano! You'll hit my cat!"

"I'll be careful, honey. Just get your little boy back so he don't get any on his clothes. Drano makes that rat blind!"

"Are you crazy?! No Drano! No. *Linda get back!*"

"Lady? Ma'am? Hey! Lady!" said Cesar. "Let me—"

PAANNGGGGANNGGG.

Cesar's ears were ringing so hard that he wiped them with his hands to see if they were bleeding or gone. They were both still hanging on and there was no blood. There was no rat either, though. It had exploded. The rat had burst in a splash of bright rodent blood, and Linda the cat had streaked from the scene like a rocket. Cesar looked around at the survivors of the explosion, who were all as stunned as he was. The little boy was taking wobbly steps in the direction of the late rat, and the lady was hitting her left ear with the heel of her hand. Henry had taken off his glasses and was staring at Cesar.

"Help that man! You got to help that man! He got hurt!" Cesar and Henry and the woman stared up at the lady hanging out of the upstairs window. "Him! That man! Over there!" She was pointing behind the group on the ground. They turned around. Arthur Battle was sprawled backward on the pavement close to the house; a .45 pistol lay beside him. The policemen, still fuzzled by the explosion, walked slowly over to Arthur.

"Arthur?" asked Henry. "Hey, Uncle Arthur? What happened?" Arthur was heaving himself up on his elbows, shaking his head slowly from side to side. Henry squatted at his side. "What happened to you, man?" Cesar squatted beside Henry.

"You okay, Mr. Battle?"

"OOnnnff," said Arthur. Cesar picked up the pistol and felt it. It was warm. He sniffed. It had been fired. He stared at Mr. Battle. "Henry," said Arthur, who was starting to get his wind back, "Henry, did I get him?" Henry looked mystified. Cesar showed him the .45.

"Man, did you *shoot* that rat? Was that what happened?"

"Yeah. Ooohhh!" Arthur rubbed his right arm. "I forgot about the kick on that bad boy. Ain't used it since Korea."

"Man, you are *crazy!*" said Henry. He smiled at his uncle.

"Is he all right? What happened?" Cesar looked up. The lady who had done all the screaming was peering down at him. For a second or two he just stared at her, his mouth hanging open. He had not really seen her in all the excitement over Linda, the rat, and Arthur Battle's rescue operation. This was a beautiful woman. The sunlight was streaming through her brown curls. Her cheeks were red from excitement, and she was half-smiling. Cesar, who was still squatting beside the fallen uncle, started to lose his balance looking up at her. He caught himself and stood so that she was looking up at him.

"He's fine, I think. Or he will be. He shot your rat."

"*My* rat?"

"Oh. The rat. The one that was there."

"I know. It wasn't mine. It was chasing my son."

Cesar looked down at the little boy, who was staring at Arthur's .45.

"Hey! Hey! Y'all! I called the police." The lady upstairs was yelling at them. "She say they be right here and you don't supposed to go away. Is he all right? You want me to call the rescue?"

Jesus. She called the police. "No. No, don't do that, ma'am. Thanks. I think he'll be all right."

"He hit that old rat pretty good, didn't he? You know, I think it's terrible the way we got rats down here. They're so big. He woulda kilt that cat if he could."

"Yeah, he was pretty big," said Cesar. And then he turned back to the woman. "Did he bite your son, ma'am? What happened?"

"No, he didn't bite me," answered the little boy, still staring at the pistol. "I just didn't see him under the box and then I picked it up and he ran out." The woman shuddered.

"How's he doing, Henry?" Cesar had to stop staring at the woman.

"He's better." And then, "Uncle Arthur, what the hell are you doing running around with that gun? You could've killed someone."

"Don't be telling me what to do, boy. I heard this lady screaming and . . . and . . ."

Cesar realized finally that Uncle Arthur was suffering as much from an afternoon of drinking as from the stupendous sound and recoil of the .45.

"Artie?" Cesar looked up. Elsie McDonald was peering around the corner. She saw Arthur on the ground and ran to his side. "Artie, what on *earth?* Baby, what *happened?* Are you all right?"

"Oh, no," Arthur moaned softly.

"Elsie, would you take him back to the house?"

"But Henry, what happened to him? Is he hurt?"

"I don't wanna go home," said Arthur. "I'll be all right."

"Elsie," said Henry, "take this old man home and keep him off the porch. There's gonna be police here in a second and I don't want him around."

"What'd you call the police for, stupid? *You're* the police. So's your friend." Elsie was indignant. "And I want to know what happened to my big baby here!"

"He thought he was back storming the beach in Korea, Elsie. He shot off his old .45 at a rat. Now get him out of here before the patrol gets here. And I didn't call them. Someone else did."

Elsie looked at Cesar and Henry as if they were a couple of stupid third-graders, and then, with Henry's help, she pulled Arthur to his feet. "Are you dizzy, baby?" she asked. Arthur just grunted. "Don't look all evil at me, Arthur. I'm just trying to take care of you. I'm not trying to steal your billfold. You come on with me before the police come and see a crazy old drunk man out shooting rats. Come on."

"Go!" said Henry firmly. Arthur let Elsie lead him out. He was still rubbing his shoulder as he left.

"Did she say you're the police?" The lady and her son were staring at Cesar and Henry. Cesar nodded. "And that man, Mr. Battle, he's your uncle?"

"Henry's uncle. Yes."

"I did figure that out," said the lady. "Doesn't he live over on Abigail?"

"Right," said Cesar. "We were there with him. Heard you screa— calling for help."

"Oh, I was screaming all right. Did you see the size of that rat? He would have killed my cat. Where *is* my cat? Sidney, where did Linda go? Oh! There's the police-men!" She was looking over Cesar's shoulders. Cesar turned and saw Vern Raterman and Lucius Carrier.

"I'll handle it," said Henry.

"Keep it simple," said Cesar.

"God, you must think I'm really stupid," Stella said to Cesar.

"About the rat? Hey, those big ones scare me, too."

"But I'll bet you don't scream like a maniac when you see one. I don't either, usually. I just got scared for my son and then for my cat."

"Yeah. Well."

"It was really nice of you to come help like you did. Your friend, too."

"Would have gotten here faster, but we kept getting caught in dead ends."

"Sidney, go see if you can find Linda. Go see where she's hiding. You know . . . what do I call you? Officer?"

"Cesar Franck."

"You're kidding! No . . . sorry . . . do you know about the composer? Of course you do. God, I'll bet you get sick of the music jokes."

"I don't get a whole lot. I guess he isn't really famous, Mrs. . . ."

"I'm sorry. I'm Stella Hineman. But are you related? To Cesar Franck?"

"Well, my dad said we were. I guess we are."

"That's really fantastic."

Are you getting bored, Mrs. Hineman? Is there a Mr. Hineman? What are you doing on a street like this? Am I too short for you?

"Well, if you're all right, Mrs. Hineman, I guess I'll see how my partner's doing."

Stella Hineman started to laugh. *"Mrs.* Hineman. Mrs. Hineman is my *mother.* That made me feel like a ghost or something. I'm not married."

"Oh. Listen, I'm sorry. I just thought—"

"I know. I've got this son. But . . ." Stella's voice trailed off.

But it's none of my business. "Listen, I'm going to check on Henry there. If you've got a shovel or something, I'll get rid of the rest of that rat for you."

"You will? Oh, that is *really* nice. I can't . . . I just really don't like to touch them. Not even with a shovel. I'll get one for you."

Cesar joined Henry and the other policemen. "Everything cool, Henry? How ya doin', Vern, Lucius?"

"Not bad, Ceez. Yeah, Henry was telling us how he shot that rat and I was telling him I was sure glad it was him, since I don't feel like doing any more reports today. Did you know he was such a good shot?"

"I knew he was good, Vern. I just didn't know he was up there with Clint Eastwood."

Vern thought that was hysterical. Lucius looked real bored. Stella came back with what looked like the first shovel in the world. Cesar went looking for pieces of rat.

As Cesar was scraping up the last scraps, a woman's voice came over the wall from the alley. "Stella! Hey, Stella!"

"What?"

"Stella, it's Sandy. Is Chips in there with you?"

"No. He was here a while ago. I don't know where he went." Stella made a face at the woman that the woman couldn't see but Cesar could.

"Well, listen, if you see him, tell him to get his buns home. Tell him the air conditioner is here and I want it installed tonight or else. You got that?"

"I got that, Sandy."

"You want to come over to the house and smoke?"

"Sandy!"

"What? You coming?"

"Sandy, you know I gave up smoking. I haven't had a cigarette for—"

"I wasn't talking about—"

"And I've got company right now. The police are here."

"Oh."

"I'll tell Chips if I see him."

"Right. Thanks, Stella."

Cesar heard the woman's footsteps as she hurried down the alley. He scooped up the little mound that was all he could find of the late bad rat and carried the shovel over to a beat-up garbage can. There was a little damp spot on the shovel, so he ran it under a tap by the basement door.

"That is really nice of you. I don't think I could have done that. I *know* I couldn't. So much for liberation." Stella smiled at him, which made the sickening rat removal okay.

"Cesar, I've got to get back," said Henry. "And these guys are leaving too."

"Wait up. I'm coming too." Cesar put down the shovel. "Need anything else?" he asked Stella.

"No. That was the worst thing, and you got it. Thanks. Thank you, too," she added, waving at Henry.

Cesar looked over his shoulder as he left the backyard. Stella had picked up the shovel. She waved it at him.

4

WHOEVER WAS IN charge of the weather cranked the heat up another five degrees Saturday night. The humidity was close to saturation. The air smelled bad throughout the city, even on the fringes. The only way it could have been worse was if it were Friday when every last displaced Kentuckian was on I-75 heading home for the weekend. They all have to wait for each other to cross the river where the expressway chokes down from six lanes to two, and the valley that channels the interstate through the city from north to south always fills to the top with a sour fog of exhaust, sweat, and bad tempers on Fridays. As it was, there being no wind for weeks, most of Friday's fog was still hanging around, although it had broken into clumps, which were slowly rolling around the city, knocking over emphysema victims like ninepins.

At 10:00 P.M., when the heat was at its peak, people were coping in different ways.

Cesar Franck was in the coolest spot in his house, the basement. He had shoved a few boxes around and made bumping noises so that his mother would think he was straightening up instead of doing what he was doing now, which was lying on his back on an old studio couch, looking up at the ceiling and thinking about Stella Hineman.

Lillian Franck, Cesar's mother, was lying on her back

on her bed with the fan sweeping back and forth over her substantial and undressed body. She had taken a bath with half a pound of baking soda and patted herself dry. Even with the air conditioner running, little beads of sweat were starting to form on her chest. She was working on *The Winds of War*.

Henry Chapman had discovered that the coolest place in his house was in the middle of the living-room floor. There was a slow but steady draft from the entry hall to the fireplace, and he had fallen asleep in his boxer shorts with the air moving slowly over his skin. Henry's Saturday evenings did not normally begin to take shape until 11:30 P.M.

Arthur Battle had decided he was in no shape to go to Elsie McDonald's house to watch the fights, so Elsie had gone all the way back to her house in Kennedy Heights to get her Sony portable and stop at Kroger's for groceries. She had fixed Arthur a big supper and laid out a lot of snacks for the evening, but she left the kitchen a wreck. She wasn't going to miss the fights for anything. Elsie made Arthur set up the TV outside behind his house even though it was cooler inside. Inside smelled too much like Arthur's dog, as far as Elsie was concerned.

Stella Hineman had moved her sewing machine to the very front of her house and parked it under a window, which was wide open. She had turned off all the lights in the house except for the little one on her sewing machine, but that was enough to attract a million bugs, since Chips had never replaced the screens on her house. The house next-door had a stereo on full blast.

Chips Reber was out in back of his first-floor apartment, wrestling an enormous air-conditioning unit into the window of the back bedroom. It was a two-man job, but Sandy had gone out to visit a girlfriend who lived in the Regency, where the air conditioning was state of the art. It was dark behind the house. Chips had rigged a work light, but he had had to hang it too low and he couldn't see what he was doing. He was soaked with sweat and not coping very well.

Greta Grimes and Nancy Sharp sat in Greta's kitchen under the ceiling fan drinking iced tea and smoking marijuana that Greta's brother had sent up from Hopkinsville, Kentucky. There were going through mail-order catalogs looking for cool cotton dresses like the ones their grandmothers wore, but everything looked too hip. Their husbands were sitting on the front stoop watching the Saturday-night people cruise through the neighborhood.

Theresa McDowell was on the phone to her mother in Lexington. She had the lights off and the windows open. Every time a car would go past blasting stereo soul music, her mother would ask, "Theresa, what *is* that you're listening to?" Paul McDowell was downstairs in a madras bathing suit and flip-flops dusting the furniture for the third time that day. Two of the senior partners had announced their intention to take the tour. Paul was sweating profusely.

Alan and Emma Howard had made a furtive trip to Swallen's that evening to buy a small portable air conditioner, which they had installed in their back bedroom, where it could not be seen by their neighbors. They were enjoying the sensations produced by the friction of dry skin upon dry skin.

Sister Clare and Louella Dwyer were still in the Truth and Beauty Outreach Center lettering signs for tomorrow's protest. They did not normally like to be on Central Avenue that late, but Dick Speers had said he would be in to help. He had come in, but he was on the phone and hadn't lifted a magic marker all evening. Stephen Rankin was still on the Apple. He had not left the building since his arrival at noon.

Ron Diehl was in Fairmount getting drunk on beer.

Sonny Werk stood at the basin in his room washing a pair of underpants prior to going out for the evening. He had coated his hair with Dippety Doo and braided it into eighteen plaits so that it would behave tomorrow. He was wearing his basketball shoes and nothing else. From time to time he would turn to catch his reflection in the mirror on his chifforobe. He genuinely did not care about the heat.

Elizabeth Sackville was warm, but she chose not to perspire. She sat in her box at Music Hall, where she was making her first appearance in the dress Great-grand-mother Probasco had worn to the Taft inaugural ball. It was also the dress in which her great-grandmother had sat for Sargent, and Elizabeth had replicated the hairdo in the picture. She had nudged her seat around so that she presented a perfect ninety-degree profile to the photographer from *Town and Country* who sat in row G, some eighteen feet away. Although her eyes were trained on Maestro Levine's fluffy curls and her expression indicated total fascination with Mahler, Elizabeth's mind was several blocks away in Dutchtown.

Betty Perrett, Juanita Anderson, Stone McCullough, and Roscoe Terry had never left the BandK Poolroom. Roscoe and Stone had long since forgotten their afternoon fight and were sitting across from each other discussing times past. They were both experienced drinkers and therefore able to stay drunk but not too drunk for the evening. Betty and Juanita had joined in a game of Tonk. Juanita was cleaning up. Betty was holding even. John Lindsey had fooled around with the air conditioner until it kept up with the caloric output of the BandK just about perfectly. In fact, Mr. Lindsey's customers were far more comfortable than the crowd at the May Festival in Music Hall, where the monster coolers, running full blast, were losing the battle and letting the temperature go up six degrees per hour. Elizabeth Sackville was the only concertgoer to bring an ostrich-feather fan. She was using it now, creating a minor sensation.

At 11:30 P.M. Chips Reber lay dead, pinned to the ground underneath a 16,000 BTU Airtemp window unit. The temperature was still in the lower nineties.

At 12:17 A.M. on Sunday, a cool wind began to blow, quickly picking up speed and force, and at 12:52 it began to rain.

5

"GUS, THAT'S A truck up there."

Oh, Jeez.

"Gus, it looks to me like that truck's stopping. What's he stopping for?"

So he can turn his rig around and aim it at us.

"No, maybe he's not stopping. Maybe he's slowing down. Is he slowing down, do you think, Gus?"

"I don't think so, Mom."

Lillian Franck leaned forward in the passenger seat of her son's Camaro. "I don't know how you can tell he's not, Gus. You know he's got air brakes like on the buses."

What do air brakes have to do with anything?

"He can stop on a dime, Gus."

"Mom, he's four blocks ahead of us. Believe me, if he does anything I'll be ready."

Lillian leaned back about a sixteenth of an inch.

"That's right, Mom. Relax."

Cesar Auguste Franck, who was Gus only to his mother, felt his mother's look of distrust.

"Mom, if you want to worry about anything, you should be worrying about that semi that's behind us, the one that's about six inches off my bumper."

"Aaannhh!" Lillian gave off a throaty little squeak as she twisted around to see her murderer. There was no

46

one behind them. Clear all the way back to Eighth and State.

"That's not funny, Gus."

"Yeah, well, you should relax. I know what I'm doing. Believe me. I drive every day."

"You're a good driver, Gus. I didn't say you weren't a good driver. It's—"

"I know. It's this car. The lowest car they ever made. The car most likely to get its top cut off under a semi."

"No, the car's okay. I just—"

". . . wish I would take a look at Fred's car because Kathy says it's real safe."

"You should."

"I have. It's about six times as big as I need."

Cesar's brother-in-law went in for full-size Buicks.

"You turn on Central, Gus."

"I told you, I saw the place yesterday."

"Don't park anyplace dangerous, Gus."

"I'm going to park in the garage behind Music Hall. Is that safe enough?"

"When did they put a garage behind Music Hall?"

"Couple of years ago."

"I don't know, Gus. It's a tough neighborhood."

"You've got a police escort, Mom. Remember?"

"You never wear your uniform. How's anyone supposed to know? Lock your door."

"Mom." Cesar started to laugh. Then he took a look at his mother and stopped. "Mom, it's—"

"Gus, watch the road. There's a stoplight. It's what?"

"What? Oh. It's Sunday morning."

"So?"

"So the kind of guys who chop up old ladies and their sons are all in bed hungover. They're on a night shift. All of them."

"I never read that."

"Did you ever read about a mugging on Sunday morning?"

"I don't—"

"Take my word for it. I'm in the business. The bad guys are all in bed."

"But you don't know what time we'll be getting out of here, Gus."

You got me.

"Now where are you going? Is that the garage? Did you miss where you go in?"

"Yeah."

"Look. There's no walls. Anybody can just get in and slash your tires."

"It'll be all right."

Cesar nosed the Camaro up to the entrance and took a ticket. The lower level was nearly full. That was a surprise. He pulled in beside a big white Mercury.

"That's a nice car, Gus."

"And the guy left it here and he doesn't have a guard on it, so see? We're gonna be all right." He got out, walked around, opened the passenger door, and pulled his short, plump mother out of the low seat. She stood and smoothed out the bottom of her dress. "You look great," said Cesar.

"You think so? I don't know. I should have worn a pants suit." Lillian fished her bag from the car, hooked the straps over her arm, and squeezed it with her elbow. She watched closely as Cesar locked and shut the door, then she tried the latch. You can't be too careful.

The detective and his mother worked their way through the rows of cars until they found an exit that put them out on Clark Street.

For a moment the two of them stopped and blinked. The Camaro and the garage had been shady, and, in the rush from breakfast to the Westwood Reformed Church and back, and then to get to the house tour, neither one of them had noticed the weather. It was beautiful.

The previous night's wind had swept away the huge blanket of smog, sending the sulfur dioxide and the lead flakes off to Georgia or Canada to feed the fish, and what the wind had missed, the rain had washed away. The sky was deep blue. Little white fake-looking clouds rolled overhead, and the temperature was in the midseventies.

"I didn't know it was supposed to be like this," said Lillian. She sounded like the weather was a trick.

"You want me to report it to somebody?" asked Cesar.

"Watch your mouth, Gus."

They walked along, following other couples who, by their clothes and color, seemed to be headed toward the house tour. As they turned the corner onto Central Avenue, they began to hear crowd noises.

Protest. A damned protest.

Cesar groaned to himself.

"What's going on, Gus?"

"I don't know, Mom." Why didn't we stay home? I could've had a nap. I could've washed the car. I could've watched animal programs on TV. Anything but a protest.

"Look, Gus, they've got signs. What's going on?"

Nukes. Whales. AIDS. Unemployment. Whales. Take your pick.

"Maybe we should go back to the car."

"Mom, we're down here. Come on. It's just a protest. You won't get hurt."

"I don't know," muttered Mrs. Franck, and she hugged her purse until her elbow went white.

It wasn't a big protest. Cesar had seen plenty bigger. Abigail Street was blocked off with a lot of potted plants where it intersected with Central Avenue, and the protesters had mounted a straggly picket line between the plants and the traffic on Central. There weren't more than twelve or fifteen marchers. All but three of them were white. Cesar recognized Sonny Werk and a couple of faces from when he had had to be the duty police representative at community meetings. He felt the twinge of a headache, same as when he was at the meetings.

"Stop a second." Lillian yanked her son's arm. "I want to read the signs."

They read. GENTRIFICATION IS GENOCIDE. HISTORICAL PRESERVATION IS HISTORICAL RAPE. POOR PEOPLE WANT HOUSING, NOT HISTORY. GENTRY OUT! THIS IS OUR NEIGH-

BORHOOD, NOT YOURS. DUTCHTOWN FOR THE PEOPLE. WE DON'T WANT BMW'S. STOP EVICTING SENIORS, and NO WEST-WOOD IN THE WEST END. The last one made Lillian go stiff.

"What is this junk?" she asked. "What are they talking about? What do they . . ." Her voice was drowned as the marchers picked up a cry of "Noooo *Gentry!*" and batted it around. Cesar felt his mother pull on his arm again. She was dragging him away from the marchers and toward Abigail Street. "Officer Franck! Officer Franck!" Cesar heard the voice of Sonny Werk through the chanting, but he ignored it.

Cesar handed the tickets to a woman in an old-fashioned dress. "Sorry about that," she said, glaring furiously at the marchers. She was saying the same thing to everyone entering the street.

"Who was that calling you, Gus?"

"I think it was Sonny Werk."

"That communist? The one that's always on television? Why does he know you?"

"I don't know if he's a communist. I had to go to meetings with him."

"He should be ashamed of himself. They should all be ashamed of themselves. That hair looks stupid. What's gentrification?"

"That's what they're calling it when people move into old neighborhoods and start fixing them up."

"Like Fred's sister?"

"Yeah."

"You're kidding! What are they talking about? What's wrong with fixing up a neighborhood? Do you know what a slum this was?" She looked around at the old limestone and brick town houses that lined Abigail Street. "Looks to me like it still is. I thought it was going to be all fixed up."

"It is. You should have seen it a couple of years ago. A lot of the buildings were boarded up. It was real dirty."

"It doesn't look fixed up to me."

"Yeah, well it's mostly on the inside, I guess. See the plants? That's how you tell. Oh, and the burglar alarms."

"I can see the plants." Half of the buildings had rain forests in the front rooms. "Where's the alarms?"

"See those things that look like loudspeakers? Up there at the top . . . in the corner." Every building with a rain forest had a burglar alarm.

"Hunh," said Lillian. "What do you know." She looked at the program the ticket lady had given them. "Are we supposed to do this in some sort of order?" Cesar tried to take the program away, but she hung on, peering at the little map. "Which one's Fred's sister's?"

Cesar pointed down the block, but his mother was too short to see over the cluster of people in front of them. "Show me on the map," she ordered. He pointed to the Sharps' house.

"And we're right here," he added, pointing to a spot marked as *The Freihofer-McDowell House* on the map. "We're supposed to start in there." They stepped up onto the McDowells' walk and joined the line waiting to get in.

"I knew Marcella Freihofer. I wonder if this is her old house. She could talk your arm off. Except this was all colored when I knew her. Maybe it's where she was born."

"Must run in the family. I know a cop named Freihofer and he likes to talk too."

A man in a blue blazer and gray pants was taking tickets at the doorway. "Hi!" he said. "I'm Paul McDowell." He took their tickets with a big smile and lots of eye contact. "I hope you enjoy the house. My wife's inside to answer any questions, but if she's busy, I'll give it a try." He laid a firm hand between Cesar's shoulder blades and shoved him gently through the vestibule and into the house.

"Are we supposed to know him?" asked Lillian through her teeth. Her son shrugged.

"Oh, look, Gus. This is nice."

Cesar looked. They had stepped into a front hall that reached halfway back into the house. There was a long staircase running back along the wall to the left, and two big doorways on the wall to the right. The walls were light beige. Mr. and Mrs. McDowell had lined the hall with a lot of pictures of birds in thin silver frames.

"Look at the birds, Gus." Cesar stepped up and looked at a bird. "These are real popular," said Mrs. Franck, who worked in the accounting department at Shillito's Department Store. "I was looking at mirrors the other day and they had a whole lot of these in there with them." She usually spent her lunch hours in the store.

"You like my birds?" asked a perky voice behind Cesar. The accent was from somewhere south of the Ohio River. He looked around. A woman in a chartreuse skirt and a yellow button-down shirt was smiling at Lillian and Cesar. "I'm just crazy about them," she said.

"They're real nice," said Lillian. "Is this your house?"

"It sure is. That was my husband who took your tickets at the door. We're the McDowells. Why don't you all go on in and take a look around? It's getting a little bit crowded out here. You be sure to ask me if you have any questions. I just love talking about the house." She herded the visitors through a tall doorway and into the front room.

"OOOoohh!" said one of the visitors. "I *love* it!"

Cesar wasn't sure he loved it. What he was sure was that one or both of the McDowells loved chartreuse and bright yellow. They liked vegetables, too. Their big front room, a sixteen-foot cube with nine-foot windows looking out on Abigail Street, was filled with green and yellow slipcovers, green and yellow curtains, and green and yellow knickknacks. There were a few places where they had settled for white, like the walls and ceiling. Every level surface had a porcelain bean or peapod or an ear of corn. There was a big china squash on the floor by the sofa. And over the marble fireplace the McDowells had hung a painting of a lemon.

"This is cheerful," said Mrs. Franck.

"Do you think so?" asked Mrs. McDowell from the doorway. "We don't get much sun in here, so I wanted to pep it up a little. I just love it." She beamed at her visitors. Most of them were too busy estimating costs to smile back. Cesar eased over to a table with a bunch of fake daisies, a pot full of green and yellow jelly beans, and a photograph in a silver frame. He wanted to see the picture. It was Mr. and Mrs. McDowell hugging a beefy-looking guy with a big grin. Famous grin. Oh. The Governor. So that was why McDowell was out there glad-handing his guests. Cesar stepped over to the window to take a look at the protesters. He had to crane his neck around a big palm tree to see down to the corner, and even then he couldn't really see what was going on, but he did see a six-foot-tall blond woman in shorts and a suntan heading up the front walk, elbowing visitors out of her way. She looked pissed off, but even pissed off she looked good.

"Paul, where the hell is Chips?" She had a big voice, too. Cesar could hear her from the living room. He couldn't hear McDowell's answer. "Theresa! Theresa, are you in there?" She banged into the hall.

"Sandy! Puh-leeze! We've got visitors."

"Theresa, where the *hell* is Chips? Have you seen him? I tried to call you. What's the matter with your phone?"

"It's unplugged, Sandy. You don't have to shout." Theresa was talking in a loud whisper.

"I'm sorry, Theresa, but I've got people lined up to get in the house, Chips has his apartment locked up, I haven't seen him since last night, and I'm going crazy."

"Honey, I don't know where he is. I haven't seen him all day."

"Well if you *do* see him, tell him to get his ass down to the house on the double. And you can tell him this is absolutely the last house tour I am *ever* going to have anything to do with." Cesar heard her bang out of the front door, then watched her as she went down the stoop, two steps at a time. Lucky Chips.

"Is that who was talking?" Cesar's mother had nosed in beside him at the window. He nodded. "I don't know how she can dress like that in this neighborhood. That's just asking for trouble."

"Looks like she can handle it," said Cesar.

"Come on. I want to see the rest of this place."

Cesar followed his mother through the living room and into a second living room on the other side of a pair of sliding doors.

Wow. Just like the other room, only the picture over the mantel in here was a great big lime. Lillian clucked her tongue and headed for the kitchen.

Cesar and his mother walked around the room, stopping to look out the window. A big Irish setter looked up at them from the yard. He was chained to the tree. "What do they want with a big dog like that?" muttered Lillian.

"Campaign posters."

"I don't get it." Lillian gave Cesar a fishy look and then started seriously casing the kitchen. The McDowells had spent big bucks on white cabinets and megabucks on appliances and gadgets. At last Lillian opened the oven, peered in, and made a sour face. "I've seen enough, Gus. Let's go." Cesar took her by the elbow and steered her toward the front of the house. They passed Theresa McDowell on the way out. "Thank you very much," said Lillian. "It's very nice." Theresa McDowell waved and went back into her spiel with some new arrivals.

The Francks got past Paul McDowell and back out to the sidewalk on Abigail Street.

"Can you believe it, Gus? Did you see the oven?" Lillian shook her head at the horror of it all.

"Dirty?" asked Cesar.

"Filthy. And it was a top-of-the-line Magic Chef. Self-cleaning. Someone should tell her how it works."

"Maybe she knows. Maybe she just didn't expect the kitchen-patrol lady to drop in with the crowd today."

"Watch your mouth, Gus. Anyway, she should expect people are going to look at things like that. I mean, it's a kitchen. And I'll tell you what, not that I would ever open my house for a tour, but if I did, you can bet my stove would be clean. Where do we go now? I want to see Fred's sister's place." She peered at the little map. Cesar tugged it away from her.

"You're in luck. Next on the tour is the Cheeseman-Poffenberger-Sharp House." Cesar read from the pamphlet as they walked along. " 'A typical middle-class dwelling from the midnineteenth century, the Cheeseman-Poffenberger-Sharp house is more notable for the pleasing simplicity and almost severe symmetry of its brick facade. Built by Henry Cheeseman, the owner of a livery stable located where the J. J. Newberry Department Store now stands, it is now the home and studio of local artist William Sharp and his wife, Nancy.' "

"What about the Poffenbergers?" asked Lillian.

"I don't know," mumbled Cesar. He had spotted a little advertisement set off in a box at the bottom of the page.

"Clothing by Stella. Japanese and American Designs. Number 12 on the map." He looked for number 12. It was the house where the rat exploded.

"Gus! Gus!" Lillian whispered urgently, and she pinched her son's elbow. "Do you know that guy up there on the stoop? He's waving at you."

Cesar looked up and saw Arthur Battle. "Yeah," he said to his mother, and then "How ya doing?" to Mr. Battle.

"All right. Is that your girlfriend with you, Franck?"

Lillian stared at Arthur.

"It's my mother," said Cesar. Arthur levered himself out of his chair, hitched up his trousers, and ambled down his walk toward the gate.

"What's he want?" whispered Lillian. She whispered a lot around black people.

"A date," whispered Cesar, and then, in a regular voice, "This is Mr. Battle, Mom. He's Henry Chapman's uncle."

"Oh!" said Lillian. She liked Henry. "Nice to meet you."

"Your mother's awful pretty, Franck."

Lillian giggled. Jesus.

"You all going on the tour?"

"Right," said Cesar.

"It's real interesting," said Lillian. "You should see."

"I don't know. Maybe I will."

Cesar leaned against Arthur's iron fence and waited for five minutes while his mother and his partner's uncle flirted with each other, then he took his mother's elbow. "Come on, Mom. We've got six houses to go." He waited another three minutes while they raked the Reds over the coals, and then he said, "I'm sorry, Mr. Battle. I should have warned you about my mom. Once she gets started . . ." Lillian shot him an evil look and he shut up.

"Listen, why don't you two stop by when you get through looking? We can have something to drink."

"I don't think—"

"Maybe we will, Mr. Battle. It's real hot," said Lillian. It wasn't real hot. It was real nice. "It's nice meeting you." She stuck out a hand to shake. Arthur took her hand with both of his.

"What a nice man," said Lillian as they crossed the street. "And so polite. Just like Henry."

Cesar wondered if he was getting a headache.

"Is that Nancy?" asked Lillian. They had reached the Cheeseman-Poffenberger-Sharp house, the purplish gray building that Arthur Battle had pointed out yesterday. Nancy Sharp stood at the top of her stoop, taking tickets.

"That's her," said Cesar. He had picked up the tickets from her yesterday after he cleaned up the rat.

"I haven't seen her since the wedding. She doesn't look pregnant."

"Maybe she's not."

"She is. Kathy told me." Kathy, Nancy's sister-in-law and Cesar's only sister, was never doubted in the way Lillian doubted her son. Kathy was married and had children.

"Hi!" Nancy waved to them. "Come on in. Long time no see! Not you, Cesar. I saw you yesterday. How've you been, Mrs. Franck?"

As soon as he stepped in, Cesar started to figure how he could get out again. In the first place, he had seen the house, or at least the downstairs, when he picked up the tickets. In the second place he heard Fred Kuhne, his brother-in-law, sounding off somewhere close by. "Mom, if you don't mind, I'm—" Somebody standing behind him had kicked his knees forward so that he started to collapse. "Cut it out, Kathy." He didn't have to look around to know it was his sister. She grabbed the fat in the small of his back and pinched hard while she said, "Mom, he's trying to run off. I can tell. Make him stay."

"Quit it," snapped Cesar, but his sister continued to pinch. He reached back and grabbed her arm.

"Cesar, don't be rough with your sister. I'm sorry, Nancy, I don't know what's the matter with him."

"You want to see the house?" asked Nancy. She put an arm on Lillian's shoulder and started the tour. Cesar stayed behind and scuffled with his sister until they started bumping into an old couple who had come in the front door. "Excuse me, ma'am," said Cesar, ducking behind the lady and heading for the door. He beat it out, leaving Kathy to go snitch to their mother.

Aaahh, freedom. Cesar pulled the map out of his pocket and looked at it, although he knew where he was headed. He wanted to make sure he had the name right. He was at the corner of Abigail Street and Hinckley Alley. He took the alley north to Franklin, turned right, and stopped in front of Stella Hineman's house. He stared at it for a couple of seconds, and then stooped to read a sign taped to the gate. It said, *Fashions. Please come to the backyard. Stella Hineman.* He pushed through the gate and walked down the little gangway between Stella's place and the house next-door. When he got to the end, where he could see the backyard, he stopped again.

Stella had rigged clotheslines at crazy angles all over the yard; they were tied to the fences and the wall of the house next-door. She had hung up dresses and blouses and skirts with old-fashioned wooden clothespins, and everything was flapping gently in the breeze. She stood talking to two women who looked like models. They were a lot taller than Stella, and they both wore shorts and safari shirts. Stella had on a dress like Lillian used to wear when she hung out wash before she got the dryer. It was blue and covered with little yellow flowers, and it buttoned down the front. Stella had left a lot more unbuttoned than Lillian ever had. She was talking to the models, holding up the bottom of a long gray dress, and laughing. She looked beautiful. Cesar didn't feel like he was going to have a headache anymore.

Stella finally noticed him. She frowned for a second and then seemed to recognize him. She flashed a big grin and then turned back to the models and pointed out several of the dresses at the end of the yard. The two lanky women wandered back to look at them and Stella came up to Cesar.

"Shopping?" she asked.

"Uhhh." What's the matter? Can't talk.

"How does it look? What do you think?"

"Uhhh . . . nice!" And then he said, "No rats!"

"Shhhh!" she whispered. "You'll scare off the customers."

"Oh, Jeez. I'm sorry. How's it going?" asked Cesar, whispering. "How's business?"

"Lousy, so far. People just started coming in. I think they're going to have a hard time finding the place."

"You should have put a sign up."

"I did. It's on the corner across from the McDowells'. I've even got arrows in the alley pointing to the door." Cesar looked at the back fence and saw an open door leading to the alley. He could have saved half a block.

"So what are you doing back in Dutchtown?" asked Stella.

"Brought my mother down. She wanted to see the houses. We've got relatives, sort of."

Cesar told her about the Sharps and his sister. Halfway through, he realized he had a really dopey smile all over his face and he blushed. But he kept talking so he could look at Stella.

"How much is this?" called one of the models, holding up a great big dirty-brown blouse.

"Sixty-five," said Stella.

"Can I try it on?"

Stella nodded. Cesar started to talk, but stopped with his mouth hanging open. The woman was taking off her safari shirt right there in the yard, and in a few seconds she was wearing nothing but her shorts and topsiders. Her breasts were small, but they were still breasts, and they were right out there in the open.

Stella looked over. "Models and dancers," she said, shaking her head. "No shame." Cesar tried once again to speak, but once again he was interrupted. For the second time in twenty-four hours and on the same block as before, he heard a woman screaming in terror.

"Chips! Oh, *God!* Chips! For God's *sake!* Help! Someone! *Help!*"

If this is another damned rat . . .

Cesar had ducked under the clotheslines and out Stella's alley door and was sprinting down the alley parallel to Abigail Street, following the direction of the screams. He came to a two-story garage behind one of the houses on Abigail. The woman sounded like she was on the other side. Cesar grappled with the garage door, but it was locked. He scooted over to an iron gate at the end of a garage, pushed it in, and ran into the yard.

"What is . . . ?" He stopped because he couldn't see anyone.

"Over here! Oh, God, come *quick!*"

Cesar looked at the back of the house. There was a woman crouched in a sort of dead-end space where the house was stepped back and another house butted up to it. He ran over.

What he saw first was a big air-conditioning unit. What he saw next was a pair of male legs clothed in hiking shorts and topsiders sticking out from under the unit.

"Help me!" The woman started screaming again. "Help me get it off him!" Cesar felt one of the ankles quickly.

The leg was cold and there was no pulse. "Oh, Chips!" The lady had started crying. "Chips, what *happened?*"

Cesar moved over and tried to pick up the air conditioner, but it was too big to get both arms around. He heaved up on one side. "Can you get the other side?" he asked the woman. She wiped her eyes and stood up. Cesar finally recognized her as the blond woman who had barged into the McDowells' house. Couldn't forget those legs. She grabbed the other side of the air conditioner and was able to raise it a couple of inches, but she quickly set it down and started sobbing again. "I can't . . . I can't . . ."

"Come on, Sandy. Let me do it." Cesar looked up to see who had spoken. They had been joined by a middle-aged man with a beard who seemed to know the lady. Sandy stepped out and the man with the beard got his hands under the air conditioner. Cesar and the man looked at each other and then heaved the machine upward. There was some sort of sharp flange underneath, and Cesar thought he was going to lose his fingers. Together they manhandled the big unit back into the yard and set it down. Cesar went over to look at the man on the ground. He was dead all right. From the look of him, he had been there awhile. Cesar felt the man's polo shirt. It was soaked except where it had been covered by the air conditioner. He must have been lying there since before it rained last night. Cesar couldn't tell whether his ribs were crushed or not. Cesar felt a crowd growing behind him. He stood up and turned around. The man with the beard was still beside him.

"You know him?" asked Cesar, looking at the body.

"I do. We're neighbors. His name's Reber."

"Is that his wife?"

"Girlfriend. She lives here."

"Is there a phone around I can use?" asked Cesar.

"Sure. My wife's calling the rescue squad, if that's what you want to do."

"I think we're too late for that."

"Looks like it," said the man.

"Is there somebody around who can take care of her?" Cesar pointed to Reber's girlfriend.

"I can. I know her. My wife will be out here in a second. They know each other."

"*No!*" screamed the woman. "I don't want Greta! You keep her out of here! You hear me?" And then she started to wail into her hands.

"Jesus!" mumbled the man.

The rescue squad had come and gone, and Cesar had encouraged the crowd to clear out of the yard. A couple of women had taken Reber's girlfriend into the house, and Cesar was standing talking to the bearded man when Stella came in from the alley.

"Nick!" she said. "Somebody said Chips is dead! Who killed him? What happened?"

"Nobody killed him, Stell. He had an accident. He must have been putting in that air conditioner when it fell on him. He shouldn't have tried to do it by himself."

"God! That's awful! I mean it's really terrible!"

"Pretty bad," said Nick. He was staring at the air conditioner. "Weird, though. He must have been trying to put it in backward, the way it was sitting."

And then Stella said, "Maybe Sandy pushed it on him."

The two men turned to look at her.

"Well." She stuck her chin out. "Don't look at me like I'm crazy, Nick. She's such a bitch."

"And if she didn't, anybody else could have."

"Why would anybody want to?" asked Cesar.

"You didn't know him," said Stella. "If you did, you'd understand. Everybody hated his guts. Even me."

6

"DETECTIVE FRANCK? Oh, Detective Franck!"

Oh, no. Cesar swung his chair around. Sergeant Evans was not a sweet man. He had never been a sweet man. When he used a sweet voice, you knew you were in for it.

"May we have a little talk?" asked the sergeant.

Cesar got up from his desk and trudged across the room. He sat down facing Sergeant Evans.

"Are you comfy?"

Comfy? What did I do? I'm sorry. Jeez, I'm sorry.

"Yeah, I'm okay."

"Good. I have some little questions for you. Do you have time for a couple of little questions?"

"Sure."

"Good. Here's my first little question. If you find the body of a person, and if that person is dead, and if that body has a little round hole where you don't usually find little *round* holes, what comes to your mind?"

Oh, no.

"The guy's been shot. What—"

"No, no, no, Detective Franck. Just wait." Sergeant Evans fiddled around with his chair, getting more comfortable, dragging it out. "Now. If you find the body of a person, and if that body has a fairly large, caved-in, sort of bloody place in the skull where you don't usually expect to find a big, caved-in, bloody place, what do you *usually* think?"

"Come on, Sergeant, what's the—"

"I said wait, Franck."

"Right."

"Now, what's your answer?"

"The guy was battered with something."

"Good. I'm glad you know that. Now, this next one's a little bit harder. Or it probably will be for you. Some other detectives might have a little easier time with it. Some others might not ever know the answer.

"If you find the body of a person, and that person has three wounds in the back, and those wounds aren't little round holes, but they are sort of this long"—Sergeant Evans held his thumb and index finger about an inch and a half apart—"but only this wide"—he moved his finger so that it was about a quarter of an inch from his thumb—"and those wounds are near the center of the back, slightly to the left of the spine, over the heart you might say, what might you think had happened to that person?"

Oh, Jeez. Reber?

"Stabbed."

"Oh! You know it. You do know it. I thought you did. But you know, I just had to make sure. You see, I was reading the report of the medical examiner in the matter of one Herman Reber, a guy who died of three stab wounds where somebody either was very skillful or very lucky since two of the wounds extended into Mr. Reber's heart, and what do you know? I find in the material referred to the homicide squad that one of my favorite policemen, Cesar Franck, was on the scene when Mr. Reber was found. I also find that Cesar Franck let the rescue squad shovel this guy up and dump him off at General, and doesn't make any mention of the matter of three holes where what appears to have been a hunting knife went into Mr. Reber. Why is that, Cesar? Off duty? Tired? Blinded by the sun? *What happened, Franck?*"

"Reber was stabbed?"

"Yes, Reber was stabbed. What do you think I've been talking about. What happened, Cesar? How did you miss that? When you saw him, what did you think? How am I supposed to explain this to Lieutenant Tieves? What am *I* supposed to think? What did you think he died from?"

"The air conditioner."

Sergeant Evans put his hand to his cheek and his head vibrated for a second.

"He had this air conditioner on him," said Cesar. "I thought it fell on him, you know. His girlfriend. . . . He was working on it. Well, you should have seen it. It was a great big Airtemp. I could barely lift it, and I had help. Believe me, it was big enough to kill you if it fell on you." He looked hopefully at the sergeant. "Didn't you ever try to put one in?"

Sergeant Evans shook his head and stared at Cesar.

"So I thought. . . . The girl was going to pieces. . . . I . . . I should have checked."

"Right. You should have checked. You're going to check. It's your case, Detective Franck. You clean it up."

"Sure."

"Can you do it?"

"Whattaya mean, can I do it? Sure."

"You won't forget what a stab wound looks like?"

"Come on, Sergeant. They were in his back. He was *on* his back. And it looked to me like his ribs were caved in. Did the report say anything about his ribs being caved in? I mean regardless of whether he was stabbed, that sucker weighed a ton, and it fell on him and it was enough to kill a guy, believe me."

Sergeant Evans glared at Cesar for a couple of seconds. "I don't know, Detective Franck. Read the report. All I know for sure is that the examiner says he was stabbed to death and that you're assigned. Go."

I still say that Airtemp could kill anybody.

"I'm going."

    * * *

Cesar walked. It was only a couple of blocks from District One to Abigail Street. He wished it were a lot farther so he could figure out just what the hell happened. Jeez. The guy had a piece of machinery as big as a Chevette sitting on him. Who's going to say, "Remember to check for stab wounds as soon as we get this six-hundred-pound load off his chest"? Sure as hell not Sergeant Evans. He'd be huffing and puffing to get the damned air conditioner off just like anybody else. Lieutenant Tieves? He would have been too busy comforting the sharp-looking widow. Except she isn't a widow. She's a girlfriend with a dead boyfriend.

Cesar was heading south on John Street. The buildings on his left were just like the ones on Central and Abigail, only none of them were fixed up yet. Since they looked across the street to the projects, they would probably be the last to get the treatment. What a dumb place to live. It's just asking for trouble. Reber was lucky that that was the first bad thing that happened to him. Okay. Not so lucky. But there are a lot of nice, safe neighborhoods, lots of nice suburbs with plenty of houses that don't need fixing up.

He turned left onto Abigail. The mobile lab was parked a little way down the block in front of Reber's building. Cesar looked up into the Sharps' front window. A couple of cats were sitting in the greenery, and they gave him the evil eye. There was a white wino standing in the little front yard of the house next to Reber's. He was watching the guys from the lab, offering his advice from time to time. When Cesar passed him, he started singing "The Tennessee Waltz."

Cesar turned into Reber's yard and headed for the back. Before they recognized Cesar, the guys from the lab started to yell at him to stay out. One of them, Don Leicht, straightened up from where he had been squatting by the big Airtemp and came over.

"This is a weird one," he said, pulling out a Merit and lighting up. "What were you doing here? I heard you found the guy."

"I didn't find him, Don. His girlfriend did."

"The one in there?" Don squinted up at Reber's building and Cesar nodded. "She is a babe, Ceez, a real babe."

"Did you talk to her?"

"Just for a second. She wanted to know what we were doing. And listen, she had one of those short robes, you know? Just barely covers her butt. And spaced out on something. I tell you, they don't make widows like that real often."

Cesar agreed. "What have you found? Anything?" he asked.

"Couple of prints. Probably his. It was a new unit, I guess. There was a plastic wrapper in the garbage. We're taking it in. Sucker weighs a ton. I can see why you thought it killed him. Damn near killed me trying to lift it."

Leicht was always complaining about something.

"How about the knife?" asked Cesar.

Leicht took a drag off his cigarette and shrugged. "It's not in the yard. We're taking the garbage in with us. I've got a couple of guys out in the alley. Be surprised if they find it. Would you drop it?"

It was Cesar's turn to shrug. The guy didn't take the air conditioner with him, but that was different.

"No," said Leicht. "You'd have to be really dumb to leave something like that around."

"Hey, Don. You don't have to be smart to be mean."

"Sure, but you really have to be stupid not to get rid of a piece of evidence like that."

Cesar didn't feel like arguing. Leicht was just running his mouth to keep from working. Cesar let him talk but tuned him out. He looked over in the corner where Sandy had found Reber and tried to remember exactly how Reber and the air conditioner had lain before he got so helpful and moved it off. The cooling unit was covered up now.

"Hey, Don," Cesar interrupted, "can I take a look at the air conditioner for a second?"

"Sure." Leicht flicked his cigarette over the fence and into the alley, then walked over and pulled the cloth off the Airtemp.

Two of the corners were smashed in. One worse than the other. There were a couple of scratches. Reber hadn't put the control cover on yet, and the cord was still coiled and tied up.

"We found a little bit of cloth stuck here." Leicht pointed to one of the sharp, uncrumpled corners. "Green nylon, looks like. What was he wearing?"

"Tan shorts. White T-shirt."

"Nothing green?"

"Nope," said Cesar.

"Well, we'll take a look at it," said Leicht. He made it sound like a favor instead of his job.

"Thanks," said Cesar. He walked over to the spot where Reber was lying yesterday. The concrete pavement that covered the half of the yard closest to the house continued in to the corner where Reber must have been working. It was cooler where Cesar stood. He looked up. Reber's building was three full stories, and the ceilings were high, so it must have been forty feet up to the gutter. Maybe more, since the first floor was four or five feet off the ground. Cesar got a little dizzy looking up the wall. There was a little patch of blue sky at the top of the shaft, but the sun probably didn't get in real often. His eye traveled back down an iron downspout. Somebody had painted within the last few years, but rust was already starting to work through. He looked up at the wall of the building next-door. One window on each of the second and third floors looked out into the skinny cut-out corner of Reber's house. He turned around and looked across the backyard. Reber's garage ran nearly the width of the yard. The upstairs windows were dirty and it looked uninhabited. He could see a little bit of the alley through the passage running beside the garage, the one he had come through yesterday. The garage cut off most of the view of the houses on Franklin Street. He turned back around. The ground-floor window stood open in the short wall of Reber's house. Somebody—Reber probably—had rigged a short platform under the window. Cesar stepped up and peered over the sill. He was looking into a bedroom. Messy. Stereo gear all over one wall. Mirrors on the sliding closet doors. Big plants. He figured this was the spot for the air conditioner.

Cesar turned around and looked down at the pavement, trying to remember how the Airtemp and the body had been situated. Reber had been lying on his back, his legs pointed out toward the garage. And the window unit had sat squarely on his chest. Balanced, almost, now that he remembered. Jeez. That should have told him something. He had just assumed that the air conditioner fell on him. Well, that wasn't completely dumb. Cesar was pretty sure he noticed those crumpled corners yesterday. It must have fallen sometime. He looked down at the chalked circles on the pavement. If those were bloodstains in the circles, he sure hadn't noticed them. Why should he? There were all kinds of stains and dirt on the concrete. As he was stepping down from the platform, he heard voices from the alley.

"Hey! Hey, you! Hold it! Hold it there!"

"Me? What? Hey, what is this?"

"Just hold it."

Cesar jogged through the passageway by the garage and out into the alley. Two cops were holding the guy with the beard who had helped Cesar lift the burden from Chips Reber.

"What's going on?" asked Cesar, and then he told the cops, both young, who he was.

"Take a look at that," said the bigger cop. "We were out here looking for a knife and this guy came through from John Street right past us. I almost didn't see it."

Cesar looked. He remembered the guy's name now. Nick. A hunting knife was sticking out of the pocket of Nick's hiking shorts.

"Where'd you get that?" asked the big cop.

"Let me handle this, all right?" The guy was getting on Cesar's nerves. "Where'd you get that?"

"L. L. Bean," said Nick. He wasn't real happy with his situation.

"Can I see it?" asked Cesar.

"Sure." Nick fished it out and handed it, grip first, to Cesar. Cesar held it carefully at the edge of the finger guard. The knife looked like it had been around. The leather on the handle was worn smooth in spots, and the blade had been sharpened many times.

"You sure this is yours?"

"I'm sure. It's got my initials on it."

Cesar brought the knife up to his eyes and turned his head sideways. There was a faint *NG* scratched into the handle, and the mark was old.

"How come you're walking around with it?"

"Well, I'm not looking to stab anybody with it, that's for sure," said Nick. He shot a dirty look at the big cop. "I found it back here in the alley. It's been missing for months. Somebody took it out of my house."

"Did you have a break-in?"

"No. One of our upstanding neighborhood residents took it at a meeting. We had a meeting at our house."

"Where did you find it?" asked Cesar. Nick pointed to a spot down the alley in the direction of Central Avenue.

"It was lying right out in the open, right beside that fence."

Nuts. If that wasn't Stella Hineman's fence, it was pretty close.

"But somebody must have just dropped it last night or the night before. I go through here a lot, so I would have seen it. Can I have it back?"

"Sorry." Cesar shook his head. "Got to hang onto it for a while."

"Hey, wait a minute! It's mine. What do you want it for? I just got the damned thing back."

Cesar handed the knife to the smaller man, who looked like he might be Detective Schmidtmeier's younger brother, and the policeman put it in a Baggie.

"I guess you haven't heard about Reber," said Cesar. Nick shook his head, so Cesar told him the bad news. Nick's mouth hung open the whole time.

"Jesus," said Nick when Cesar had finished, and then, "Jeeezus!" He seemed to have remembered something that upset him even more, and he went over to lean against Reber's big old garage door. He stared down at his feet.

"You know something about it?" asked Cesar.

"What?" Nick looked up at the detective. "Oh. No. I was just thinking about how I'm going to tell his son. My stepson. My wife." He looked back down at his shoes. "Chips was my wife's first husband. We've got custody of their son. It was bad enough telling him his father was dead. Now I've got to tell him he was murdered."

Cesar stood in Reber's front yard. He had let Nicholas Grimes go back home after he found out where he lived and that Grimes was an architect working out of an office over his garage. "Carriage house," was what he called it. That was probably what Reber called his garage too. At first Cesar thought that was a phony thing to say, but then he realized that every last building on Abigail Street was built way before cars hit the streets.

He was putting off going in to see Reber's house and girlfriend. He wondered about Grimes and Reber and what it was like to have your wife's first husband hanging around, living on the same block with you. And he remembered that Stella Hineman said everybody hated Reber. And that made him remember that Grimes said he found the knife behind Stella's house and he didn't want to think about that, so he rang Reber's doorbell.

Cesar peered through the pattern of vines and flowers that decorated the pane in Reber's door. It was dark in the entry hall, but he could make out a pair of long bare legs coming down the staircase. He pulled away from the door and was looking out toward the street when it opened. He turned back to see Sandy Schott in a pair of shorts like Grimes was wearing, and, for that matter, like Reber was wearing when he died. She was even wearing a white T-shirt. Cesar introduced himself.

"Oh!" she said. "You were really a policeman yesterday? When . . . ?" She stopped and pulled a Kleenex out of one of her sixteen pockets and dabbed at her eyes.

"Yes, ma'am. I'm really—"

"Come in. Let me close the door."

He stepped in and blinked. The hall was very dark after standing in the morning sunlight. It was cool, too. Why did Reber need an air conditioner?

"Come on. I live upstairs."

Cesar followed her trim behind up the long staircase. There was thick carpeting underfoot. He slid his hand up the cool wide wooden handrail and tried not to think unprofessional thoughts about the backside in front of him. Finally he took his hand off the handrail and watched Sandy's feet. Which were in sandals. Which were tan. With polished toenails. Jesus.

She led him through a dark paneled door at the top of the stairs. "Get back, Anwar," she said to something that was snuffling and jingling on the other side of the door. "He won't bite," she said to Cesar. Oh shit. A big Doberman was working his head past Sandy, obviously on his way to take a big hunk out of Cesar's belly. "Dammit, Anwar! Get back. We're trying to come in." Sandy grabbed his choke chain and dragged the dog with her into the room. Anwar stepped on Cesar's foot to make sure that Cesar knew he weighed at least as much as the detective. Looked like he was in better shape, too. "Get in the kitchen," she snapped. The dog walked out slowly, looking over his shoulder at the policeman, and then, chains clanking like crazy, settled down under a table where he had a clear view of Cesar's throat.

Sandy shifted some magazines and papers from a sofa and sat down, waving Cesar into the other end. She dabbed at her eyes and said, "I'm still trying to understand about this stabbing. The guy downstairs said"—she stopped to blow her nose—"said that it wasn't an accident, that somebody killed . . ." She started to sob. Cesar waited, and in a few minutes she had stopped. She pulled a pack of cigarettes from between two sofa cushions and lit up. "Are you conducting an investigation?"

"Yes, ma'am."

"Just you?"

"Well, the guys downstairs are looking for any evidence that might help us. But, yes. This is my case."

"Oh." Sandy took a long drag off the cigarette and sucked it all the way to the bottom of her lungs.

"Do you—" Cesar started to ask if anyone was staying with her when she finally blew out her smoke and then interrupted him.

"I guess I'm not surprised. Not really." She leaned back in the corner of the sofa and looked straight into Cesar's eyes. "These people down here are the meanest bunch I've ever seen. I wouldn't put anything past them. Nothing. They've had it in for Chips from the time he got here, and when they couldn't get to him, they tried to get to me. And I can tell you why, if you want to know."

"Sure."

"Greta. Greta Grimes." She stubbed out her cigarette. "You're going to hear a lot of shit about how Chips was doing the wrong thing for the neighborhood and all kinds of bullshit about the way he rehabbed his buildings, but it's all just that. Bullshit. They had it in for him from the beginning because of Greta."

"Greta Grimes? She's married to Nicholas Grimes?"

Sandy nodded and reached for another cigarette.

"And she was—"

"Chips's wife. *Ex*-wife," snapped Sandy.

"And they had a son."

"H.P."

"And he's with Mrs. Grimes."

"He's with Greta. *Of course.* The most wonderful mother in the whole world." She glared at her dog. "Bitch."

The dog whined, but he stayed under the table.

"Do you—"

"The whole neighborhood—and I mean *everybody*—thinks she's so wonderful and they hated Chips, but let me tell you, Greta Grimes is a bad-tempered, selfish, hypocritical bitch. And I *know* she had something to do with this." All of a sudden, Sandy, who had seemed angry but in control, started to cry. Buckets. Big sobs. And Cesar sat there wondering why he didn't feel any worse, since he usually embarrassed himself by getting teary-eyed when a widow let loose. He stayed on the sofa while Sandy stomped over to a bookshelf for a fresh Kleenex. The dog stood up and started to growl. "Oh, Anwar, shut up." And she stopped crying. "He probably thinks you're making me cry."

"Miss Schott, I—"

"Did you know . . . ? You couldn't. Chips was trying to get joint custody of H.P. His attorney was working on it. It was my idea. I don't see why *she* should go around acting like she's the only one who knows what's good for him. She wasn't any better a parent than Chips. But oh God, you would have thought she was Mother Theresa around here."

"So you—"

"I think you ought to go over and arrest her. Or her husband. Or both. I can tell you right now they had something to do with Chips getting killed. And they'll act so terrific and surprised and they'll tell you *I'm* crazy, and everyone on the block will leap to their defense, but you ask, just ask them if they got a letter from Chips's attorney and see if that doesn't shake them up. Bastards."

No sobs. Just smoke.

Cesar had opened his notebook and was writing. Sandy said, "That's G. R. E. T. A."

"Right," said Cesar. "Now would you mind telling me anything you know about what Mr. Reber was doing Saturday night? Were you here?"

"No. I was with a friend out in Hyde Park. Mimi Collins. She lives in the Regency. I was there until the rain started and it started to get cooler. It was too hot to stay here. That's why Chips was putting in that god-damned air conditioner."

"Don't you have central air? It feels like it."

"Oh, it's not bad now, but that's because it's not too bad outside. And the high ceilings help. But it was just unbelievable Saturday. I went out to Mimi's right after supper."

"What happened when you came back?"

"I went to bed. Well . . . I looked for Chips first, but his door was locked and he didn't answer, so I came up here."

"Does he li— Did he live downstairs?"

She nodded. "We had our own spaces. I have to have my own space. He was fixing this up as three apartments, and he let me have this. He stayed downstairs since he . . . Just a second." The phone was ringing. Sandy ran out into the kitchen to answer. She was out of sight, so Cesar didn't even pretend not to listen.

"Yes? . . . What? . . . What . . . Oh! It's you . . ." And then there was the ear-splitting sound of a shriller and the bang of the phone into its hook.

"Creep!" yelled Sandy. "I hope I blew your eardrum wide open!" Anwar whined. "Not you, stupid." She came back into the living room. "God, I hate that son of a bitch. I hope I really hurt him."

"Obscene call?" asked Cesar.

"Some pervert has been calling about twice a week ever since I moved in here. And it's the same stuff every time." She shuddered. "What a sicko. I wish Chips had caught him before . . ." Her voice trailed off.

"It's hard to catch them, Miss Schott."

"I know. But Chips was working on it. He said he had a way. I don't know how."

"I'm sorry. I know they're a real pain. That whistle ought to help."

"It hasn't so far. I think he knows it's coming," she said. Cesar tapped his pen on his notebook, bringing them back to Saturday night.

"Did you have any idea where Mr. Reber was on Saturday? Had he planned to be out?"

"I don't think so. But he was in and out a lot. I mean it wasn't a big deal that he wasn't in. He had a lot going. So I just came up here."

"And then you were looking for him on Sunday? I thought I saw you at one of the houses across the street."

"Oh? The McDowells'."

"Right. And your house was supposed to be open?"

"Not mine. Just Chips's apartment. I didn't want anybody in here, but he wanted people to see the building and the kind of apartment he could make. He was going to fix up some more, and he wanted the advertising."

"So he owned other buildings around here?"

Sandy nodded. "He's got the one across the street with the bay that's already fixed up and rented, and a couple more on that side that he was fixing up. Oh, and three on Franklin Street."

"That's a lot of property."

"Oh, he was really into it. He had a couple of buildings in Avondale, but he got rid of them. He thought this was going to be really big. I guess it is."

"How long had he been down here?"

"I don't know. Three years, I guess. He was going great guns, though. Which is another reason everybody hated him. He was too successful."

"A little jealousy?"

"For sure. Only everybody *said* they just didn't like the way he did things. I mean he caught all kinds of shit from the idiots down here. *Including* Nick and Greta. But he also caught it from the Victorians and the poverty workers and even from people who should have been *glad* to have him down here. Chips was the only one who was starting to make money off of this place. Everybody else on the block was too busy fooling around with wallpaper and brass doorknobs to get ahead. Really stupid. And the poverty workers. God! Those idiots wanted his ass in jail. They're nuts. All of them."

"Displacement?"

"You got it. They actually tried to get him into court. You would have thought he was throwing old ladies out into the street every day before breakfast."

"Who are the Victorians?"

"Preservationists. They've got an office over on Central Avenue. They're not as disgusting as the poverty workers, but they've got a huge pile of money."

She thought for a moment.

"You better take a good look at Sonny Werk."

"Why?"

"You know who he is?"

Cesar nodded.

"Well, that maniac actually had pickets down here once. Chips threw a couple of them off the sidewalk and you would have thought he had done something really serious. Sonny went nuts. Threatened all kinds of things. But Chips bought him off."

"How?"

"Well, I told him it was really stupid, but he gave a bunch of money to Sonny's dumb-ass outreach center. Oh, and a computer."

"No kidding."

"Yeah. He had an Apple and he wanted a Lisa, so he wrote the Apple off his income tax. And that shut Sonny up for a while, but he went crazy again when Chips bought those last buildings across the street."

"What happened?"

"It was silly. Stupid. There were a couple of welfare families in there that hadn't paid any rent for months. The buildings were in an estate. Well, when Chips bought the place, he went over to see them about the rent. They said they didn't have to pay . . . that Sonny told them they had some kind of rights. Well, of course, after they didn't pay the back rent or the first couple of months after Chips bought the buildings, he had them evicted. What was he supposed to do? He was losing money, for God's sake. And, get this, he had even offered to move them over to Franklin Street, where they wouldn't have to pay so much. But Sonny went nuts anyway. Called him fifty times a day. But Chips must have shut him up somehow. He hasn't called for a week."

"Then it's okay with Sonny?"

"Well." Sandy lit up again and started fooling around with her toes. "Chips might have leaned on him a little."

"What do you mean?"

"You know. Leaned."

"Threatened him?"

"Not exactly. It's just that Chips liked to know things about people he had to deal with. And sometimes he knew things that were kind of surprising. Like that."

If you mean blackmail, why don't you say so?

"So maybe you should check and see what Sonny was doing Saturday after you check up on the Grimeses, who'll probably lie anyway. And you just watch; everybody on the block will back them up. The assholes."

Cesar stood up. "I'll be talking to most of the neighbors, Miss Schott. Believe me, I'm used to hearing a lot of different views. I'm just interested in finding out what happened." He picked up his notebook from the sofa. "Is there any way I can get in to take a look downstairs? I'd like to have a look around."

"I don't know how. I don't have a key. Chips had it. He wouldn't make a copy for me."

Cesar looked at her.

"I lose things," she said.

He crawled in through the window. It wasn't easy. The platform that Reber had rigged just put Cesar's chin at the level of the sill. He scuffed up his shoes and scraped his stomach, but he got in.

It was funny. Even with all of Reber's hotshot furniture and electronic gadgets, there was the same feeling in the apartment as there was in any dead person's house. People never expect to get murdered. Or almost never. They always leave a place expecting to come back. Nobody straightens up for the death squad.

Reber's bed was unmade. There were clothes on the floor and on the armchair. Cesar stuck his fist into the waterbed and watched it wobble. Then he walked around the bedroom, nosing into things.

The closet held about six thousand dollars' worth of leather sport coats, leather bomber jackets, and even a couple pairs of leather pants. There were thirty or forty shoes scattered on the floor in no order, but they were all expensive-looking. Guccis.

There was marijuana in a plastic bag on the wooden cube that served as a nightstand. There was also a space-age remote control for the television and VCR on the wall across from the foot of the bed. Cesar fooled around with it until there was a whirr from the recorder and a hum from the TV.

Holy smoke!!

Sandy Schott was stark naked. Right there on the screen. He walked to the end of the bed and sat down, never taking his eyes from the television. It was here. Right here in the room. There was the nightstand and the waterbed and . . . holy smoke again! There was the late Chips Reber. Naked as a jaybird and primed for action. Cesar looked around for a second and spotted the camera sitting on a tripod back beside a big chest of drawers. He snapped back to the screen. Unbelievable. He had never seen anybody in real life look like Sandy Schott doing what Sandy Schott was doing. And Reber! How could he do that in front of a camera? Holy smoke. Cesar thought he heard a noise in the front of the apartment, so he dived for the remote control and started punching buttons like a madman. For a while he was stuck with "The Price Is Right," but he finally got the whole system to shut down.

He found his way to the front door and fiddled with the locks until it opened. Sandy Schott was standing in the hall hanging on to Anwar.

"You got in," she said. Cesar nodded. He couldn't talk, looking at her and remembering her video antics. "I've got to take him out." Anwar was nearly dragging her out of the front door. "Let me know if you need anything. Okay? And if the phone rings upstairs, could you try to get it?" Cesar nodded again. "Terrific."

He closed and locked the door and looked around. He was in Reber's living room. It was the same size and shape as the McDowells', but Chips didn't go in for green and yellow and vegetables. Chips was into modern. Two identical eight-foot-long sofas faced each other on either side of the fireplace, and between them were two polished marble cubes instead of a coffee table. Each of the cubes had a couple of pieces of Mexican-looking pottery and nothing else sitting on top. The cubes sat on a woolly rug, also maybe from Mexico. Reber had bought two of those floor lamps that start from the floor and, eighteen feet of chrome later, end in a light bulb that floats over your head. Three big trees sat in purplish-brown pots over by the front window. It looked to Cesar like they needed water. The long leaves were droopy and dull. Cesar went to the window that wasn't blocked by plants and looked out. The buildings right across the street looked abandoned. Halfway down the block he could see Arthur Battle's house, but Arthur wasn't out front. Henry said he was retired. He turned around to look at the living room again. Chips hadn't gotten around to hanging any pictures. The light brown walls were completely bare. The only decoration was the thick white woodwork around the doors and windows, and a wide plaster molding running around the ceiling. There were no bookshelves, no whatnots, no consoles, no desk. Who wants to read if you've got Sandy Schott on tape?

Cesar circled the big couches and went into the next room. More modern. Big chrome-and-glass dining table and six seats that looked like they came out of a customized van. That was it except for a little statue on the mantel. He walked over and looked. Naked lady.

The kitchen was space-age and big. The side-by-side fridge looked small under a fifteen-foot ceiling. Reber had bought enough cabinets for two kitchens. For that matter, he had two sinks. The cabinet doors all rolled or slid instead of opening like real cabinets. Very slick.

Black countertops. Brown quarry tile on the floor. The door on the built-in microwave stood open. The box from a package of Stouffer's lasagna lay nearby on the counter, and over on a breakfast counter sat the tray that used to hold the lasagna. There was a dirty fork in the tray and two empty Miller cans next to it. A magazine lay open on the counter. Cesar flipped it over; *Popular Computing*.

He found the hall leading to the back rooms. The first room must have been for Reber's son. There was a single bed, a fifteen-inch color set, a ten-speed bike that looked like it was just out of the store, a soccer ball, a punching bag, a pile of Atari cassettes. There was also a lot of dust.

Bathroom next. This guy had too much money. Or terrific credit. Jacuzzi, of course. Sauna. Shower. Two basins. All built into tile-and-marble walls and floors. The toilet needed cleaning, though. So did the basin. The soap-and-whisker crud was a half inch thick.

Somebody was banging on a door someplace. Cesar went back to the kitchen and opened doors until he found one going out into a stair hall with a door to the outside. He opened it and let Don Leicht come in.

"She told me you got in," said Leicht. "I'll tell you, if she didn't have that Doberman with her . . ." He rolled his eyes and looked pained. Maybe he thought he looked sexy.

"She's something," said Cesar.

"Hey," said Don, looking around the kitchen. "Who'd of believed there was stuff like this down in the ghetto! This must have cost a fortune!"

Cesar agreed. Leicht took a fast stroll through the front rooms, whistling in amazement. He stopped to stroke the breasts on the little statue in the dining room. "No way I could bring something like that in the house. Margie would bust it over my head." He came back into the kitchen, where Cesar had been waiting. "It don't look burgled," said Leicht. Cesar shook his head. "What about in back, where the window was open?"

"Looks okay," said Cesar. "There's a lot of electronics back there. They don't look torn up." He led Leicht back through the hall. Leicht stopped to check out the bathroom.

"Oooohhh!" he moaned in agony. "That guy had that girl and this bathroom in one house! What a way to go!"

"Come on, Don."

"Did you see this?"

"I saw it."

"I could die happy with a setup like this."

Cesar pried him out of the bathroom and took him to Reber's bedroom, and of course Leicht had to carry on for a while about the bedroom and what he could do with it, so Cesar nosed around to see what he had missed while he was watching video funtime.

He had missed the computer and everything on a big drafting table. Sandy said something about an Apple and a Lisa, and the computer said it was Lisa. He didn't know how to turn it on, much less run it. There were a couple of green account books on the desk along with a million papers and stacks of computer paper. Cesar was starting to get into the accounts when Don found the magic buttons.

"Oh, God! No! Oh, *Christ!* No! I don't believe . . . oooh! Cesar, will you *look* for Christ's sake?! Oooohhhhhh!"

Cesar didn't have to look.

"I saw it, Don."

He went back to the account books. One of them seemed to be rents and building expenses. There was an entry for Stella Hineman. The other book wasn't so easy to figure out. There were a lot of coded entries and initials and a few names like Luis and Ramon. He flipped through a few more pages and found names like Pete and Arn and then there was Stella again. Cesar closed the journals and picked them up.

"Don. Hey, Don." Don was hypnotized. "Hey!"

"I think I'm dying."

"Yeah, right. Listen, are you and your guys going to go over this place?"

Leicht nodded without taking his eyes from the TV screen.

"Well, I'm leaving, okay?"

Leicht nodded again.

"Don, if the phone rings upstairs, she wants you to get it, okay? Did you hear me?"

"I heard you, Ceez. Answer the phone. Right. See you later."

"Right."

7

IT WAS CESAR'S turn to pick where to eat lunch, so he and Henry were at the Queensgate Frisch's. Henry was pouting because he hated Frisch's, or said he did, but he always finished a Buddy Boy platter with no problem. Sometimes he had strawberry pie, too, but he never stopped pouting. That wasn't fair, because Cesar never pouted when Henry dragged him up to some hole-in-the-wall up on Burnet Avenue or out in Madisonville where the menu was always full of soul food that looked to Cesar like it had been cooking since slave days. And if you really wanted to get into it, Cesar never made Henry go up to the Price Hill for overcooked white people's food. Frisch's was for anybody who needed tartar sauce.

Cesar spent a good three minutes going over the familiar menu even though he knew he was going to have a Big Boy platter with onion rings instead of fries. Henry always spent at least ten minutes over the soul-food menus and then always ordered whatever the waitress told him was the special.

The waitress today was Bonnie, which meant they had to talk fast since she did her job on the run. She wouldn't stop and shoot the breeze for anybody, not even Henry. She ran. When she had taken their orders and whipped their menus out of their hands, Cesar started to tell

Henry about his morning. He already knew about Henry's morning, which had started late and gone downhill.

As soon as Cesar described Chips, Henry recognized him as the man who had offered to take Arthur's house off his hands as well as the man who got slapped on the sidewalk Saturday. He was telling Cesar about the connection when Bonnie raced up with their platters. Cesar nearly had to tackle her to slow her down so he could order some extra tartar sauce. Henry looked out the window, ashamed of his colleague.

Cesar was interested in Uncle Arthur and the house offer, but not half as interested as Henry was in Sandy Schott and the action-filled videotape. He simply could not hear enough, but the thing about Henry was that he wasn't interested in what they did. Nobody did it better than Henry, so he had nothing to learn. He was just fascinated with their doing it for the camera.

"Ee ab a zoonglenz?" asked Henry.

"Mmmff?" asked Cesar.

Henry chewed and swallowed his massive bite of Buddy Boy and repeated, "He have a zoom lens?"

Cesar caught a blob of tartar sauce working its way down his chin before he answered, "Beats me. How could I tell?"

"Close-ups."

"Oh." Cesar chopped up an onion ring and drowned it in catsup before he said, "Must have."

They ate for a while, Henry imagining, Cesar remembering. Then Henry said, "You better go see Uncle Arthur. The man knows everything that goes on on that block, even with white folks."

"I was going to ask you about that. He wasn't outside this morning."

"He wouldn't be. Gets up early and goes out."

"What for?"

Henry dumped two Sweet 'n Lows into his coffee and said, "He patrols."

"Walks around?"

"Sees everything. Goes for miles." Henry sipped his

coffee and then smiled to himself. Finally he said, "He used to drag me around on his walks when I went down and stayed with him. He'd talk to everybody that was up. Tell me who lived where, what they did, who was tough, who was crazy, that sort of stuff."

"Old cop on the beat, hunh?"

"He used to." Henry started laughing. "He used to go in peoples' *yards* if they weren't up. Just to see what was happening. Look at their trash. I wouldn't go in because I thought folks would come out and shoot us, but he'd just bust right in. He even used to wake people up if their yards was a mess. Get them out of *bed*. Told them they were attracting rats." He laughed again. "Nobody stopped him. Never. You go see him. Tell him I told you to."

So, after dropping Henry off at District One, Cesar drove back to Dutchtown. He took a little detour down Franklin Street to see what kind of places Reber might own. He took a peek at Stella Hineman's house, too, but she wasn't out. He got caught in the one-way traffic on Central Avenue and wound up at District One before he got headed back down John Street on the way to Franklin. The gents in the craps game at the east end of the project got a little nasty on his second trip past, but he didn't want to play.

This time Arthur Battle was out on his stoop. Cesar waved and drove up the block until he found a spot in front of the McDowells' place. Arthur came down to his gate to meet Cesar.

"How you doing, Frank? I thought I recognized that Camaro."

"Fine. I guess I ought to wash it."

"Clean car runs better."

"That's what they say. You got a minute, Mr. Battle?"

"I got a lot more time than you, boy. Come on up and sit down."

Cesar remembered the chair from his last visit, so he

sat down carefully. It was still a thrilling ride to the bottom.

"Henry called me," said Arthur. "He said you're on the case for the fella across the street."

"Right."

"Why didn't they put Henry on it?"

Why didn't you teach Henry how to ask straight out like you do? "Rotation. I was up next."

"Henry says the boy was stabbed in the heart."

"That's right, Mr. Battle." Cesar figured that he was going to have to fill Arthur in on the details if he was going to get any information out of him. So he did.

"Well," said Arthur when Cesar had finished, "isn't that something. And you thought that air conditioner mashed the breath out of the boy. Well."

Cesar waited.

"You know," Arthur finally got started, "it don't surprise me, Frank. It don't."

"How's that, Mr. Battle?"

"Well, in the first place that boy was a show-off. All those gold chains and that Corvette. Boy sort of looked like a white pimp. That always brings the sharks around. And then I got to tell you that I think he was dealing a little."

"Reefer?"

"No, I don't think reefer. Cocaine, more likely. I know he liked to snort sitting right out there in his car, but I've seen him plenty of times when white folks come through in nice cars and pull over to talk to him and it sure looked to me like he was dealing with them. Nice cars. All the time. None of these Price Hill punks looking for reefer in a hot rod. More like your German cars. Sports cars. People with money."

"You ever actually see any transactions?" asked Cesar.

"No. Boy tried to be cool. Always keep things close to him. But you know, you live down here long enough, you get to know it when you see it. You're a policeman. You know what I'm saying."

"I know what you're talking about."

"See? And I'll tell you what else. That boy did an awful lot of dealing in cash. When he bought those buildings over there on Franklin Street, he paid cash. Then he bought these buildings here on this block and he put cash down. Couldn't pay all cash like he did over there. These buildings cost more, don't you know, but he put cash down.

"Now I carry some cash around. I don't like to be without it, you know, but I don't have that kind of cash on me. It ain't right."

"You've got a point, Mr. Battle."

"You want something to drink, Frank?"

"No, thanks."

"I got to get me something. You sure?"

"No, thanks. Really."

Cesar sat and soaked in the scenery, waiting for Arthur. Abigail Street on a quiet Monday afternoon was a far different place from the steamy Saturday evening site of rat explosions and murder. It was different from the confusion and crowds of the Sunday walking tour. There were just a few parked cars and very little traffic. The sidewalks were empty. The weather was still good. From his perch at the top of the stoop Cesar could see the entire block by simply turning his head. It wasn't such a bad place on a morning like this. The old town houses didn't look nearly as bad as the rows of tenements farther east in Over-the-Rhine. In fact they looked kind of nice. They were all about the same size and shape. They all had little bits of front yards, some of them with tough old bushes in front. One or two of them had a mulberry tree. Cesar fell to thinking what the street must have been like when it was new and the houses belonged to regular families. Nice, probably.

And then it turned into a slum. Everybody moved out to the suburbs and left the street to the blacks. There used to be hundreds of blocks like this where the expressway and the projects were now. All filled with blacks. If you were black, you lived in the West End. Right here. Couldn't go anyplace else. And most white people stayed the hell away. Cesar's mother and her friends talked about Linn Street as the most dangerous street in the world. The first time Cesar drove down Linn in his uniform, he was sure he was going to get sniped at every corner. Scared shitless.

But while it wasn't much like the corner of Harrison and Montana, the center of Westwood where Cesar grew up and where he still lived, Linn Street was nothing like the vision his mother and her friends had given him. It was a street full of people doing their business. Black people and black business, sure, but mostly stuff you could understand.

And now the whites were coming back. Not to the projects. Not to Linn Street. But here, and on Dayton Street, and Freeman. What did they want? Chips Reber had enough money to live in Westwood, or even Hyde Park. Why would he want to come down here and mix it up with the natives? And Stella Hineman. Why would a really beautiful girl like that—

"I got you a Coke, Frank. Go on, take it."

"Thanks. Looks good."

Arthur settled back into his chair. "Henry told me to tell you anything I might have seen Saturday night that might have something to do with that fella getting hisself killed, but, you know, I can't think of anything right off. Old Elsie came back and brought her TV so we could watch the fights out in the backyard, and between Howard Cosell and Elsie, there wasn't much getting through. You heard Elsie. She thinks she knows all there is to know about the fights and she likes to tell you about it, so that's what I was listening to. And I didn't get out of the yard. About the only thing I did do was come up this way every now and then to stretch my legs out."

"See anything?"

"Nothing to talk about. I didn't see Reevers or that Corvette he drives. He mostly uses the alley anyways. Parks in back in his garage. Now I did see that white lady that's got the big old Packard. She came through."

"Who's that?"

"Don't know her name, Frank. I just know what she looks like, and her cars. Most days she comes down here in a white Packard convertible and that is a fine car. Smoothest ride you'll ever take. She's got a Jaguar, too. But she was driving the Packard Saturday night. Came through slow and stopped in front of Reevers, but Reevers didn't come out, so I don't know what she was doing. Looks like she was dressed up too. But she was the only thing out of the ordinary. Everybody else just slid on through."

"You didn't hear any fights? Anybody yelling?"

"No. Nothing to pay any attention to. Just the usual Saturday yelling. You know how that is."

"I sure do," said Cesar.

"No. Aside from that lady coming through, there wasn't nothing special happening. Not that I heard. And, like I said, she comes around. I think she must work someplace around here."

"What about Reber? Can you think of anything he's done to get in trouble? Did he get in fights?"

"Is that his name? I've been saying Reevers."

"Reber."

"Well, I thought some about that, too. I told you I think he was messing around with drugs, so you know that. About the only other thing I can think of is he got some people pretty mad at him when he bought that house down the street and those places back there on Franklin. I didn't pay much attention, you know, not when he kicked out the trash down the street. There was a bad crowd in there. Thieves. They had a girl was a whore. And they took to yelling about how he shouldn't be kicking them out. Brought that Sonny Werk in to stir things up. But I was glad to see them go.

"Now, he did treat a family over on Franklin bad. I didn't like that. Nice people. Kind of slow, but nice. I think they always paid their rent on time. Kept the place clean. Nice people. But he went and kicked the rent up on them to where they couldn't pay, and they had to leave. But they didn't make a fuss. So maybe you could check up on these folks from up this block. Adams is their name. Adams. Except they're probably all in the workhouse by now. Ought to be."

"Anyone else?" asked Cesar.

"I'm thinking. But, you know, I want to tell you, all this shit about coming in and kicking folks out down here is just phony. I been watching, and except for Reevers, all the white people that moved either bought themselves old raggedy torn-up places that nobody was living in or else they paid a fair price to the people that owned them. They haven't done any kicking out in the streets except what I told you. They're pretty good neighbors. They've got the block looking a whole lot better than it was. It was real run-down a couple of years back. Got so bad I almost sold this place. But I'm glad I didn't. It's better now."

"It's really pretty quiet. I was just—"

"You know who you ought to talk to, Frank, is Miz Cornbuster across the street. Next-door to Reevers."

"Cornbuster?" asked Cesar.

"Something like that. That's what I call her. It's a German name."

"Which house? The one on this side?"

"No, no. The other one, with all the carving on it. She's an old German lady runs a rooming house. Got it mostly filled with old hillbilly winos, except she's been clearing it out so she's only got a couple now. No, I don't know the people on this side too well. Young couple. White. But I've been knowing Miz Cornbuster a long time now. She was here when I bought this place back in 1955. She's old, and her English is kind of hard to understand sometimes, but she stays on top of things. She's not deaf. Why don't I take you over there? I'll introduce you. She gets kind of suspicious if she don't know you."

"Would you mind?"

"Mind? No! Be a pleasure. I've got to take Sheba out anyway. You just wait here while I get out of these house shoes."

While Arthur went inside, Cesar stood up to stretch.

He walked down the stoop and followed a narrow walk that branched off halfway to the front gate. He peered around the corner of the house and into the side yard. Arthur was lucky. Years ago somebody had planted a couple of hard maples beside the house. They were huge now, almost filling in the space between Arthur's building and the house next-door. There were no windows on the neighbor's house, and Arthur had a garage stretching across the back of his property, so it was private as well as shaded. He had three more of the soft sprung yard chairs grouped around a low metal table near the back of the house. That must have been where Arthur and Elsie watched the fights. What a life.

Cesar heard the front door closing, so he went back to the stoop. Arthur had put on a pair of army boots. He was followed by a big, slow-moving dog.

"This is Sheba," said Arthur. "Poor old Sheba's about lost all her teeth, she's so old."

"She's got some shepherd in her, doesn't she?"

"Shepherd and collie. Half and half."

"Smart dogs," said Cesar.

"Real smart," said Arthur. "Come on, Sheba." Sheba took the steps real carefully. The men let her set the pace as they hit the street. Sheba was in no hurry.

"That's Reever's place." Arthur pointed to a building on his side of the street. "He's got it all fixed up and rented now. I hear he was getting big rents; four hundred and fifty dollars for a one-bedroom." He shook his head in admiration. " 'Course he put in all new kitchens and plumbing." They crossed the street, passing Chips and Sandy's building, stopping in front of the next house. "This is Miz Cornbuster's," said Arthur, and he pushed open the gate, letting Sheba go in first. Cesar followed.

The building looked pretty crummy. Nobody was taking care of it. The front of the house, which seemed to be covered with carved stone, had been painted a dark red years ago, and it was starting to peel, revealing patches of even older brown paint. And there was brown dust on the red paint. A heavy cornice at the top stopped any cleaning a heavy rain might do. The downspouts seemed to be solid rust.

"She can't take care of things too well anymore," said Arthur. He had seen Cesar's look of appraisal. "Used to be she could get some of the winos to do a few things for her, but not anymore. I guess she's too old to try." He stepped up into her entry and banged on the right half of her double door.

They waited a good five minutes. Twice Cesar turned around to leave, but Arthur told him to wait. Finally he saw one of the curtains move behind the pane in the door, and the locks began to clank and rattle. Finally the door opened.

Miz Cornbuster used a walker. She leaned on it and peered out at the men in the entry.

"Is that you, Battle?" she asked. Only she still had a German accent, so she said, "Iss det you, Bettle?"

Arthur greeted her and introduced Cesar as Frank, a detective on the police force.

"What's he want? I don't have crooks here anymore."

"He's not looking for crooks, Miz Cornbuster. He's trying to find out who killed your next-door neighbor."

The old lady opened the door a little farther and inched her walker around a few degrees so that she was aimed at Cesar. "What do you mean killed?" She peered up at him. Then she said, "He was crushed. They told me."

"Somebody stabbed him, Miz Cornbuster. They found the holes."

The old lady slowly raised a hand and placed it on her bosom. She shook her head slowly. "What a place!" she said. "What a terrible place this is now."

"Can he come in and ask you some questions?" asked Arthur.

"Sure," she said, and then she started to back and turn. It took a while. She muttered throughout the process, "What a place. What are you supposed to do these days? My God."

"Miz Cornbuster, I'm just going to leave Frank here

with you. Sheba's expecting to get back outside," said Arthur.

Miz Cornbuster stopped and looked over her shoulder at Arthur and then at Cesar.

"You'll be all right," said Arthur. "This boy's a policeman. He won't do you no harm."

"All right, Battle."

Cesar promised Arthur he would check back with him and thanked him for the Coke, and Arthur and Sheba left for their walk. Cesar followed the old woman as she worked her way into her front room.

It was dark. The granddaddy and grandmother of all wandering Jews had taken over the two front windows, which were dirty. Neither of the two old standing lamps was lit, but Cesar had been in enough old peoples' apartments to know that there was no bulb brighter than forty watts in the house anyway. The lady stopped in front of a big overstuffed chair and waved him into it. She moved on to a wooden rocker and slowly settled in. Cesar had started to stand, intending to help, but she shook her head.

"Oh," she said, "when you get old . . ." She shook her head.

Cesar took out his notebook and asked, "Do I have your name right? Is it Cornbuster?"

"No. It's Kornbrust." She spelled it for him. "Hilda Kornbrust. Miss."

"Sorry. I must have heard wrong."

"That Battle. He never gets it right. You know none of these blacks speaks German. None of them." She shook her head in disgust. "But Battle's pretty nice. He keeps his place clean. Some of them . . . I don't know. This used to be a good place to live. Now . . ."

"It looks to me like it's coming up a little," said Cesar.

"Maybe. Maybe it is. I don't know." She looked toward the window, and Cesar guessed that she was remembering a different place. Finally she looked back at the policeman. "So. You want to know about the boy next-door."

"That's right, ma'am. I'd like to know if you heard or saw anything last Saturday. Something that might help us clear it up. We know that Mr. Reber died sometime before midnight, but that's about it right now."

Hilda Kornbrust shuddered. "See what I mean about this neighborhood? It's changing. It used to be that the blacks only killed each other. They all the time stab each other with their knives, but they used to leave the white people alone because of the police, but now . . . now here they stab a white man on his own property."

"Uh, Miss Kornbrust, we don't know for sure that a black man had anything to do with this yet. We don't have any eyewitnesses. That's why I'm here."

"You don't think it was a black man?"

"I don't know. Could be."

"But you said he was stabbed, this boy. They always like to stab."

"Well . . ." What could he say? The lady's opinions were probably eighty-five years old.

"What did you say his name was?" asked Miss Kornbrust. Cesar spelled it for her.

"See, he never introduced himself to me, so I don't know it. I don't see him unless he goes in and out sometime when I'm on the stoop, and he's always running, so I don't know too much about him except his wife sometimes says good morning. But that's all."

"Did you see him working last Saturday? He was installing an air conditioner in his back room."

"Oh, no. I couldn't see that. I got a chain-link fence and bushes and then he put up that wooden fence, so I can't see in his yard if he's in the back. So I don't even know when he's working back there. Anyway, I don't go in the back too much anymore."

"Were you back there Saturday? Did you maybe hear anything?"

"No. Saturday my niece was here after supper to pick up some washing and we talked for a while, but then I go to bed. I don't watch no television."

"Is your bedroom in back?" asked Cesar.

"No, it's this next room through there." She pointed at a pair of sliding doors in the wall opposite the front windows. "It's quieter in there."

So. Nothing.

"Now maybe you should . . . What's your name? I already forgot what Battle told me. I'm too old."

"Detective Franck, ma'am."

"Maybe you should talk to Gene upstairs, Detective Franck. He's in the room over my kitchen, so he can see in the yard of that house. Maybe he sees something. I don't know 'cause he don't tell me but if you want to go up there and ask him . . ."

"I would. Is he there now?"

"Sure. He only goes out to the store. You just go up there. You go up the stairs and back and knock at the first door, but you gotta knock loud sometimes. He sleeps a lot." She started to get up.

"I think I can find it, ma'am. Don't get up."

Hilda Kornbrust leaned back with a sigh.

Cesar groped his way up the stairs. It was a little lighter on the second floor. He looked up and saw a dirty skylight. He heard country wailing coming from a radio somewhere. It got louder as he neared Gene's door. Cesar knocked, knocked again, and then knocked his knuckles raw.

"I'm coming, God damn you, I'm coming. Quit beating on that door." Great. One of those guys.

His name was Eugene Standriff. Cesar found that out after waiting for Standriff to grapple with his locks, peer out, and look at Cesar's badge. Standriff turned his radio down, and they sat opposite each other at an old dinette table.

Standriff, who wanted Cesar to call him Gene, turned out to be the guy Cesar had seen that morning, supervising Don Leicht and his crew from Miss Kornbrust's front yard. He was your standard retired alcoholic. There was no guessing his age. He looked about seventy-five, but the really serious alcoholics start looking that way at forty. He had spiky gray hair that looked like he cut it himself, and he had about three days' growth of beard. His old-fashioned undershirt hung off of his shoulders, tired and dirty. The skin on his shoulders and arms had lost any tone it had gallons and gallons ago. It looked as if you could pull it off without much trouble; he might not even feel it. But his eyes were still alive; they were light, clear blue, and he had laugh lines. He had scars, too. Fight scars, falling-down-drunk scars, maybe even battle scars, but you could still see the laugh lines.

Cesar told Standriff what he was doing and asked if he had seen or heard anything going on next-door last Saturday night. And Standriff had.

Standriff had been in his room the whole night except when he went to the bathroom. He told Cesar that his funds were running low because his disability check was late, so instead of going out to socialize, which was what he called drinking in a bar, he had brought in a bottle of Mad Dog and spent the evening alone. At some time, he hadn't looked at the clock, he heard somebody banging and hammering outside.

"It was terrible," he said. "I couldn't hardly hear myself think. Just bang, bang, bang. That's all I could hear. So I got out of the bed and went to look out the window, and there was that fellow from next-door just a-banging away like it was daytime even though it was dark out."

"How did you know it was him? Could you see his face?"

"Oh, I know him when I see him. He's got that curly hair, you know, and—"

"What did he have on?" asked Cesar.

"Short pants. He was always running around in short pants." Standriff made a face as he fished for a Pall Mall. "Now, I don't wear those short pants myself. Not since I was a little boy. But he wears them all the time in the summer."

"What about his shirt."

Standriff took a deep, unfiltered drag and blew it up at the ceiling. He was starting to get into this recollection stuff. "Well, now, let me think. Seems to me he must have had on a T-shirt. Not like this, not an undershirt. The kind with sleeves, you know."

"But you didn't see his face," said Cesar.

"Now, hold on a minute, Officer. I didn't say that."

"You did see his face?"

"What happened was I went to the window and started in to yelling at him to stop. And if you need to know, what I said to him was 'Stop that hammering of a night' and he said 'What did you say?' and I said, 'Stop that hammering of a night. Can't nobody sleep with that hammering,' and he was looking up at me, see, to see what I was saying and I seen his face. So yessir, I did see his face. Clear as my hand."

Standriff held up the hand with the Pall Mall. It was shaking.

"But you said it was dark out."

"He had a work light, Officer. Like for working on your car. Had it strung out to where he was working."

"So what was he doing?" asked Cesar.

"Well, sir, I believe he was going to put in an air conditioner in that back window of his. You can just sort of see it from here."

Cesar got up and went over to the window. He was looking down on the spot where Sandy had found Chips Reber, and where he had climbed in Reber's window. He could barely see the window.

"And the reason I know that," Standriff went on, "is that he had a air conditioner sticking out of that window where there wasn't one before."

"So what was the hammering?"

"You know, I don't know *what* he was hammering. He had himself some kind of step stuck in up against the wall and he was banging on something underneath the machine, but I couldn't tell you what. But when I told him he better stop that hammering, he did."

"He stopped?"

"Yessir, he did. He didn't hammer no more. Said he was through, but you know I don't believe that. I think he didn't want to tangle with me." Standriff leaned back in his chair and reached out to smash the Pall Mall into an ashtray.

"Was he alone, Gene?"

"Yes, sir, he was. Wasn't nobody with him."

Well, shoot. "How about later? Did you hear anybody go out or come in? Anybody talking."

"Well now, Officer, I went to sleep pretty soon after he stopped all that banging, and I have to say I sleep pretty good, so if I heard anybody, it probably didn't bother me none."

Cesar closed his notebook and scratched his head.

"Now don't rush off, Officer. Just wait a second."

Standriff looked as if he was trying to remember something. Hard work for him.

"There. I remembered. I told you there wasn't nobody with him, and there wasn't. Not with him. Not in his yard. But it seems to me there was somebody going through the alley when I was talking to that boy."

Aaaahh.

"And if you'll sit still for a minute I'll try to remember which way she was going."

"It was a woman?"

"I ain't sure, but I think so."

"White or black?"

"Well, this is funny, but I ain't sure about that either. See . . ." He made Cesar stand up and go to the window with him. He smelled ripe. "See, all the light there is in that alley comes from that one streetlight, and it's too far away to do much."

"So why do you think it was a woman?"

"Well, if it wasn't a woman, it wasn't a very big man. But you see, I couldn't see her hair."

"Why not?"

"I don't know." Standriff squinted his eyes and thought. It made him lose his balance. "Seems to me she must have had on some kind of hood. I believe that's why."

"Oh. Had the rain started?"

"Did it rain?"

"Yeah. There was a real rain. Thunderstorm."

"Well, I must have slept through it. No, it wasn't raining then. So I don't know why she had that hood up. That *is* kind of funny, ain't it? It was real hot."

"You remember anything else? What about other clothes?"

"Pants. Had on pants."

"What color?"

"I couldn't tell you, Officer. They was dark. Might have been blue jeans, but then again, might not."

"You said she had a hood on. Was it a coat? Jacket?"

"Must have been a jacket. I remember she had a sort of big backside to her. Oh, and I'll tell you something else. She was walking away when I saw her, and it seems to me she had something written on the backside. You know, like on a baseball jacket."

Cesar pumped for another five minutes, but Standriff had already gone a lot further than either one of them expected, and the effort was getting to him. His shake was getting worse. Cesar packed up and started to leave him to his cure. Then he asked, "Are you the only person living here? Besides Miss Kornbrust?"

"Oh! No, I ain't. I should have told you that. There's another fellow lives in the next room, and his name is Stanley Goodin, and you might want to talk to him, only he ain't in. But I better explain about him."

"What?"

"Stanley's been in the asylum out at Longview most of his life, but they've got him out on a release now. Only he ain't all there yet. But he's a real nice fellow. He is. Real gentle. He won't hurt you."

"Good. When'll he be back?"

"Stanley don't come till real late. He works, you know. Cleans up in restaurants after they close. If you want to find him, you'd best come of a morning. He'll be in then."

There was a new smell. It hit Cesar as he worked his way down the dark staircase. Miss Kornbrust's house had the smells he expected in a home for old men and winos—dust, sweat, fried bologna, grungy bathrooms—but here, over all of that, was the scent of gardenias. It hadn't been there when he came in. As he reached the bottom of the stairs he heard voices in Miss Kornbrust's living room. She had company. He knocked on the door and waited. He followed Miss Kornbrust and her walker with his ears as she dragged her way to the door and opened it a crack.

"I'm leaving, Miss Kornbrust," he said. He couldn't see much more than her nose and a little bit of her white hair.

"Okay."

"I'd like to come back and talk to your other roomer, okay?"

"Sure. Okay. You come back tomorrow." She closed the door on him.

8

CESAR STOOD BLINKING in the sunlight after the gloom
of Hilda Kornbrust's house. As his eyes adjusted, he
found himself staring at a very long white convertible
parked on his side of Abigail. He strolled down Miss
Kornbrust's walk and out onto the sidewalk toward the
car. God, it was long; it took up two normal parking
places. A Packard. A Packard with a red and a black
stripe on the quarter panel. He looked around to see if
anyone was watching and then pushed down on the front
fender. Sure enough, there was a quiet *whirr* from someplace inside the car as the self-leveling mechanism brought
the rear of the car down to compensate. You could only
do that to a Packard. He stepped back and leaned against
Chips Reber's fence to take in the whole car. It said
Caribbean behind the front wheel. What a beauty. He
stepped up to peer inside. There was nothing loose in the
car that might identify the owner except for a pair of long
white women's gloves. Other than that, it was a sea of
white leather with a little black trim and a dashboard that
probably weighed more than Reber's air conditioner.
They knew how to do things like that in the fifties.

He looked around to see if the owner was returning,
but he had the street to himself.

What now? The lab truck had left Reber's. He didn't
want to talk to Leicht anyway. Leicht would only be able

to talk about "The Sandy Schott Show." He decided to try the neighbors on the other side.

The card on the mailbox said *Alan Howard and Emma Wells Howard.* There was another card taped below that said *The Sentimental Fool.* White professionals, for sure. The recessed entry was clean and freshly painted, the brass was shiny, and he had seen big plants in the window as he came to the door. He looked for the doorbell, but all he found was a brass knob in the doorframe with *Pull* engraved in the center. He pulled and heard a bell jingling back somewhere in the house. He waited. No one came except a cat. The cat bumped against the door a couple of times and complained, but Cesar couldn't help. He stooped down to read a small card between the glass pane and the lace curtain stretched behind it. *If no answer, come to the Sentimental Fool, 1180 Central, Mrs. Howard.*

Okay.

He must have gone past it a thousand times, but he didn't know it was there. Who was going to look for a dress shop in one of the dumpiest blocks of Central? Cesar didn't look for dress shops all that often anyway.

He had walked over. His car was doing okay parked where it was. Arthur and Sheba were keeping an eye on it from Arthur's stoop. Arthur had pointed to the Packard and said, "That's the one," and Cesar had nodded.

Now he was standing outside the Sentimental Fool. Apart from a bar up the street, it was the only storefront open for business. The Howards had done a lot of cleaning. Every other window on the block was covered with an inch of dirt and dust, but the Sentimental Fool was gleaming. Some of the other stores were totally empty, a couple were filled to the ceiling with old furniture and space heaters. One window had a sign that said *The* TRUE *One and onley Tabernacle of* THE LORD *with* US *Bishop Mary Presiding,* but there was another sign under it that said *Moved to 516 E. Twelfth come worship with us.*

He couldn't figure out what sort of store it was. There

were two display windows. In one there was a dummy standing beside a kitchen table with chrome hairpin legs, the kind of table Lillian Franck had assigned to the basement fifteen years ago when she got the Early American dinette. She said the table was thirty years old even then. There were a couple of mixing bowls and a Betty Crocker cookbook on the table. The dummy was wearing a housedress like the one Stella had on yesterday, a blue apron, and high-heeled shoes, and there was a cigarette tucked behind one ear. The other window contained a dummy wearing pleated shorts, a halter top, and a yachting cap. She was standing beside a mint-condition man's balloon-wheel twenty-six-inch Schwinn with a tank and a horn button. There was no price tag on the bike. He pushed open the door and went in.

A woman stood behind a glass counter halfway to the back of the long, narrow shop. She was bent over, peering into a stand-up mirror, doing something to her face. She looked up when she heard the door and then went back to her mirror. "I'll be right with you," she said. She puckered her lips and stared intently at her reflection. Cesar ambled back toward her. There were chrome-plated pipe racks on either side of him jammed with dresses and blouses. The rack on the left said *Period— never worn;* the one on the right said *Fakes.* He stopped when he got to the counter. The woman seemed to be gluing some kind of little black patch that looked like a mole near the left corner of her mouth. She finally took her finger away from the patch and it stayed. She straightened up. "What do you think?" she said, and leaned on the counter looking sultry.

How do you answer a question like that? The woman had had her black hair cut into a DA. She didn't look like Elvis, though. She looked like Cesar's cousin Joyce in her graduation picture from 1956. She had on a sleeveless blouse, which was open pretty deep, and she had tied a small scarf around her neck. Her lipstick was fire-engine red.

"Umm. Sharp!" said Cesar at last. The woman lowered her eyelids and reached back to feel her haircut, making her breasts stick out right at him. Jeez. She opened her eyes wide again to check the reaction and then started to laugh. "I'm trying to look smoldering, not scary," she said.

"Oh," said Cesar.

The woman looked back in the mirror and started to laugh again. "I was sure I was going to look just unbelievably desirable as soon as I got this beauty mark on. I guess not."

"Would you be Mrs. Howard, ma'am?"

"Emma," she said.

Cesar introduced himself, explained what he was doing, and asked if she had seen or heard anything happening in Chips Reber's yard Saturday night. She hadn't. She made the usual shocked comments about Reber, although she didn't seem the least bit upset, and then she told Cesar that her husband had, after years of pleading on her part, installed an air conditioner in their bedroom late Saturday afternoon. They had spent the evening putting the air conditioner to various uses, she said. When Cesar finally understood, he blushed. "And then I went to sleep," she said. "Hard. It was the first good night's sleep I've had since it got so hot. It was wonderful. But," she went on, "my husband always revives afterward, which means he's usually hanging around downstairs or outside for a couple of hours. He's the one you want to talk to."

"Does he work here too?"

"No," said Emma. "This, for better or for worse, is mine. Just mine. No, Alan's a lawyer. He's an assistant city solicitor. Parttime. He has his own practice, too. But the city job's the one that pays. Alan spends a lot of time preserving things."

"Please?"

"He's become a rabid preservationist. Ever since we moved into Dutchtown. Which is fine, I suppose, but he doesn't make a cent off of it. You could go over to City Hall and see him right now, if you want to. He won't mind. I do it all the time. He's never doing anything important."

That's for sure. "If you don't mind, Mrs. Howard, I'd rather catch him at home. I'm going to be around the neighborhood for a while. What time does he get home?"

"Well, he's out of there like a shot at five and then he stops in here to pick me up, and if I'm not too confused we usually get out of here by a quarter past. Try five-thirty."

Five-thirty was fine with Cesar, since he would rather stay up until three in the morning than show his face in the Research Evaluation and Budget office.

"How's business?" he asked Emma as she saw him to the door.

"You would ask," she said, rolling her eyes.

That bad?

"Actually, it's not that bad. I mean it was terrible to start, and of course I'm undercapitalized like crazy. I'm blowing a tiny inheritance on this. But since the suburban brats have discovered me, I'm hanging on. It all turns out to be very New Wave. Of course that wasn't what I had in mind. I just wanted to sell the kind of things I like to wear, but I don't argue with it. Actually, what's selling best to the grown-up ladies is Stella Hineman's things. She's a neighbor who designs and sews. Nifty things."

"I met Miss Hineman."

"You did? Oh, of course. You must be talking to everybody. Isn't she nice?"

"Oh, yes. Very nice. I mean she seemed real nice. When I was talking to her. Right."

What's the matter? Can't talk.

"Is . . . is . . . does . . . How long has she been sewing?" asked Cesar finally.

"Oh! Do you sew?"

Jeez, lady, no. I just want to talk about Stella. "No, ma'am. I just thought it was interesting. That's more like New York than Cincinnati."

"Well, actually she's more like Tokyo these days, but

you have a point. I don't know. I think since she was a girl."

"Well," said Cesar. And then, "I'll see you at five-thirty then."

Emma Howard smiled him out the door and headed back to the counter, but Cesar came back inside and asked, "How much is the bike? The one in the window."

"Isn't that nice? I could have sold it fifteen times this month. But it's my husband's first preservation effort. He'd part with me before he'd part with his Schwinn."

"I don't blame him," said Cesar. Then he realized how insulting that was. "I didn't mean that, ma'am. What I meant was—"

"Never mind, Officer. I understand."

When he got out on the sidewalk, Cesar looked at his watch. Four-thirty. An hour to kill until Alan Howard got home. He decided to forget any more interviews until then, and he started up Central Avenue. This was a good time to poke around the neighborhood and see what went where.

He couldn't get over Emma Howard. She was about the last woman he would expect an assistant city solicitor to marry. Most of the solicitor's staff thought they were the local equivalent of the White House staff, so you would expect their wives to be sorority types or else corporate lawyers. But Emma Howard was like nothing he'd ever met. And while you might expect to see an up-and-coming lawyer on a six-hundred-dollar ten-speed, you sure as hell didn't expect to find him cruising around on a Schwinn with balloon tires.

Cesar heard overdriven speakers crunching out soul music. He had reached Abigail Street. The music was coming from the BandK poolroom on the opposite corner. There were a couple of afternoon drunks standing in the door. One of them waved at Cesar and he nodded back. He looked across and down Abigail and spotted an alley running behind the BandK, parallel to Central Avenue. Unless it was a very screwed-up block, that alley would intersect the one that ran behind Reber's house. And Stella's. He cut across to the alley.

When he turned into the alley, he bumped into a ten-year-old black kid taking a leak against the fence behind the BandK. The kid nearly jumped a foot when he saw Cesar, and he splashed all over himself. He took off running toward Franklin Street, tucking himself back in as he went. Fom the smell of it, about a thousand guys had also relieved themselves in the same spot recently. Cesar figured it was a favorite with BandK patrons on their way home.

There was a lot of crap in the alley—the usual Pampers, tires, and automobile seats—but he had seen worse. He could still see the shiny little bricks that they used to pave the alleys with. And the broken glass wasn't ankle deep. He figured this was probably a pretty quiet block, with so many abandoned stores and houses around. He looked at the backsides of the buildings facing Central Avenue. They looked worse than the fronts. Most of the buildings were two stories high, with wooden porches on both floors. The porches hadn't seen new paint since the Second World War. They all sagged in the middle. One or two had separated from the bricks and were hanging out over the backyards. Cesar didn't know what was holding them up. The BandK was only one story high. He looked over the back fence and saw a black woman in a white dress through the door. She was cooking something. She must have felt him watching, because she looked out to the alley. When she saw it was nothing but a pudgy-looking white guy, she went back to her cooking.

The building on the other side of the alley seemed to be in the middle of a renovation job. The bricks had been cleaned, but the windows hadn't. He didn't hear or see any signs of life inside. He moved on down the alley. There was a building a few doors from the BandK that looked a little cleaner than the rest. He looked over its fence. The backyard had been swept, and there were bars on the window. The door had a new lock on it. Even from that distance he could tell that the lock was a good one. At first he thought the building hadn't been painted, but after a second he realized it was a fresh paint job. Who would pick colors that looked like old paint?

The next couple of buildings were clearly abandoned. He had reached the intersection with the alley running parallel to Abigail. It was empty. He decided to go all the way to Franklin and then come back.

He stuck his nose over the next fence and nearly had it torn off.

BAUBAUBAUWURRRAUUUWOOOFOOOF!!!

Ohnoohnoohnoohno! A damned pit bull!

Cesar flattened himself against the fence on the opposite side of the alley and felt to see if his face was there. It was. It had just *seemed* like the big fighter had jumped down his throat. It actually probably got no closer than two or three millimeters. Cesar knew for sure that he had felt its hot breath on his eyelids. He leaned against the fence until his legs stopped shaking. Then he pulled himself together and walked toward Franklin Street on the edges of his rubber soles so as not to irritate the doggie.

The house on his left faced Franklin Street and seemed to be occupied. It was covered with aluminum siding, and there were blue plastic curtains in the two square windows that looked out on the alley. The last building on his right, which faced Central Avenue, seemed to be occupied too. It had no back fence, and the back wall was almost on the curb. There were lights on inside. Cesar stepped out onto Franklin and then turned toward Central. When he got to the corner he saw the sign hanging over the last building. Truth and Beauty Feeding Program and Rap Center/Outreach Program. Home of Sonny Werk. He quickly ducked back down Franklin to the alley. No time for Sonny today.

What did Sandy Schott say? Something about Chips Reber leaning on Sonny. Why did she have to say that? Maybe Henry would handle Sonny as a favor. Sure.

Cesar walked slowly back through the alley and turned

at the intersection, heading for Reber's garage. He was following a cat. The cat took a quick look over her shoulder and decided that Cesar wasn't dangerous. She trotted on without breaking stride until she came to a tenement facing the alley, jumped up to a windowsill and from there to the top of a fence next-door.

"There she is, Mom." Cesar heard a child's voice from the other side of the fence.

"Linda, get down from there. Get down *now!*" It was Stella Hineman. Linda looked back at Cesar and then jumped down and out of sight. Cesar opened his mouth to speak and then shut it. He didn't know what to say, so he just stood there and listened. There were two children with her today. It sounded like she was playing some kind of war game with them. There was a lot of laughing and whooping and gun noises. He stood there and eaves-dropped until one of the boys fell off of something and they went inside for BandAids. He moved on down the alley.

When he recognized Reber's garage on his left, Cesar backtracked to check out the Howards' place. They had a carriage house too, but it wasn't as wide as Reber's and it ran the entire width of the property. The big sliding door had a little door cut out in the middle to give access. The Howards had hung a big padlock on the sliding door and put a new lock on the little door. Cesar peered through a filthy window near the corner of the building. There were flowerpots in front of the window, so he couldn't tell much except that there was no car inside.

Don Leicht had sealed off the gate to Reber's back-yard. Cesar rattled the lock. It held. Reber had covered the garage windows with newspaper. Cesar fiddled with the garage door until he got it to move aside about half an inch so he could see inside. Reber's Corvette was still inside, surrounded by old stoves, counter units, basins, and commodes. He heard something move and looked down in time to see a rat scooting under the door and into the garage.

Hilda Kornbrust's carriage house looked like it was ready to cave in, which was too bad, because it was the biggest one on the alley. She had had somebody nail sheet metal over all the windows, but they didn't cover up the carved stone frames. Maybe the building could be saved.

Cesar reached the next intersecting alley, the one he had run through on his way to rescue Stella from the rat. The alley separated Hilda Kornbrust's property from the Sharps' house. The Sharps' lot wasn't any wider than the Howards', maybe even narrower, although it still had its own skinny carriage house. There was a plain board fence running from the garage to the corner of the house. Cesar stood there checking out the gutters and downspouts, which were in pretty good shape considering that William Sharp was an artist. Somebody was rapping on a window. He looked until he saw Nancy Sharp waving at him from upstairs. She disappeared, and a few seconds later he heard a door opening, and then Nancy came out through a gate in the fence.

"I thought that was you," she said.

"It's me," said Cesar.

"What are you doing? Are you on duty?"

"I'm trying to find out what happened to your neighbor."

"You mean who killed him? I heard he was stabbed. Alan Howard told Bill. Isn't that awful? Did Sandy do it?"

"I don't know much of anything yet. Why her?"

"Because she's such a bitch. She's a monster. They were the perfect couple."

This was pretty funny coming from Fred Kuhne's sister. Fred was big on sounding like a judge. He never called a spade a spade.

"Did you know them pretty well?" asked Cesar.

"Better than I wanted to. She was always over here borrowing something or complaining about how Chips wouldn't take her to Mexico whenever she wanted to go. Oh, and telling me all about their sex life. I mean. I know it *all*. Frankly, I couldn't stand her, but I never know how to tell anyone to get away and leave me alone."

"What about him?"

"I didn't know him as well. He was pretty busy. Actually he was very hardworking. Probably trying to get away from Sandy as much as possible. But he—"

Nancy stopped and stared at Cesar. He stared back at her.

"Would you arrest me?" asked Nancy finally.

"I don't know. Why?"

"Oh, I don't know. Well . . . I was going to say that he had really good grass all the time and then I remembered you were a policeman besides being Fred's brother-in-law. But he's dead. Chips."

"Right. So he sold marijuana."

"That's what I hear," Nancy said dryly. "Ooops. That's my phone!" She ran through the gate, waving at Cesar. He couldn't hear the phone himself.

9

CESAR PULLED THE Howards' doorbell and listened for the tinkle. This time he heard a person coming instead of a cat. Emma Howard let him in. She had changed out of her work clothes and into a bright yellow sun suit. It was impossible not to notice her legs. They were short with old-fashioned curves and she had tied on a pair of red wedge sandals.

"What do you think?" she asked, posing in the doorway.

"Nice," said Cesar. "Looks nice."

"How about this?" She reached behind the door and came up with a beach ball. She posed again, this time with the ball up over her head and a big smile.

Maybe this was what Connie Francis was always trying to look like.

Emma threw the beach ball back into the hall, startling a huge light-gray Persian cat. The cat made a pissed-off noise and scrambled through the door at the end of the hall.

"Come on in and sit down. I'm through asking you about my clothes. You're entirely too frank." Emma led Cesar from the hall into the living room. The layout seemed to be pretty much the same in every house on the block. "Have a seat," said Emma. "Alan is upstairs changing. He'll be right down." Cesar sank into a big soft club chair. "Can I get you something to drink? I've got some iced tea."

Cesar started to say no thanks and then realized that he was parched. "That sounds good," he said.

Emma Howard headed for the kitchen, swinging her hips. She was about fifteen pounds overweight compared to most women her height, but she didn't seem to care. He didn't either.

Cesar got comfortable. The chair he was sitting in was one of a pair on either side of the fireplace. Both were covered in the kind of flowered upholstery material that Lillian had been hiding with slipcovers. The hearth was buried under magazines. A big leather sofa faced the fireplace, its back to the hall door. The Howards had hung floor-length flowered curtains on the large front windows, and, it finally hit him, there were no big plants. He looked around. There weren't even any small plants. The afternoon light came slanting into the room, filtered by a scraggly mulberry tree in the front yard and by the curtains. The windows were open.

"What do you take?" Emma Howard was back with a pitcher of iced tea and some glasses on a tray. She had brought sliced lemons and a bowl of sugar lumps and he asked for both. They sat around and beat up their lumps without talking. As he took his first sip, he heard Alan Howard coming down the stairs. Howard strode into the room and around the sofa, heading for Cesar. He had changed into a pair of shorts and moccasins, but he was still wearing his buttondown office shirt. He had a drink in one hand. He held out the other and said, "Alan Howard."

"Detective Franck," said Cesar as they shook hands.

Howard dropped himself into a corner of the sofa. Emma got out of her armchair and went over to sit close beside him. Too close for her husband. He tried to back away from her a little, but he was trapped by the arm of the sofa. "What are you *doing?*" he asked. Emma Howard looked puzzled and slightly hurt. But Cesar saw that she was snaking a hand along the back edge of the cushions. "Ow! *Emma!* Quit it!" Emma had grabbed a handful of her husband's behind. Cesar wondered if it was an old game. "Emma, do you mind?" asked Alan. "This detective is here on business."

"Sorry," said Emma, but she started to work her hand back under her husband. He trapped it and pinned it to the cushion.

"Emma tells me we've got a murder on our hands," said Alan.

"That's right, sir."

"That's unbelievable."

"It really happened, Alan," said Emma.

"I didn't mean that. I meant it's terrible."

"Terrible," said Emma.

"Emma, will you try to be serious? I'm sorry, Detective Franck."

Cesar shrugged.

"Emma says you want to know if we saw anything going on at Chips Reber's house."

"I had to tell him what we were doing, Alan." Emma smiled at her husband and rumpled his lawyerly locks.

"What?" asked her husband. Then he said, "Oh. Oh."

"I'm sure he won't tell anyone else, Alan. You won't, will you?" she asked Cesar.

"I don't think so, ma'am."

"Not for my sake," said Emma. "I have no shame."

"She really doesn't," said her husband.

"And now I'm pregnant. The world will know what we do."

"Congratulations," said Cesar.

"But not from that particular act," said Emma. "It was earlier."

"Emma, if you don't care about embarrassing me, you might think about this poor man. Give him a break. Please."

"Right. So"—Emma tried to look serious—"you want to know what else we did?"

"Actually, Mr. Howard, I'm more interested in what you might have seen or heard next-door. Your wife said you stayed up later than she did and that maybe you went outside for a while?"

"I did. I'm not used to the air conditioner."

"Tough for you," said Emma. Howard ignored her.

"So I got dressed and went for a little walk."

"Did you see Mr. Reber?"

"I heard him. He was banging around in the backyard. Working on his own air conditioner I know now, but I didn't know what he was doing. I stepped out into the alley for a minute, but I didn't go look in his yard."

"What time was that?"

"Eleven, maybe?"

"Was anyone in the alley?"

"Not that I saw."

"Did you hear anyone besides Mr. Reber?"

"No. Yes. Yes, I heard Gene-the-wino over at Hilda's."

"While you were in the alley?"

"No. I came back into the yard. I was going to go sit on the front steps, but I heard Gene start yelling at someone to shut up, which took a lot of nerve since he had his own radio going full blast."

"Did you hear what he said?" asked Cesar.

Howard nodded. "He said, and I quote, 'Stop that god-damned hammering of a night.' So I knew he was yelling at Chips. What was interesting was that Chips stopped. I don't know how many hints we've all dropped to get him to shut up, but we were obviously going about it the wrong way. Gene's the first person to get it right."

"Did Mr. Reber work a lot at night?"

"Yes, he did. He was a real asshole about it."

"That's one of the reasons we got the air conditioner," said Emma. "The noise."

"I have to tell you that Chips Reber was not one of our favorite people," said Howard. "The noise was just one of his many less desirable features."

"Like what?"

"Like—"

"Like the way he treated Greta and H.P.," Mrs. Howard cut her husband off. "He was a real son of a bitch to

Greta and he treated H.P. like a piece of cute talking real estate."

"That's his ex-wife?"

"Greta is, yes. H.P.'s his son."

"They had problems?" asked Cesar.

"Always," said Emma. "I don't know what ever possessed Greta to marry him in the first place. Have you met her?" Cesar shook his head. "She's lovely. Absolutely lovely. Completely unpretentious, a wonderful mother, funny, generous. I have to tell you she's one of my best friends, so I'm not completely unbiased, but even if I didn't know her she would still be one of my best friends."

"Emma, you're not making sense," said Howard.

Thank you.

"Yes, I am. He knows what I mean. Anyway, that's the way she's *always* been. Even when she was married to Chips. But Chips was the exact opposite. He has always been Mr. Conspicuous Consumption. He's pretentious, gross, conniving, and mean." Emma paused to suck an ice cube into her mouth and chew on it.

"You said something about their son? You said he got some real estate?" asked Cesar.

Emma spit the ice cube back into her glass angrily. "I said he *treated* H.P. like a piece of real estate, and that's the truth. How could any father—"

"Emma, you're getting crazy," said Howard. "But she's right, Detective Franck. I know we're not actually parents *yet,* but you don't have to be a parent to know that children aren't supposed to be bargaining chips and they aren't supposed to be cute little pets that talk, but that's the way Chips dealt with H.P. I don't like to speak ill of the dead, you understand—"

"Doesn't bother me a bit," said Emma.

"Just . . . just lay off a little, Emma. Okay?"

"Why? Why should I lay off that crass coke merchant just because he's dead? I always thought that was ridiculous."

"We don't know that he sold coke," said Howard.

"Yes, we do. That's bullshit. Sandy Schott told us. She was always saying we could get it at a really good price from him—when we were still speaking to her."

Cesar was distracted for a moment as he watched a man and a woman come through the Howards' gate toward the front door. Shortly after he lost sight of them he heard the front door open and a woman say, "Yoo-hoo! Anybody home?" He had heard the voice before.

"In here, Theresa," said Howard.

The McDowells, the people with the blinding living room across the street, stopped in the doorway to the living room. Theresa stood in front and slightly to the left of her husband. She barely reached his shoulder. He stood holding his suitcoat on two fingers so that it hung down his back, and rested a hand on his wife's shoulder. McDowell still had a tie on, but he had loosened it and unbuttoned the top button of his shirt. Ask not what your city can do for you . . .

"Oh, you've got company! I'm sorry," said Theresa. And then she looked closer at Cesar. "Do I know you? I think I know you."

Cesar stood up. "I was on the tour yesterday. I saw your house."

"Of course!" Theresa sounded thrilled.

"Guys, this is Detective Cesar Franck of the Cincinnati Police Division Homicide Squad," announced Howard. "I think I got that right."

"That's right," said Cesar.

"A *detective!*" Theresa sounded thrilled again. Her husband elbowed her aside and reached over the sofa to shake hands with Cesar. He had a great grip.

"I just want to say I think you guys do a terrific job. Terrific," said McDowell.

"But what are you doing here?" asked Theresa. "Are you going to buy a house?"

Cesar sat down and let the Howards fill the McDowells in on the neighborhood murder. He watched McDowell's face as he took in the news. McDowell seemed to have trouble figuring out where murder fit in with a promising political career. His wife was just plain fascinated. He must have decided that murder came out on the minus side, because he stood up, bringing his unwilling wife up with him.

"I can't tell you how shocked I am, Detective Franck," said McDowell. He had made his voice deeper and put on a very serious expression. Did he think Reber was some sort of relative of Cesar's? "I wish I had some sort of information to give you, but my wife and I were at home all Saturday night getting ready for the house tour, and I'm afraid we didn't hear a thing. Not a thing." He started to tug his wife toward the door.

"Well, *Paul,* why do we have to run out?" asked Theresa. "He's going to think we're guilty or something." She looked exasperated at Cesar. "We're not your culprits, sir. I was talking to my mother Saturday, and then my daddy got on the line and he wanted to talk politics, so I made Paul get on the downstairs phone and we talked until the rain started and I made everybody get off so we wouldn't get any lightning through our ears. And that's the truth. You can ask my daddy."

Cesar believed her.

"Don't you want some iced tea?" asked Emma. Theresa looked like she wanted to stay.

"We've got to run," said McDowell. "We just wanted to touch base." He stopped, thought of something, and then strode firmly over to Cesar and shook his hand. "If there's anything I can do for you, you just let me know."

Right.

Alan Howard waited until his wife had closed the door behind their neighbors, and then he leaned toward Cesar and said, "Paul has political ambitions."

"Oh," said Cesar.

"They're nice people, though. Really."

"He's getting worse," said Emma from behind the sofa.

"I'm probably keeping you from dinner," said Cesar.

"Don't worry about it," said Howard. "Anyway, I want to try to be a little more helpful about Chips."

Cesar leaned back and listened as Howard and his wife told him about Greta Grimes's good and bad husbands, about squabbles over Chips's and Greta's son, and about Chips's fast dealing in the world of slum real estate. But even with nudging from Cesar, they couldn't come up with anything that sounded directly related to a stabbing. The Grimeses were known to all their friends as an extremely peaceful and reasonable family and wonderful parents to H.P.

"But," said Emma, looking at her husband.

"But what?" asked Alan.

"Should I tell him?"

"Tell him what? What are you talking about?"

"The fight." Emma turned to Cesar. "They had a little fight Saturday."

"Mr. and Mrs. Grimes?" asked Cesar.

"No, no, no. They never fight. Greta and Chips."

"Oh," said Alan. *"That* fight."

"Which wasn't really a fight. It was just that Chips was his usual obnoxious self and Greta let him have it across the chops, which was wonderful. She should do it twice a day."

"I really don't think it was very serious, Detective Franck," said Alan. "Certainly nothing that would lead to real violence."

You'd be surprised.

"Just another one of his custody letters," said Emma. "Chips loved to have his lawyer send bullshit letters. He was that kind of sweetheart."

Cesar looked at his watch. It was seven o'clock and his stomach was starting to growl.

"Oh! I forgot to tell you something," said Emma as Cesar closed his notebook. "I think Chips was making obscene phone calls." She looked defiantly at her husband. He looked exasperated at her. "Alan thinks I'm wrong, but I don't know how he knows, since he never hears the calls."

"Have you been getting a lot?" asked Cesar.

"One a week, I'd say. And he always says something

to let me know he's seen me recently. That he knows me. It's horrible."

"Why do you think it was Reber. Did he—"

"She thinks it was Chips because she didn't like him. That's why. There's no way to know for sure," said Howard.

"I wondered," said Cesar, "because Miss Schott said she's been getting calls too. She got one while I was talking to her."

"She did?" Emma Howard didn't like that news. "Oh."

"Told you," said her husband.

Alan Howard walked along with Cesar on his way back to the car. "How do you like it down here?" asked Cesar.

"Terrific," said Howard. "Except in the summer. It gets kind of noisy."

"Had any problem with break-ins?"

"No. We really don't. Just the occasional murder." They both thought that was kind of funny.

Then Cesar asked him about the Packard convertible.

"You mean the Caribbean?"

Cesar nodded.

"Beautiful, isn't it? I wanted to buy it, but the woman who owns it knows what she's got."

"Who is she? Do you know her?" asked Cesar.

"Yes, I do. Very well. Her name's Elizabeth Sackville. She's the president of the Consortium for the Nineteenth Century. I'm the treasurer. We have a small office on Central Avenue."

"Oh." Cesar thanked him and forgot about ever owning that car. Then, as he climbed into his dirty Camaro, he remembered the Schwinn and asked again about it.

"You like that?" asked Howard. Cesar nodded.

"Yeah," said Cesar.

"Well, I do have a lead on an even older one with a horn that works. If that works out, I might consider selling mine."

"Let me know," said Cesar.

* * *

He could have walked it in less time. It was just that he wasn't sure that he was going to go there, and anyway, he didn't want to tell the Howards where he was going. So he drove to Central and then left again a block later onto Franklin and then parked in the first spot. He was maybe three hundred feet from the Howards' living room. He sat in the car and tried to think of a good excuse for dropping in on Stella Hineman, couldn't, and got out anyway. This time he took a good look at her house. The houses on Franklin were smaller than their neighbors' on Abigail. Cesar looked at the whole street. It looked crummy. Smaller.

Stella's house was typical. It wasn't more than twelve or fourteen feet wide. The front door and window were cramped. The house was brick that had been painted a cream color; the trim was painted a sick-looking brown. But she had washed her windows. That helped a lot.

Her front door was open. He checked the screen door, which turned out to be unlatched. There was no bell. "Anybody home?" he called.

"Just a minute! I'm in the kitchen." Stella came to the door wiping her hands on a dish towel. Her son hung back in the door from the kitchen.

"You know, you ought to lock your door down here," said Cesar.

Oh, *Jeez.* What a way to start out.

"Who . . . oh! It's you! I didn't recognize you. Come in."

"Thanks. You know, I'm not kidding about the door. It's not like you're out in the suburbs."

Quit it. Shut your mouth.

"What are you, the door inspector? Are you here to arrest me because I forgot to latch the door?"

"I didn't mean to criticize you, Ms. Hineman. I just thought you might not—"

"Look, just call me Stella, okay?"

"Sure," said Cesar. "Can I call you Sidney?" he asked the boy.

"Yes," said the boy.

"I'm Cesar Franck."

"Sid! Did you hear that? His name? It's Cesar Franck! Do you believe it? Go put on our record. Go get it!"

The little boy was looking at Cesar as if he were Johnny Bench or Ronald McDonald. He finally tore himself away and ran around a corner and upstairs.

"You won't believe this. It's his all-time favorite record in the whole world. It has been for years."

"What is it?" asked Cesar.

"Wait. Just wait. You'll hear." Stella stood looking at the ceiling, so Cesar looked at the ceiling too. At last they heard the record start. They continued to stand looking at the ceiling until Stella looked at Cesar with a smile.

"Do you believe it? It really is his favorite record. It's his second copy. He wore the first one out."

"Really. Hunh. What . . . what *is* it?"

"You don't know? You really don't know?"

Cesar shook his head.

"It's the D Minor Symphony." She waited. Cesar looked at her. "By Cesar Franck," she said at last. "You really don't know what it is? Haven't you ever heard it?"

"I don't know," said Cesar. "Maybe."

"Okay, Sidney!" Stella called at the ceiling. "Turn it off." A few seconds later the music stopped. Cesar looked at Stella and forgot to talk. She looked at him, waiting to see what he wanted. Finally she asked, "Did you want something?"

"What? No. Oh. Yes. Sorry. I was . . . I've been in the neighborhood all day. I had to talk to people about Mr. Reber."

"Oh. Are you on that case?"

"Right. So I thought I'd stop in. Let you know what I was doing."

"Okay. Good." Stella waited for more.

"And . . . so I just thought if you had anything to say . . . or maybe if you had seen anything . . ." She was starting to laugh. *Oh, shit. What a dummy.*

"Detective Franck, if I had seen somebody stabbing Chips Reber, I would have told somebody. I might have waited until they were finished stabbing him, but I'd tell the police. I know my duty. Anyway, I spent the whole night sewing right there in front of the window. You can ask the nosy neighbors who sat out there and ran their ghetto blaster until they got rained out."

"Hey, I didn't think—"

"I know you didn't. And if I think of anything helpful, I'll get in touch."

Right. I'm leaving. I'm sorry. "Um . . . how did you do? With your dresses." You smooth talker.

"Yesterday? Terrible! Who wants to buy dresses when you can go look at a corpse?"

"Yeah, I guess that would be a problem."

"I mean even *I* went over to look."

"People can't help it, I guess."

"Especially when it's a worthwhile cause."

"What do you mean?" asked Cesar.

"Like Chips Reber."

"Hey! The guy is dead! Somebody killed him!"

"So?" snapped Stella.

"What do you mean, 'So?' You know, it's kind of strange the way everybody down here thinks it's okay that a guy gets murdered. I noticed that."

"I told you yesterday. Everybody hated his guts. He was a real bastard. All right?"

"I don't think it's all right," said Cesar. "You got a problem with a guy, you find some way to settle it. You don't just wipe him out. I think it's really strange that all you professional people coming down here are always talking about how the blacks behave and then you talk about how it's all right when somebody you don't like gets killed. You guys have a real double standard, you know."

"Are you from Westwood?"

"What do you mean, am I from Westwood? Yes. I am."

Cesar glared at Stella.

"I knew it," she said.

"What's that supposed to mean?"

"You're just exactly like everybody up there. No kidding. I thought you were probably Westwood the first time I saw you."

"So? What's wrong with that?"

"What's wrong with that is that everybody up there is so smug. They think that's the only way to live and that anybody who lives any other way is some kind of hippie freak communist. They're stupid! All the time running off their mouths about black people when they don't even know any."

"What are you talking about? I know plenty of black people. We've got black cops now, did you know that?"

"Okay, so you know black cops. Big deal. You still wouldn't want to live anyplace near them, right? You wouldn't even think of living in a place like this even though it's three blocks to the police station, just because it's also right in the middle of a bunch of black people, right?"

"Look, I live in Westwood because that's where I've always lived, all right? I didn't pick it. And that's the same for a lot of people. They were born there. Is there something wrong with that? And I didn't say anything about *your* living down here. I don't care about that."

"You didn't have to say anything," said Stella. "I could tell. You walk in here and start screaming at me about locking the door as if there's a thousand rapists getting ready to charge into my living room. You sound just like my father when he comes down here."

"Your father's not so dumb."

"Who said he was dumb? He's just prejudiced. Just like everybody in Westwood."

"Hey, do you even know what you're talking about? Have you ever even been out there? I'll bet you haven't. I'll bet you've never once been there."

"You'd lose. I grew up there."

"No kidding?"

"No kidding. What do you say to *that?*"

"What are you doing down here?"

Stella laughed in his face again.

"What's so funny?" asked Cesar.

"Nothing. You are."

"I am?"

"Did you come over here to yell at me or can we sit down and talk?"

Oh Jeez, I've been yelling at her. What a dope. "Oh, listen," said Cesar. "I'm sorry."

"It's okay, but can we sit down?"

"Sure!"

"You want a beer before I sit down?"

"Oh, no. Thanks."

"I'm having one. Are you on duty?"

"No, I guess not. Okay, sure." Cesar sat down on Stella's sofa, stood up and removed a GI Joe from under him, and sat back down.

"I'm glad to hear you're off duty," said Stella from the kitchen. "I'd hate to think this is the way you grill your suspects. You want a glass?"

"Can's fine."

Stella came back in with two Hudepohls, handed one to Cesar, cleared off the other end of the sofa, and sat down. She took a sip of her beer and then grinned at him.

"What? Did I do something?" asked Cesar.

"No. It was just funny getting you pissed off."

Funny?

"I have to ask you," said Stella, "do they make you wear a mustache or do all the cops just do it to look like a cop?"

Cesar touched his mustache. He hadn't thought about it. He'd had it for years. "I don't know . . . No! They don't make anybody wear a mustache. Plenty of guys don't."

"How many?" laughed Stella. "Six? No kidding. Every last policeman in Cincinnati is blond, wears a mustache, and has a big butt from eating in Frisch's all the time."

Cesar squirmed in his seat.

"Am I right?" Stella laughed again.

"I don't know. I never thought about it."

"Look at you. You're blond. You have a mustache."

"Okay. And I weigh a little more than I used to."

"Come on! I was joking. Don't get your feelings hurt. You probably think I drive a Volvo, don't you? Admit it."

"I hadn't thought about it." That was true.

"Well, I don't. I don't even know how to drive."

"You're kidding! I thought my mom was the last person in the world who didn't."

"Nope."

"How come?"

"I hate it. I don't want to know how."

"What do you do, take the bus?"

"And walk. I walk a whole lot."

"That's supposed to be good for you."

"I don't do it for the exercise. I don't do anything for the exercise. But I should tell you—to be fair—there *are* three Volvos over on Abigail. Some of my best friends drive them."

"They're good cars. Or they're supposed to be. I don't know anybody who has one."

"Everybody drives a Chevy, right?"

"I don't know! How am I supposed to know what everybody drives?" She was going to see his Camaro. There was no way around it. Get her off the subject. "How did you wind up down here? Are you into old houses?"

"I'm 'into' cheap and getting away from Westwood."

Oh. "Is this your house?"

"It's rented. From Chips Reber. Or it was. I don't know who I rent from now. I wonder if I rent from H.P.?"

"Is he Reber's only kid?"

"Only one I know about."

"He's probably your landlord then."

"Which means I'll be paying Greta. Good. I hope that's right."

"Did you know Reber real well?"

"No! I stayed away from him as much as possible. It was bad enough having to pay him the rent. I told you I couldn't stand him. He was always trying to hit on me. He really thought he was sexy. I hate that."

Good. Good. "Do you . . . have you ever heard anything about his being involved with drugs?"

"What's that supposed to mean?" Stella set her beer down on the table sharply.

"Well, I heard he may have been dealing a little."

"You did? So. Is that a big deal? Are you going to start checking out everybody to see if they've got grass in the house?"

"What are you talking about?" asked Cesar. "I just want to know if—"

"If we're doing dope down here, right?" she interrupted. Stella's face was turning red. "You cops. You really make me sick, you know? All you want to do is bust people for dope. You can't imagine anyth—"

"What are you talking about? Who said anything about busting anybody? You got a guilty conscience or something?"

"See? See?"

"No, I don't see. You're the one who got all jumpy. I was just asking about Reber. I need to know if—"

"Look at what's in your hand!"

Cesar looked. He was still holding the Hudepohl. He stared at Stella.

"That's a drug," said Stella. "It's all right for you and your cop friends to go out and get blind drunk on beer, but just let someone smoke a little marijuana and you're all over them. Sure, Chips Reber may have sold some cocaine, but that wasn't what made him a bastard."

"Look, ma'am, I was just—"

Stella interrupted him with a whooping laugh.

"What? What did I say?" Cesar didn't get it.

"I can't believe it! You called me 'ma'am'!" She started whooping again.

Well, shit. Forget it. Cesar stood up and set his beer can on the end table.

Stella tried to stop laughing but couldn't. "You . . . you . . . you looked so *serious* and you called me"—she wiped her nose—"you called me 'ma'am'!"

'Hey, I'm sorry. I won't—" But she had started laughing again. "Well, I've got to go," said Cesar.

"You do? Oh, no. I've hurt your feelings. You're mad."

"No, I'm not mad. I just have to go. Thanks for the beer."

"You're welcome. Don't be mad," said Stella.

"It was nice talking to you." Cesar let himself out.

All he wanted to do was get away from there. But just as he was leaving Stella's gate, a woman came out of the house next-door and ran up to Cesar.

"Hey, *Mister! Mister!*"

Don't give me any trouble, lady. I can't take it. I'm whipped.

"Hey, mister. You a policeman, ain't you?"

Cesar nodded. What now?

"I thought you was. You was down here the other day, wasn't you? When that old man shot that big old rat?"

"Yes." Oh, yeah. The woman who called the rescue squad.

"I knew that was you. I told my boyfriend I bet you was a policeman. You just look like one, you know . . ."

Jesus, what is this? Two in one night!

" . . . so when I saw you going in next-door I decided I was gonna ask you if you was."

"I am."

"Are you a detective?"

Cesar nodded and started to turn toward his car.

"Is that lady in some kind of trouble?"

"No, ma'am."

"Oh, good! She's so nice, you know. And she's got that little boy and all."

"Don't worry. She's all right. Good night." Cesar headed for his car. He stopped in the middle of inserting his key. Should he or shouldn't he? He shrugged and went back to talk to Stella's neighbor again.

"Ma'am, were you out in front here Saturday night? Playing a . . . a tape recorder?"

"Oh! Was she complaining? My sister always plays it real loud. She was out here. Well, so was I, but I was in and out, you know. Your friend was doing some sewing there, but I didn't know we was bothering her. She was there all night, but she didn't say nothing. I'm real sorry."

"She didn't complain," said Cesar. "It's all right." He smiled and scooted back to the car.

"What you investigating?" the woman called after him, but he didn't answer. He got into his Camaro and laid rubber on half a block of Franklin Street.

10

CESAR GOT UP and did push-ups. He did ten and then lay on the floor for a minute, his forehead on the cold oak planks. He did ten more. Slowly. He rolled over and tried some sit-ups. He got to fifteen and then lay on his back panting. He rolled over and tried push-ups again. This time he made it to eight and then his elbows started to wobble like crazy. A little whimper escaped from someplace deep inside. He dragged himself up and looked in the mirror.

Bad news. His face was scarlet from exertion. He couldn't see below his stomach in the small mirror, but that was bad enough. When did that happen? His stomach was definitely straining at his T-shirt.

And what was this about a big butt? He turned around but he couldn't see that far down. He had to drag his old desk chair over, stand on that, and peer over his shoulder into the mirror. How big was it supposed to be, for crying out loud?

He stripped in the bathroom and checked the size in his underpants before he threw them in the hamper . . . 36/38. Was that fat? He got in the shower and turned it on full blast on the off chance that the vibrating water would blast away a couple of pounds. He scrubbed like a maniac. Okay, so he was a little soft. So what? He got out and did five deep knee bends before he dried himself off.

The scale was sitting out where he could use it, but he wasn't ready for that.

After checking his belt and finding that he was on the last hole and that at some time he had been three holes back, he decided to skip breakfast. His mother eyed him as he poured his coffee, and then she went back to her *Enquirer*.

Cesar left before Lillian. "Are you all right, Gus?" she called as he went out the door. He didn't answer her.

He had to stop thinking about the flab situation as he drove to work. It was too depressing. So he thought about Chips Reber.

Drug dealer? Probably not a big one. He seemed to spend a lot of time on his real estate. He was most likely one of the hundreds of amateurs doing the last distribution for the really big rats. That didn't mean there was no problem. Arthur Battle said he was always waving wads of cash around and even the little guys could make big money the way everybody and his brother was doing nose candy. Like Stella? What did she go so nuts about? She didn't look like a big cokehead. In fact, from the furnishings and the house she lived in, it didn't look like she had enough money for any kind of extras.

It was just getting nice before she blew up at him.

Back to Reber. If he's a big dealer, the vice squad is going to have something on him. They probably would have said something already. If he was just a little fish with a big horn, they still might know something about him.

One thing's for sure. He wasn't an obscene caller. Unless maybe he arranged for someone to carry on his work. Boy, talk about someone in line for an obscene phone call, Sandy Schott had to be the number-one candidate.

And Emma Howard was getting calls. But she was the one who thought it was Chips Reber on the line.

She sure didn't like Reber. Sandy Schott was a hundred percent right so far. Everybody liked Greta Grimes.

Nobody liked Chips Reber. Could this business with their kid be hot enough to stab somebody over? Could Greta Grimes pick up an air conditioner and set it on her ex-husband's body? Maybe she could do more than fifteen sit-ups. Fifteen. That's terrible.

So maybe Greta Grimes was a very strong woman. Could she be the woman in the alley that Gene Standriff had seen from his window? What a lead. An old drunk leans out of his window and possibly sees someone who maybe was a woman who might have been wearing a green jacket with a hood. Well, he didn't make up the bit about yelling at Reber. Alan Howard had quoted him nearly word for word. So maybe he had seen someone.

Cesar zipped in front of a bald guy in an old Dodge as they both turned onto the expressway ramp. He looked in the rearview mirror in time to catch the bald guy giving him the finger.

A Colombian hit woman? In a green hood? Nah. Colombians were more like old-fashioned mobsters—bodies in the trunk, fifteen bullets in the head.

A local hit woman? Reber screws over the Ohio Valley Cocaine Dealers' Association and they send one of their own after him? She just happens to find a knife that's been stolen from a neighbor's house and just happens to catch Reber working alone?

A neighborhood woman? Greta Grimes, the ex-wife? Theresa McDowell? Emma Howard? Stella Hineman? Was there something wrong with a mustache? There were plenty of cops that didn't have blond hair. Take the homicide squad. Lieutenant Tieves has black hair, Sergeant Evans has gray hair, Henry has black hair (of course), Carole Griesel has brown hair, and the rest of the guys . . . well, mostly it's light brown hair. And Carole Griesel and the lieutenant don't have mustaches. It's really terrible the way people generalize about cops.

He pulled into the parking lot and switched off the engine. He was getting mad about last night all over again.

*   *   *

Henry wasn't in yet. Detective Griesel was early as usual. She looked pointedly at the clock before she said good morning. What did she want? It wasn't even eight yet. Cesar grunted at her and went to his desk.

"It's polite to say good morning back, Franck."

"Good morning, Carole."

"How're you doing, Cesar?"

"Okay. How about you?"

"No, I mean with Chips Reber?"

"Okay."

"Did you know that I knew him?" asked Carole.

"No." Cesar opened his paper.

"It's a real shame. He had the most terrific body."

Bodies again.

"How do you know that, Carole? I thought there were no men in your life."

"Don't be a jerk."

"Then what? Did you lend a hand with the autopsy?"

"God, you are so gross, Franck. As a matter of fact, he was in the same health club with me. Do you know what a health club is?"

"I always thought it was a bunch of great big vibrators, Carole."

"Figures," said Carole, looking at Cesar's stomach.

Cesar went back to his paper for a minute. Then he said, "Hey, Carole, did you this? About Jane Fonda?"

"What about her?"

"It's bad. Pectoral cancer. They think it's due to overdevelopment. She's got maybe six months."

"What? Really? Where does . . . ? Oh, you asshole."

Some days there is God. Just as Detective Griesel was revealing her true nature, Lieutenant Tieves strode in. Carole started to cough. Cesar folded his paper and smiled at her. Time to go to work.

He dug through the messages on his desk and found a note from the lab. The knife that Nicholas Grimes said he found in the alley had traces of what appeared to be the blood of Mr. Herman Reber.

*   *   *

Cesar found a place to park right in front of Arthur Battle's house. He crossed over to Hilda Kornbrust's to see if he could catch the mental patient before he went out for the day. It was still early. Abigail Street was quiet.

The heat was coming back. Cesar looked up at the whitening sky. Smog. The humidity was back too, and so was the litter. The big cleanup might never have taken place. Broken pop bottles crunched underfoot. Potato-chip bags sulked in the gutters. Cesar felt like taking Stella Hineman on a little trip to compare litter in Westwood and litter in Dutchtown.

He beat on Hilda Kornbrust's door and settled in against the wall to wait for her. While he waited, he watched a black woman coming down Abigail from the direction of the projects. When she got closer, he saw that she was young, maybe eighteen or twenty, and carrying schoolbooks. He figured she was on her way to one of the downtown business schools. He smiled politely. She gave him the once-over, ending up around his belt, and then rolled her eyes in boredom.

What is this, a conspiracy?

At long last Cesar heard Miss Kornbrust clumping her walker on the way to the door. He waited patiently for her to undo the chain and back out of the way of the door.

"Morning, ma'am."

"You want to see Gene again? I think maybe he's drunk."

"No, but he said there was another man living here?"

"Yeah, there is, but he's crazy. He can't tell you nothing."

"I know. Gene told me. Is he here?"

"I think so. He's real quiet, so I don't always know. That gives me the creeps a little bit, you know. His name is Goodin. Same as the old police chief. Stanley Goodin. He's upstairs all the way in the room over Gene."

The staircase to the third floor was about a foot narrower than the one below, the handrail was thinner, and the landing at the top was smaller. The light from the skylight was brighter, though. Cesar knocked on the back door. It was opened right away.

The man standing in the door blinked in the glare of the skylight. He was smallish, pale, a little pudgy. His hair stuck out in uneven tufts. He was wearing nothing but black socks, underpants, and a green nylon pullover jacket. Printed over the chest pocket were the words *St. Anselm Softball*. He stared at Cesar and Cesar stared at the jacket.

"Hello?" said the man.

"Are you Stanley Goodin?" asked Cesar. The man nodded solemnly. "I'm Detective Franck, Cincinnati Police. Can I come in?" Goodin nodded again. "Now?"

"Sure," said Goodin. He turned around right where he was standing and then walked into his room. The jacket said *St. Anselm Softball* on the back, too. And there was a hood.

He had found the jacket in the alley early Sunday morning. Goodin had a job cleaning up at the Provence Restaurant downtown. He worked with a friend from Longview State Hospital. They had been at the Provence from nine Saturday night until three o'clock Sunday. Stanley told Cesar he didn't need much sleep. He took naps. He was up and around at six o'clock. That was when he'd found the parka.

"I didn't steal it," he told Cesar. "I found it." He looked scared.

"It's okay, Stanley. I believe you. I didn't think you stole it. I'm trying to find out who it belonged to."

"Oh! I guess I'll have to give it back when you do."

"Maybe not. We'll see," said Cesar. "Whereabouts was it?"

"On the ground."

"Right. Where? Behind the house here? Next-door?"

Stanley tried to describe where it was, but he couldn't. "I can show you!" he said.

So Cesar waited while Stanley rooted around for pants and shoes. The room was pretty much like Gene's downstairs. The ceiling was lower, but it had the same kind of second-hand bed and table and a washbasin in the same corner. However, where Gene's single wall shelf had held a pile of westerns, Stanley's shelf held about ten cans of beanie-weenies. Stanley put on a pair of black pointy shoes and a pair of tan pants that were way too big for him and led Cesar down the stairs.

Cesar could barely keep up. Stanley Goodin walked briskly and took strides that belonged to a basketball player instead of a man shorter than Cesar. "I always check it out back here," said Stanley. They were in the alley behind Reber's and headed toward Central Avenue. "In fact, I usually walk by way of the alleys wherever I go, because sometimes I find things like this jacket." He led Cesar around the corner of the cross alley that led back to Abigail Street. He slowed down and twisted his body so that his feet kept going south while his head aimed down and to the left.

"I'm looking for a nail," he said. "I'm going to know exactly where it was, because I hurt my head on a nail when I found it. There. There it is. It was sort of stuck under there."

It was the place with the tidy backyard and the good lock.

"Do you think I should put it back?" asked Stanley. Cesar shook his head.

"I'm going to have to borrow it, though, Stanley. It's evidence."

"Evidence! Wow! Evidence! You should have told me!" Stanley whipped the jacket off over his head and stuck it out at Cesar. "I didn't know it was evidence!" He was a sight, standing there in the alley with his big pants and his pudgy chest. Cesar tried to get him to put it back on, but he wouldn't. "I can go buy one at the outreach center. They've got clothes there that don't cost too much."

"The one around the corner?" asked Cesar. "Come on, I'll buy you a replacement." Stanley tried to refuse, but Cesar told him it was government policy.

They walked around the southern end of the row of businesses facing Central so that Cesar could see which one had the spiffy lock. He counted backsides as they went south and counted fronts as they went north. It was the building with a fresh paint job, the one with lace curtains in the display windows. He stopped to read the small old-fashioned gold lettering on the door—*The Victorian Centre*— and then he followed Stanley up Central Avenue to the Truth and Beauty Outreach Center.

"There's a really really nice guy works in here named Sonny," said Stanley. Cesar didn't comment. He was running out of breath trying to keep up with Stanley. Boy, wouldn't that be lousy, running into Sonny? You could lose half a day when Sonny started running his mouth.

Stanley led the way into the Outreach Center. "Woo-oohh!" said Stanley. "Chilly!" The old air conditioner over the door was cranked to the max.

Cesar hadn't been in this center, but he'd seen plenty just like it. They all had government surplus desks and a thousand signs in English and Spanish for the six Mexicans who came to Cincinnati every year on their way to the tomato fields of Indiana. And they all had outreach workers. Outreach. Go out into the neighborhood and tell everybody that there's a convenient place in their own neighborhood where they get the shaft without going downtown.

The outreach workers were out. There was a white typist in the back eating an Egg McMuffin, a white guy in a glassed-in office on the phone, and a black teenager sitting behind a tabletop computer. The guy in the office saw Cesar and Stanley come in. He hung up the phones and came up front. He was obviously Management since he had on a skinny tie and a white short-sleeved shirt. Outreach workers are supposed to wear neighborhood clothes so that they can relate. Cesar knew how it worked from all the neighborhood meetings he used to have to sit in on. Our Representative From The Police.

"Stanley," said Mr. Management. "How's it going?

How'd you lose your shirt?" He looked at the parka rolled up in Cesar's hand.

"I forgot your name," said Stanley.

"It's Dick, Stanley. Dick Speers." He stuck out a hand at Cesar. "I don't think I know you," he said.

"He's a detective!" said Stanley.

"Can we get another jacket for Stanley here?" asked Cesar.

"Sure. Help yourself. What happened to the one you had?" asked Speers.

"It's evidence!" said Stanley as he started rummaging through a box marked MENS ONE DOLLAR.

"Evidence? What do you mean, 'evidence,' Stanley?"

"You know. When the police want something, it's evidence."

"Did this man want your shirt?"

"No, no. No my shirt. It's sort of a jacket, only there's no zipper."

"Stanley, do you have an attorney?" asked Speers. He looked at Cesar as if daring him to step on a constitutional right. Any constitutional right.

"I don't think so," said Stanley, still rummaging.

"He doesn't need one," said Cesar. "He's not charged with anything. We're just looking for a jacket or something."

"Is that his?" asked Speers, pointing to the parka in Cesar's hand.

"I gave it to Mr. Franck," said Stanley. "He can keep it."

"Find anything you like, Stanley?" asked Cesar. He turned his back on Speers, who was getting on his nerves.

"Well, there's a lot of things, so I've got to decide. I sometimes have a hard time making up my mind."

"No rush," said Cesar. "You pick a good one." He walked away from Speers, who was still glaring at him, and went over to watch the kid on the computer. He walked to where he could see over the boy's shoulder.

The boy was playing a video game. Or that was what it looked like, except every now and then the action, which was taking place on a sort of grid, would stop. The little blobs that were streaking around after other little blobs froze where they were and the boy would stare at one screen and then write something down on a pad. "Whatcha doing?" Cesar asked.

The boy looked over his shoulder at Cesar and then back at the screen. His face looked about sixteen, even though he was about the size of a twelve-year-old boy. "It's a game, man."

"I figured. What is it, Pac Man?"

"Naw."

Cesar watched as he started the game up again, stopped it again, and wrote on his pad again. "Are you making up a game?"

"Yeah."

"No kidding? You know how to do that?"

"Something wrong with that? You never see a black programmer before? Figure we too stupid?"

"Take it easy. I never even saw a programmer before. I don't know how they do that stuff."

"It's simple, man. You just got to be a genius."

Cesar felt somebody behind him. He looked around and down at Dick Speers. "How about leaving him alone?" said Speers.

"It's all right, Mr. Speers. The man never seen a genius at work before."

"You let me know if he bothers you, Steve."

I'm just looking, Creep. "Where'd you learn to program? I thought you had to go to college for that."

"Not if you brilliant you don't."

"Did you just teach yourself?"

"Just like that," said Stephen, and then he relented. "No, they had a couple of computers at school and I started to learn there, only once they taught me everything they knew, which didn't take too long since they didn't know too much, I started to teach them. And they didn't like that." He laughed.

"Where do you go? Walnut Hills?"

"Naw, man. I *went* to Taft."

"You quit?"

"Let's say we agreed that there wasn't too much more that they could teach me." Stephen turned around and grinned at Cesar and then went back to his screen.

"So what's the game?" asked Cesar.

"The name is . . . are you ready for this? The name is . . . GHETTO BLASTER!!! The first black video game by black people for black people! And I am going to be *rich,* man." The kid couldn't resist an audience. He explained the game to Cesar. The grid on the screen was a bird's-eye view of the projects, including the streets and walkways. One of the little moving blobs was the car belonging to Ghetto Blaster, who was sort of a black Robin Hood. The other little blobs belonged to cops and gangsters, both of whom were constantly after Ghetto Blaster.

"Like Pac Man," said Cesar.

"Hey, man, this ain't *nothing* like no Pac Man. Look at this." Stephen showed him some of the features, but since he still hadn't figured out how to make a Pac Man game last longer than fifteen seconds, it was hard for Cesar to appreciate Ghetto Blaster. He did kind of groove on the opening screen where the kid had made the Ghetto Blaster car appear in a drawing with tires that throbbed. Stephen said he was planning on heavy sound to go along with the game. " . . . except I got this problem with the man going to come up with a synthesizer."

"What's the problem?" asked Cesar.

"The problem is the dude is *dead,*" said Stephen. "Boy went and got himself killed before we could get together on a deal."

Oh, yeah. "Guy's name Reber?" asked Cesar. Sandy Schott said something about Reber giving an Apple to the outreach center, which finally made sense now that he saw the Apple label on the computer.

"You know the cat?" asked Stephen.

"Not really, I—"

"I can't believe what happened to that dude. That's some bad shit. He was all right. I told him about Ghetto

Blaster, he said he was gonna back me with some cash. And he would have too. He wasn't no Scrooge McDuck with his money like some of these cats around here." Stephen looked pointedly over in the direction of Dick Speers. Speers was one of those guys who's always staring at you and then pretending like he wasn't. Like it's really interesting just over your shoulder. There was something really interesting just over Cesar's shoulder at that minute.

"Speers don't seem to like you too much, man. That's probably 'cause you a detective. Sonny and them don't like the police. You looking for the dude that killed Chips?"

"Hey! Mr. Franck! I found what I want!" Stanley Goodin held up a hooded sweatshirt that said ELAINE POWERS. Cesar held out a dollar to him and then turned to Stephen. "Can you read computer disks?" he asked.

"That depends on the disk," said the boy. "What kind you got?"

"I don't know. I don't know the first thing about them. They're Reber's."

"Then I can read them. No problem. Some of them I probably wrote on myself."

"No kidding."

"Hey, I don't kid the police, man. 'Specially no detectives. See, I used to do the little occasional computer job for Chips. Little business proposition. Strictly business. You bring them in and I'll fix you right up. I am the expert."

"Thanks. I appreciate it."

Cesar left Stanley at the outreach center and started back down Central Avenue. The Packard was back. He could spot it all the way from the corner. As he approached the car, Cesar saw that it was parked in front of the Victorian Centre, and he remembered a couple of things. One, the car belonged to Elizabeth Somebody who worked in the Victorian Centre, and, two, Arthur Battle had seen a Packard cruising the neighborhood the night Chips Reber died. Arthur said the Packard stopped outside Reber's house. Time to get a little information and just possibly a ride in the Caribbean. With any luck it would turn out to be important evidence that he would have to take back to the office. What a car. He walked into the Victorian Centre.

Alan Howard was inside with a woman, and somehow, within two seconds, Cesar understood that they weren't talking to each other. Something about the atmosphere. Howard was sitting at one of a pair of old-fashioned wooden desks going through some papers. The woman's perfume gave out the same heavy smell of gardenias Cesar had smelled at Hilda Kornbrust's. She was wearing an off-white blouse with big sleeves and long tight cuffs. She had an old gold watch pinned over her left breast, and her hair was piled up on top of her head. She was writing with a big black fountain pen. When Cesar walked in, she glanced at him, rolled a blotter over her work, raised her chin, and said, "Yes?"

Alan Howard introduced them. Mrs. Sackville raised one eyebrow when she heard Cesar's name, but she didn't make any smart remarks. When Cesar told her that he was investigating the Reber homicide she put one hand on her throat and drew in a little breath, but she didn't really look all that shocked. Cesar held up the green parka, which did seem to shock her a little because it looked out of place in the office, and he told her that it had been found behind the Victorian Centre. She told him that many equally vulgar, occasionally even more vulgar items appeared behind the fence, but she assured him that none of them had anything to do with anyone in any way associated with the Victorian Centre or the Consortium for the Nineteenth Century. "Unless," she added, "Mr. Howard has been disposing of some of his darker secrets in the alley." She glanced over at the other desk, and Howard glared back at her.

Then Cesar asked her if she had seen Chips Reber Saturday night when she stopped in front of his house sometime around eleven o'clock. She put her hand on her throat again. This time she did look shocked.

"What on earth, Officer! Am I being followed? Why do you know my movements? Am I under suspicion of murder? Alan, are you paying attention to what this policeman has been saying?"

"It's your problem, Elizabeth. I'm sure you can handle it." Alan Howard smiled smoothly at Elizabeth and Cesar and went back to his papers.

"Alan, I expect you to serve as my solicitor. Pay attention."

"Elizabeth, just can it. Answer the detective's questions. If he starts mentioning your constitutional rights, you can always pick up the phone and call your own lawyer."

"I won't forget this, Alan."

Alan Howard didn't seem to care.

"I seem to find myself alone, Officer. I shall have to trust you."

"You'll be all right, ma'am. The gentleman's correct. And believe me, nobody's following you. A neighbor saw your car and remembered it. It's a fairly unusual automobile."

"Do you think so? My father always drove a Packard, so they don't seem odd to me."

"Elizabeth, just answer his question." Alan Howard couldn't stay out of it.

"But I have forgotten what the gentleman asked me."

Cesar already had the impression that Elizabeth Sackville was a lady who never forgot anything ever, but he let it pass.

"Saturday night, ma'am," he prompted.

"Of course. Let me think." She put a hand to her temple and thought. "Saturday night. Yes. I did drive down Abigail Street, but I did not stop in front of Mr. Reber's house, although I was quite near. I had stopped in front of the Worth-Dupree house to admire the carving again."

"Which house is that?" asked Cesar.

"It is the house immediately to the west of Mr. Reber's."

"Hilda Kornbrust's house."

"No, Detective Franck, it's mine. I have bought the Worth-Dupree house for my own use."

So that was what she doing at Hilda Kornbrust's. Where was Hilda Kornbrust going to go? Where were Gene Standriff and Stanley Goodin going to go? Sonny Werk was going to love this one.

"Well," said Cesar, "I'd still like to know if you saw or heard Mr. Reber last Saturday. Or anybody else on the street for that matter."

She hadn't. She made it sound as if it would be sort of low-class to see anybody on the street.

"Would you know Chips Reber if you saw him?" asked Cesar.

"Unfortunately, yes," she answered. "I have, on occasion, found it necessary to meet him. Not socially. We—"

"They were fighting over the house," said Alan Howard. "Elizabeth, I can't stand it. This guy probably has plenty of work to do and I know I do, so quit dragging it out." Elizabeth Sackville opened her mouth, but Howard cut her off. "They were in a bidding war, Detective Franck. They both wanted that house. Poor Reber didn't know he was up against the local branch of the Rothschilds, but he forced her to pay more than she planned."

"Are you enjoying this, Alan?"

"It beats listening to you try to yank this poor man around."

Elizabeth Sackville reached for the bottle of black ink that sat on her desk and then pulled her hand away.

"He's quite right, Officer. I have delayed you and I apologize. I left the May Festival Saturday night and drove through Abigail Street. I did pause to admire my new house, but I neither heard nor saw Mr. Reber. Nor for that matter did I see anyone else. I left immediately and joined my husband at a party on Grandin Road. He drove his own car. Do you need any further information?"

"Are you sure you've never seen anyone wearing this?"

asked Cesar, and he held up the green parka one more time.

"It is not something I would remember," said Elizabeth Sackville with a sniff.

Cesar headed toward the BandK, where he figured the bullshit would be a little easier to take. The customers were also a lot more likely to remember something like a person walking around with her hood up on a hot summer night. And, if they thought it wasn't going to screw them or anyone they knew, they would be perfectly happy to talk.

"Heybro, whashap?" asked the drunk who was sunning himself in the doorway of the BandK.

"Not much," said Cesar, and he beat it inside before the guy could hit him up for money.

Things were calm at the BandK. Only one of the pool tables was in use. The rest of the customers were at the tables or in the booths taking it easy. The cooler weather of the past couple of days had helped, and even if today was the beginning of a new hot spell, it was too early in the cycle for tempers to get out of hand.

Cesar never felt too bad in places that catered to an older set, like the BandK did. He didn't know why the older black people didn't get real jumpy around him, compared to the younger, badder dudes, but they were always easier to deal with. There was a good case for things being the other way around, since the older blacks had lived through a lot heavier stuff than the guys in their twenties. The older people remembered segregation in Cincinnati that wasn't too different from segregation in the deep south. Some of the older guys had had to fight in segregated units in the war, and a lot of the women had spent their lives blowing white kids' noses, but he could usually count on them to be more reasonable than some kid who didn't even know there were two world wars.

Cesar worked his way back through the poolroom to the little bar, nodding at the customers. They mostly nodded back, even though they knew right off that he was a cop. There was only one customer at the bar. She was talking to the bartender, who introduced himself to Cesar as John Lindsey, the owner. The woman swiveled in her seat and crossed her legs, settling in for a good listen. It was always interesting when the police came around. Always.

Cesar told them that he was investigating the death of Chips Reber, and Lindsey and the woman looked at each other and laughed.

"It's a coincidence, Officer," said Lindsey. "Mrs. Anderson and me was just talking about Rebers."

"Johnny said he was fixing to buy this place," said Mrs. Anderson.

"Reber?" asked Cesar.

Lindsey nodded. "It's a *shame*. Thought I had found me the perfect sucker." He laughed.

"And I told Johnny if somebody hadn't kilt that dude first, he would've got it from one of these old men in here soon as word got out he was fixin' to close the only place to get a drink on this side of the projects." Mrs. Anderson let out a big whooping laugh. Lindsey started to look sad. "Hey! Cheer Up!" said Mrs. Anderson. "You gonna be glad you kept this place. All those new doctors and lawyers moving in down here got to have someplace to shoot pool and drink beer, ain't that right, Mr. Detective?" She held onto Cesar's arm and leaned way back, winking and laughing. She almost fell off the stool.

"You got to watch it there, Juanita. You're gonna laugh yourself right into the emergency room," said Lindsey. He turned back to Cesar. "I tell you what," he said, "I wish I did know something could help you. I'm real disappointed. Real disappointed."

"You ever see anybody wearing this thing?" asked Cesar, and he unrolled and held up the green parka. Lindsey shook his head, but Juanita Anderson pulled herself straight and said, "Honey, that there is from the Truth and Beauty Outreach Center. I seen it there just the other day. I was thinking about maybe buying it but I got a sweater instead, but that's where it was. At the Truth and Beauty Center. I know it. Where you get it?"

"A guy found it," said Cesar.

"Is that evidence?" asked Juanita.

"Yeah, it is."

"Woo! I am a *crimestopper!* Hey! Everybody! Call Channel Twelve and get those boys down here with that truck 'cause I am a *crimestopper!*" Juanita got off of her stool and threw a couple of powerful bumps to her audience. She got light applause.

"Are you sure you saw it at the outreach center?" asked Cesar.

" 'Course I'm sure. I saw that name on it and that's why I decided not to get it. Besides, I don't play no softball."

"Did you ever see anybody wearing it?"

"Unh-unh. Only time I ever see it was when it was in the clothing bank."

"What about you?" Cesar asked Lindsey. Lindsey just shook his head. He was looking sad again, probably thinking about his lost sale.

"Hey!" Juanita Anderson took the parka from Cesar and held it up over her head as she turned to face the rest of the poolroom. "Hey, all of y'all, listen up! Y'all ever see anybody wearing this here jacket? Somebody wake up Stone over there. Did y'all ever see this?" She waited until she had heard all the goofy responses the customers could come up with and then handed it back to Cesar. "Nope," she said, "ain't nobody seen this jacket. 'Course most of these old drunks can't even tell you what *they* got on."

"Thanks anyway," said Cesar. "That's more than I knew ten minutes ago."

"Glad to help, Officer. Anytime. You just be sure you tell the chief where you got your most important information. From Mrs. Juanita Anderson at the most famous and best poolroom on Central Avenue." Juanita pinched John Lindsey's cheek. He looked like he was going to cry.

*   *   *

Why didn't those clowns at the outreach center say where the jacket came from? They saw me standing there holding it all the time I was in the center. What the hell did they think I was doing with it?

Cesar marched back to the Truth and Beauty Center without even stopping to look at the Packard.

The outreach workers and the social workers had come back to the center, and one of them, a black woman, recognized the parka right off. But even though she seemed to have responsibility for the clothing bank, she couldn't remember anybody buying it. Neither could anybody else. All that anybody knew was that it had come in with a load of clothes collected by a church out in College Hill and that they had been delivered sometime the week before. While Cesar was prying that information loose from the workers, Dick Speers stood outside the office door with his arms folded and a you-had-better-have-a-search-warrant expression pasted on his face. Stephen was still glued to his computer. He had pasted a big *Do Not Disturb Or Else* sign on his work table. No one was disturbing. As Cesar started to leave, Speers walked over to join him. Cesar waited.

"You know, you're lucky Sonny Werk wasn't here to see this," Speers said, only he mumbled out of the side of his mouth so Cesar had to make him repeat it twice before he finally understood.

"Well, I'm sure Mr. Werk understands I've got a job to do," said Cesar.

"*I* understand," said Speers. "You probably don't know this, but I was accepted as a police recruit several years ago, so I know what you have to do." Speers gave a far-seeing look through the front window, then said, "Sonny didn't have that experience. In fact, the only experience he's had with the law has been negative, so he wouldn't be happy to have you in here."

"Well, I'm going, so he ought to be just fine." Cesar pulled the door open and got one foot out on the sidewalk. Speers was sticking close behind. How did he turn out to be such a close buddy?

"I trust you're not limiting your investigation to low-income persons," said Speers.

"Why?" asked Cesar. "You know something about the crime?"

"No. Nothing specific."

"Because if you do, you ought to be telling me right now."

"I'm merely concerned about any possible discrimination."

"What are you talking about?" asked Cesar. "Discrimination my—"

"Against poor people. I'm sure you've assumed that this is a black crime."

"No," said Cesar, "I haven't." He started to walk away from Speers.

"No need to get upset, Officer. But you *have* been conducting your interrogation in an agency for the poor."

"Sir, you don't know where I've been, all right? So just—"

"What about the BandK? Word gets around in this community. You just came from there. Why don't you start looking at some of Reber's middle- and upper-income friends? You know violence is *not* limited to poor and minorities."

"I'm aware of that, sir." There was no way he was going to give Speers the satisfaction of knowing that he had spent half the time on this case in middle-class offices and living rooms.

"Are you aware, then, that Chips Reber had plenty of enemies among the white people on his block?"

"Whether I am or—"

"The same professional types who claim they are bringing stability to a neighborhood when they are actually disrupting an intricate and well-established balance—"

"Sir, I—"

" . . . which has its own validity. It's actually more valid for poor people to be here than for any of these young professionals. As far as the poor are concerned, these young professionals are a greater enemy than any other force for evil in this—"

"Mr. Speers." Cesar had had enough. He had also been to enough neighborhood meetings to know the verses to this particular hymn. "Mr. Speers, I've got a long day ahead of me, a lot of work to do. So unless you've got some specific information that might help me with my investigation—"

"I understand," said Speers. "And if you need any help, Officer, call me. I'll handle Sonny for you. It'll save you time."

"Thanks. I'll remember that."

"And I'll do some checking on that jacket for you. What does it say?"

"It says, 'Saint Anselm Softball.' "

"I'll be discreet, don't worry. We're always discreet about the clothing bank. We have to be. Low-income people are sensitive about having to buy used clothes. That's needless, of course. They're perfectly good. We don't accept clothes that aren't in good shape. You could wear them and nobody would notice. I guarantee it. As a matter of fact, I got this tie from the bank." He held up his inch-wide iridescent green tie. "And Sonny never gets clothes anywhere else. He pays for them, of course."

Wacko. One minute he's down on you, the next minute he's ready to ride shotgun. He must be Sonny's Carole Griesel.

Forty-six seconds after leaving Dick Speers in front of the Truth and Beauty Center, Cesar stood on Stella Hineman's front stoop, knocking on her screen door. It was unpremeditated. If he had premeditated, he would never have gone back to see her. "Is your mom home?" he asked Sidney, who had come to the door with Linda the cat cradled in his arms. Sidney walked into the back of the house without answering, leaving Cesar to wonder if he had been snubbed or if it just wasn't Sidney's day to talk. He surreptitiously tested the screen door and was pleased to find it locked. Stella came to the door.

"Oh, it's you," she said. "Come in. Wait, let me get this lock undone." She fiddled with the latch.

"Thanks, I can't stay," said Cesar. "I just wanted to see if I could take you to dinner tonight." He hadn't known he was going to do that either.

"Are you kidding? No, you're not. I'm surprised."

"I thought maybe we could talk better."

"It would have to be better than last night," said Stella.

"Can you make it?" asked Cesar.

"You know, that really sounds nice? I'd love to, but I've got this problem."

"Anything I can do?"

"Can you get a baby-sitter? That's the problem."

Lillian? No.

"It really is a problem down here," sighed Stella. "None of the white people has any kids . . . definitely no teenage daughters . . . and all of the black teenagers have their own kids."

"How about—"

"Look," Stella said, "why don't you just eat here? I'll fix something."

"That's a pain in the neck for you."

"No, it's not. Let me see what I've got." Stella headed for the kitchen, but Cesar stopped her.

"I'll bring something. I'll bring carry out."

"Don't bring carry out, bring groceries. I hate carry out."

So he ate carry out for lunch.

11

WHAT CESAR HAD was four-way and a cheese coney. It all worked out. He parked on Court Street and bought steaks at Avril's and potatoes and stuff for salad from the market stands and candy from the candy store and then he remembered there was a Skyline just across Vine, so he picked up the chili, and everything fit in the Camaro just fine, even though Lillian said it was a tiny car, and he still had time on the meter.

He put the groceries in the office fridge and ate at his desk while he read his messages. The worst one was on top. Carole Griesel had taken it and she must have loved it. The mayor's office had gotten a call from Sonny Werk complaining about Detective Franck of homicide searching his outreach center without a warrant and harassing his employees and a poor person without cause. Cesar guessed that the poor person was Stanley Goodin. The mayor and Stefanie, the mayor's chief aide who made the call, wanted to know what was going on, and was it really necessary to harass Sonny Werk?

There was also a message from Cesar's sister, Kathy, reminding him that Sunday was his nephew's birthday and he should remember to bring a very nice present. And there was a call from Sandy Schott. He pushed the messages aside and worked on the cheese coney.

Henry came in and sat at his desk behind Cesar. He

had picked up a turkey dinner from some church in Walnut Hills. He looked at Cesar's lunch and shook his head. Cesar looked at the Baptist carry out and shook his head too. There was enough for three people, but Henry never left anything on the plate. Cesar filled Henry in on the Dutchtown news while they ate. Henry didn't have any news. He was working on your basic family murder with sixteen eyewitnesses.

Henry wanted to know if Cesar had run across any more interesting videotapes. Cesar told him no but he had run into a great investment opportunity, "Ghetto Blaster." Henry wanted a lot of details that Cesar couldn't give him. He did tell Henry that the computer genius seemed to be on the level and could do with enough money for a synthesizer and that the game probably did need sound effects. Henry sucked on his teeth and looked out the window, which meant that he was thinking about money and the possibility of parting with it for a while. Henry didn't like to do that. But he did like a gamble once in a while and if it might make a couple of new black millionaires . . .

"Jeez, it *stinks* in here. What are you guys *eating?*" Detective Griesel adding to the smog.

"Autopsy," said Cesar. "Want some?"

Detective Griesel gave him the finger and said, "Lieutenant Tieves wants to see you in his office. It's about *the mayor.*"

"Ooooh," said Cesar. "I'm scared."

"You ought to be," said Carole. "He's been studying height-to-weight charts, too. Have fun."

"Come on in, Cesar. Close the door." Lieutenant Tieves sat behind his desk in his litter- and germ-free office. Sergeant Evans sat in one of the guest chairs too, but he never looked as germ-free as the lieutenant. "We had a call from the mayor's office."

"Right. Carole left me a message."

"Sit down, Cesar. Make yourself comfortable."

Impossible. Absolutely impossible. The office was all hard surfaces. Nobody ever got comfortable.

"Now," said the lieutenant, "I know you haven't been harassing anybody and I know the mayor knows that we know the difference between gathering information and conducting a search on private property—"

"Lieutenant, all I did was—"

"You don't have to explain, Cesar. I have every confidence in you. I just thought we might have a talk about Sonny Werk and where he may or may not stand in the scheme of things."

Sergeant Evans had turned himself away from the lieutenant and felt free to cross his eyes over the last statement.

Lieutenant Tieves stood up and tucked his starched shirtfront into his trousers, emphasizing his youthful waist and flat stomach for the benefit of his thicker staff. "Nobody has to tell me what kind of a guy Sonny Werk is. I've seen him in action and I know what he stands for and I don't have any use for him or his projects. So don't get me wrong. But Sonny, as far as the mayor and council are concerned, has a definite and legitimate activist role to play."

Sergeant Evans broke into a coughing fit.

"Are you all right, Sergeant Evans?" The sergeant nodded and held his breath. "Good. Sonny Werk is more than just the voice of the poor; he is starting to be a definite political consideration. If you've been watching the news, you know that he's been running a successful voter-registration drive in Over-the-Rhine." Cesar nodded. "You certainly know that he's been able to organize substantial opposition to redevelopment of some of the old neighborhoods."

"I saw one of his protest marches Sunday," said Cesar.

"Then you know what I'm talking about. Good. Now I want you to know that in no way do I approve of Sonny Werk or the way he goes about his business, but considering the fact that he has become the most visible leader of a growing movement, and that he may figure substantially in future elections, I want you—and everybody in the squad, for that matter—to treat him with the respect you would give any other community or political leader."

Sergeant Evans choked.

"Problem, Sergeant?" asked the lieutenant. Sergeant Evans shook his head. "What about you, Cesar? Any questions?"

Cesar had a whole lot of questions, but he knew the lieutenant wouldn't think they were funny.

"No, sir, I think I understand. I just want you to know that I didn't even see Sonny Werk today. All I did was interview this guy from Longview who's living over in Dutchtown, because he found this jacket that maybe belonged to whoever killed Chips Reber. That's it. And the only reason I was in Sonny's agency was to buy the guy a replacement because he really seemed to like the jacket. That's all I did. Except that it turns out the jacket came from Sonny's clothing bank, so I asked some questions about that. So I don't know where he's coming from complaining to the mayor, sir."

"Cesar, I told you I had every confidence in you, all right? And I meant that. You wouldn't be working for me if I didn't. But if you're going to move up in the division, you're going to have to be a little more sensitive to some of the issues out there in the community."

Say it. Say politics, for crying out loud.

"Sonny Werk doesn't like the police. You should know that."

"I know that, Lieutenant. But I'll tell you what. Whenever I went to any community meeting that he was at, he spent half his time crying for more patrols in his neighborhood. No kidding. He wanted them pulled out of other neighborhoods and assigned downtown to protect his winos."

"Now that's what I mean, Cesar. You can't call them winos."

"Okay. Alcoholic people."

"I'm not joking, Cesar. All I need is for you to call the alcoholics 'winos' around some reporter. You think Sonny's yelling now, but he hasn't even gotten started."

"What am I supposed to do, Lieutenant? I'm investigating a homicide that happened a block away from his agency. I've got to talk to people down there. I've got to—"

Carole Griesel opened the door and interrupted Cesar. "Sir, I've got a reporter on the phone for you. It's about Sonny Werk. He called the paper."

"Tell him I'll get back to him in five minutes, Carole." Lieutenant Tieves looked gravely at Cesar. "You see what I mean, Cesar? You're going to be in the paper when you don't need to be. A little discretion would have prevented this. That's all. You're going to have to start paying attention to the bigger picture."

"Right, sir. I'll work on it. Is that all, sir?"

"That's all."

Sergeant Evans followed Cesar out of the lieutenant's office. Carole Griesel flashed her professional smile at them, and Henry looked questioningly as he crammed his disposable dishes into a full wastecan. Cesar headed for the washroom and Sergeant Evans followed.

"What a lot of shit!" snapped Cesar, standing at the urinal. "What a load of first-class horseshit!"

Sergeant Evans, who was two urinals over, shook his head. "Relax, will you?"

"Relax?! After I get reamed out for doing my job? Will you tell me how the hell I am supposed to guess that that overgrown fruitbowl is going to call the mayor's office when I didn't do anything? Nothing! I'm telling you! And he sits in there and tells me he has complete confidence in me and then turns around"—Cesar punched the flush lever hard with his fist—"and tells me I should use more discretion when I'm busy not doing anything wrong. What's *with* that guy?"

"Use your head, Cesar," said Sergeant Evans as he zipped up. "Use your head." Sergeant Evans began to scour his hands. "He doesn't like calls from the mayor unless it's to congratulate him. He likes to bat a thousand all the time."

"Yeah, but—"

"Look, he knows you didn't screw up. He's not stupid. But besides not wanting any trouble from the mayor or the manager or any of the loonies on city council, he doesn't want to get involved with Sonny Werk."

"Hey, I don't either!" said Cesar.

"See? Who does? The guy is crazy and the reporters all love him. He'll say anything. He don't care. He's trouble any way you look at him. So the lieutenant gets jumpy. What are you going to do? Cry?"

"Who's crying? I'm pissed off."

"You don't have to shout, Cesar. Just take it easy. You're not in any trouble."

"Not yet I'm not. But I want you to guess who in this city dresses himself from his own clothing bank where this jacket which maybe was worn by Reber's killer came from. Just guess. And guess who I'm going to have to talk to about whether he helped himself to a Saint Some-body's Softball jacket."

"Werk, huh? Well, well. You got yourself a little prob-lem, Cesar. I have to say you've got a problem."

Cesar walked back to Dutchtown.

He had dropped the parka off at the lab, where they were going to see if it matched the threads they'd found stuck to the corner of the air conditioner, and then he had stopped in to talk to Marv Bolte in Vice. Marv was all right. He worked his ass off, but he never got too caught up in the undercover work. At least not to the point where he thought he was both Starsky and Hutch, like some of the younger guys. Marv had been checking around for Cesar. All he had found out was that the cocaine dealers knew who Reber was but that they hadn't heard any noise about his getting mixed up with any of the heavies. He was a very small fish who liked people to think he might be a much bigger fish, but nobody trusted him. Marv was going to keep looking and listening, but he didn't think that anything major was going to show up.

And then, when Cesar checked in at the office on his way out, there was a box of roses on his desk. A dozen red roses. So of course there was a lot of crap from everybody in the room about what he must have done to deserve them. Except that Detective Griesel didn't say anything. She was probably jealous. Cesar read the card and told everybody that it was from a woman, but he didn't tell them who, and he didn't tell them what the card said. They were from Elizabeth Sackville, and the card said, "With most sincere gratitude for your attack on Sonny Werk."

Now what in God's name was he supposed to make of that?

He was on his way to talk to the Sharps and the Grimeses. Cesar glanced down Franklin Street as he crossed it, but he didn't have any excuse for checking out Stella until tonight, so he kept walking until he got to Abigail.

Nancy Sharp let him in. She got all flustered when she saw him, and Cesar couldn't figure out why, since he was family. Then he remembered that the last time he saw her she sort of admitted to getting grass from Reber. She probably thought Cesar was going to turn her in.

Cesar didn't like marijuana. Everybody got used to smoking marijuana and scoffing at the drug laws, so they thought it was okay to move on to coke, which was why half the economy was flying off to Colombia and why baseball wasn't the way it used to be. Drugs made a mess. But he wasn't about to pinch Nancy Sharp for smoking grass, and he told her so.

"Are you sure you're not gonna haul me in?" Nancy gave a nervous little laugh.

"I'm sure. Just don't tell anybody you told me, okay? Can I come in?"

"What? Oh! Sure. Come on back to the kitchen. Do you want to talk to Bill? He's back in his studio."

"In a minute. Where's the studio?"

"It's over the garage. Didn't you see it on the tour?"

"I must have missed it," said Cesar.

Nancy Sharp led him to the kitchen, which was the last room on the ground floor. She pointed to a stool beside an island in the middle of the room, so he sat down while she made coffee. He put his elbows on the island and then took them off since the butcher block on the island was greasy. He sat and waited and tried not to be obvious about spotting the gas goop all over the pottery sitting on the tops of the hanging cabinets. You really only have to wash that stuff a couple of times a year—four, say—and you don't get that buildup.

Nancy told him that she thought the killer was somebody from the projects. She said that nobody on the street had ever had a break-in but that young guys from the project were always coming through Abigail and the alleys and they were always looking in at the houses. A lot of times they made threatening remarks. As far as she was concerned, that was the only real drawback to living where she did, but it was a big one. And besides, she said, it was a stabbing.

Cesar drank his coffee, which was pretty good even though the cup wasn't quite clean. He told Nancy that he had seen a lot of stabbings and enough of them were perpetrated by white people that you couldn't always assume. Nancy got embarrassed. He also said that Reber had about six million dollars' worth of consumer electronics in his bedroom and they hadn't been touched. Reber's diamond pinky ring was still on his pinky and his gold chains were still around his neck and his gold stud was still in his ear when he was found, and Cesar didn't think that fit your usual ripoff murder. There was also the matter of the air conditioner the killer had left on Reber's chest, which had never shown up in any MO he'd ever seen. At least not in the projects. Nancy thought all of that was real interesting.

Cesar asked her where she had been Saturday night and if she had heard or seen anything going on around Reber's house.

No. She and Bill had been over talking to Nicholas and Greta Grimes until a little after ten. She and Greta had stayed in Greta's kitchen and the men had stayed out on the stoop. H.P. had been in bed. They might have heard Reber hammering but there was always some kind of noise at night, especially in the summer. They hadn't paid any attention to Reber's place when they'd walked home.

"Was anyone else there?" asked Cesar.

"Just us."

"So you left the Grimeses alone?"

"Yeah." Nancy took a second to realize that she had left her friends without an alibi, then said, "But you'll see. They're not violent people. I'm a thousand times more violent than either one of them."

Cesar calmed Nancy down and asked her how well she knew Reber.

"I didn't really *know* him, Cesar," she answered. "He really wasn't the kind of person . . . well, he wasn't really what we wanted down here."

"What do you mean?" asked Cesar.

"Oh, you're going to think I'm a real snob. Kathy's talked about you."

"You can't believe what she says."

"I'll tell her you said that. Anyway, what I mean about Chips is that he's . . . he was exactly wrong for what we're trying to get going here. He comes along with an indecent amount of money and he starts buying places left and right and kicking people out of their homes, which gets *Sonny Werk* on our case, which is *exactly* what we don't need. And not only does he buy up these places; he gives them the old Mount Adams treatment. You know, with the saunas and the jacuzzis. Except for Stella Hineman's and the Speerses' places. He hasn't done *anything* for them."

"I thought Jacuzzis were real popular," said Cesar. He was still hoping for a Jacuzzi adventure before he got too old.

"Well, they *are* nice. What I mean is that he just charged into the buildings and started carving them up into rental units for singles. And we just really don't want the singles scene."

"Oh. Did you say the Speerses live here?"

"Over on Franklin," said Nancy. "Why, do you know them?"

"I met a guy named Dick Speers over at the outreach center today."

"That's him. Isn't he a creep?"

"I really didn't get to know him, Nancy."

"He's gross. Just gross. I think he looks like a pervert. In fact, I think he's the one that's been making obscene calls all over the place."

"Really? Have you been getting them too?"

"Yes." Nancy shuddered. "They're so disgusting."

"Why do you think it's Speers? Do you know his voice?"

"Oh, he disguises it, and I can't swear to it. I don't know. I suppose he just looks like someone who'd do that."

"You've got to have a little more to go on than that."

"Of course." Nancy stuck her finger into her coffee cup and stirred the little puddle that was still in there. Then she looked up and asked, "Are we through?"

"I guess so. Unless you can think of anything that might help me. Like did you ever see people going in and out of his place?"

"You want to see Bill about that. He's the big snoop. He can see up and down both alleys from his studio. Over the fences, too. You want to go up there now?"

"Sure." Cesar rinsed his cup out at the sink, set it next to a pile of unrinsed dishes, and followed Nancy out a side door and through the skinny little yard back to the garage. Cesar glimpsed the Sharps' van and several mountains of junk before he and Nancy started to climb a skinny flight of stairs. Each step sort of squished under his weight, so he gripped the handrail—which promptly came out of the wall.

"I never come up here if I can help it," said Nancy as she helped Cesar shove the handrail back into place. "I'm sure I'm going to die on every step. I don't know how Bill stands it." They reached a crowded little landing, and then Nancy threw her weight on a door and led

Cesar into her husband's studio. "Company!" she yelled. "Wake up!"

Bill Sharp's studio was a single large room with windows on three sides. The ceiling sloped up, following the roofline, so that it went from nine to fifteen feet high. With all the windows, and a skylight made from a camper top, the room was full of light. Nancy led Cesar between stacks of boxes and canvases and window frames and broken furniture until they came to an open space. She led Cesar around the gigantic canvas that was rigged into a vertical framework and at last they found William Sharp.

As Arthur Battle said, Sharp looked kind of like a hippie. He had hair to his shoulders and a bald spot on the back of his head, and he had a long beard. He was wearing filthy coveralls, Birkenstock sandals, and a Sony Walkman. He seemed to be completely caught up in the music or his painting because he didn't even notice Cesar and Nancy. Nancy stepped between her husband and his painting.

"Whooa!" Bill hollered. Nancy had startled him.

Cesar looked at the painting. It was a big slice of cantaloupe. Sharp must have been responsible for the big lemons and limes at the McDowells'. Or else that was what artists were doing now. Cesar didn't know a whole lot about it.

Nancy pointed at the Walkman earphones until her husband understood that she wanted them off. He wiped his hands on a rag and rejoined the world.

"You remember Cesar, Bill. He's Kathy's brother."

"Sure. The detective, right?" He shook hands with Cesar and then waved at the big cantaloupe. "Whatcha think?" he asked Cesar.

Oh, Jeez.

"Great," said Cesar finally. "Cantaloupe, right?"

"Yep," said Sharp. "My latest sofa-size fruit. Can you believe anybody buys this shit?" He shook his head and laughed. "It's paying the bills, though."

"Bill, I told you you've got to quit joking about that.

Somebody's going to hear you and get pissed off," said Nancy. "He did a couple of these fruit things for a joke, Cesar, and they turned out to be real popular with decorators and he's made a lot of money with them. I think it's great."

"I'm not complaining," said Sharp. "I just don't want one in my house. They give me a headache."

"That's his real stuff over there," said Nancy, waving her arm toward a corner of the studio. "You better go over and look. He won't let you out until you do."

Cesar stepped over a couple stacks of newspapers and worked his way to the corner where Sharp's pictures were hanging. There were about ten, unframed, none of them very big, but all of them very strange as far as Cesar was concerned. The first one he looked at was of the inside of a bus. It looked almost like a photograph of a real bus, like the one Lillian rode every day, except that there were more black people, so maybe it was a 17 College Hill. But not even a 17 would have a human-sized possum and a pigeon in there with the regular riders. The possum was sitting next to a window and looked like it maybe had a headache, and the pigeon was sitting in another seat with its head back and its eyes closed. None of the other passengers was paying any attention. They just looked like they were on their way to work.

Next to the bus Sharp had hung a picture of a row of women under hair-dryers. One of the women was a big rabbit.

They were all like that. Sharp could really paint people and animals. Cesar thought all the people looked like people from Cincinnati and all the animals looked like real animals. You could see hairs in the fur. But strange. Boy, were they strange. He could see why the decorators went for the fruit.

"You don't have to say anything, Cesar," said Nancy.

"It's real interesting, though," said Cesar.

"That's the usual comment," said Sharp.

"It kind of grows on you, you know?" said Cesar. "I

mean if you don't try to figure it out." Was that a dumb thing to say?

"All right!" said Sharp. "That's all I'm looking for. What did I tell you, Nance? The only people that have a problem are professional idiots."

"In other words, they don't sell," said Nancy. "Bill, give Cesar a break. He came back here to ask you about your snooping."

"Huh?"

"What you've seen going on in the alley."

"Oh, what I've seen going on in the alley," said Sharp. "Regular slice of life, I'll tell you. If you don't see it here, it ain't happening."

"He's not interested in that kind of stuff, Bill. He needs to know what went on at Chips's place."

Sharp went over to the eastern window and looked out. "You mean like now? Hey, Cesar, catch this!" Cesar and Nancy came over and stood beside him. "That's a typical day at Chips Reber's," said Bill.

Holy smoke. Sandy Schott was stretched out on a deck chair back by the garage, where the early afternoon sun hit the yard. She had on one of the smallest bikinis Cesar had ever seen in real life and she really tested its endurance. She was well oiled. The peaks of her curves gleamed like a metallic bronze Buick.

"What a slut," said Nancy.

"Now catch the juxtaposition," said Sharp. He pointed across the alley from Reber's garage. "Ain't it great?"

He was looking at a white woman in a small backyard surrounded by a dilapidated board fence. She was thin, dressed in red pull-on pants and a white sleeveless blouse. Her hair was dark blond and she had a self-inflicted haircut. She was hanging up gray diapers on a clothesline. Even from his distance Cesar saw the lines and hollows of worry and deprivation in her face. "I didn't know there were any Appalachians down here," he said.

"She's not," said Nancy. "That's Barbara Speers."

"That's Dick Speers's house?" asked Cesar. Nancy

nodded. She turned away from the window and went back to her husband's work area.

"I can't stand to watch her," she said.

Bill and Cesar followed her back. "What about that Sandy, though?" asked Bill. "Isn't she something?"

"I don't think you should watch her either. I'm going back to the house, Cesar. Don't let Bill get going on art or anything like that. He'll keep you all afternoon."

Cesar thanked Nancy for the coffee and watched her out the door. Sharp uncovered a couple of old footstools and motioned Cesar to sit down. He pulled out a squashed pack of generic menthols from his coveralls, lit up, offered one to Cesar, who declined, and sat down.

Cesar reminded Sharp what he was there for. Sharp stretched out his legs in front of him and thought. He said that Reber wasn't his favorite subject in the alley. He enjoyed watching Sandy cavort, and he had looked forward to the day Chips installed a hot tub, something Sandy had been hounding him to get, but mostly he thought Reber was a typical playboy with a lot of money and no taste. He said that Reber had wanted an eight-foot painting of a watermelon for his hallway.

Cesar asked if Sharp had seen any comings or goings last Saturday or any day before that. Bill didn't think so. He said there was always a lot of pedestrian traffic when Sandy was sunbathing, but they were all passers-by. He said that even Dick Speers took the back way to work when Sandy was out. It was funny, though. The only way you could see into the backyard was through the alley gate, since the garage was in the way, and no one wanted to get caught just standing there. So guys would walk past and about break their necks trying for that short, sweet peek.

No, he thought all of Reber's callers came through the front way. There was the occasional furniture or appliance delivery through the back way. That was probably how the big air conditioner arrived. Sharp did remember one of the winos from the BandK wandering in once when Sandy was out back. She screamed, and Sharp had to help the guy out. Reber wasn't home. Sharp laughed and said the guy was really confused. The last time the guy had been in the yard was when there was still a whore working out of the back room, which turned out to have been more than fifteen years ago.

"So you have to add me to the list," said Sharp.

"What list," asked Cesar.

"You know, people that went in and out there. As a matter of fact, I went over there a lot when I was doing some wiring. I had to borrow tools from him."

"Is that gate always unlocked?"

"Yeah. He had a padlock on it for a while, but he started using the gate too much when he cleaned out the space for his Corvette, so he took the lock off. And then Sonny and Speers started using it."

"Werk? What for?"

"Oh, they were big buddies there for a while. Chips gave them a computer. He might have given some money to the outreach center, I don't know. But Sonny was in and out."

"Did he and Speers come together?"

"Sometimes. Sometimes not. Speers used to borrow tools too. Chips was nice about that. I have to admit it."

But that was it. Aside from Sonny and Speers, Sharp drew a blank.

Cesar stood up from the footstool, knees cracking like crazy. He thanked Sharp for his time and said he had to get on over to the Grimeses'.

"Can I sell you some fruit before you go?" asked Sharp. "I can fix you up with a bathroom-size banana in about fifteen minutes. Two hundred bucks."

"No thanks," said Cesar.

"Good man," said Sharp.

12

THE GRIMESES HAD an old-fashioned bell, only it wasn't like the Howards' with a knob, it was a fat brass button with a stiff spring. Cesar pushed once and got a faint, mechanical *wrrk*. He pushed again vigorously and got a healthy *WHRRRRK*. Greta Grimes answered the door. Her eyes were puffy and red, and she had a Kleenex at her nose. Cesar hadn't expected Reber's ex-wife to be as upset as his current girlfriend, but that was the way it looked. He introduced himself quietly and asked if this was a bad time to talk. She said no, and then she must have guessed his thoughts because she laughed, blew her nose, and said not to worry; it was hay fever, not grief. She invited him in.

Greta Grimes went on into the living room and Cesar started to follow, but he stopped to look at a small picture hanging in the front hall. It was an oil painting of customers in a dark old bookstore. They were all reading and poking around the shelves except for a great big fish, probably a trout, who was waiting by the cashier's desk. The fish was really lifelike. You could see all the scales.

"Is that . . . did Bill Sharp do this?" he asked.

"Oh, you must have seen his things. Aren't they wonderful? I'm the only one who's ever bought one. I'd buy them all, but my husband thinks they're ridiculous."

They sat opposite each other in matching modern leather

167

sofas. Greta pulled her legs up and sat cross-legged next to a big box of Kleenex.

"First of all," she said before Cesar could open his mouth, "I didn't kill Chips."

"I didn't—"

"Although I could have. I thought about it a lot. But I didn't. And my husband didn't either. I can't prove it, so I hope you can."

"I'm just gathering facts now, Mrs. Grimes. This isn't a—"

"I suppose you've already talked to Sandy Schott."

"I've talked to sev—"

"Did she tell you what a bitch I am? You don't have to answer. I know she did." Greta blew her nose. "I won't tell you what a bitch *she* is. You can find that out for yourself."

"Mrs. Grimes, we hear a lot of things when we're investigating a case. We don't take everything we hear seriously. People get upset."

"I'll bet. If I know her, she's over there playing up the grieving widow to the hilt."

Actually she's working on a tan.

"If you don't mind, Mrs. Grimes, there's some things I'd like to go over with you, so if we could—"

"Right. I'll shut up."

Greta Grimes confirmed that she and her husband had spent Saturday evening together with the Sharps, only she told him that she and Nancy had been smoking grass, something Nancy hadn't bothered to mention. She also said that the Sharps left before the rain started, that they were all tired from their marathon cleanup session.

"But my husband and I stayed up for a while. It was too hot to go to bed until after the rain came. And I might as well tell you, we were talking about my ex-husband."

"You had seen him that afternoon, isn't that correct?"

"Yes," Stella said glumly. "We did."

"And I understand you had an argument of some sort."

Greta looked at Cesar for a moment and then got up. She went over to a table and picked up an envelope, which she brought back to her seat.

"We did have an argument," she said after she sat back down beside her Kleenex, "but that's nothing new. It was the only way he and I ever communicated. What happened was that he did one of his favorite things to me. He let me know I had another one of his custody letters on the way."

"Did you have joint custody of your son?"

"Detective Franck, there's not a judge in this country stupid enough to give Chips Reber custody of anything smarter than a goldfish. *I* had custody. Chips had visiting rights. But he loved to drive me crazy with letters from lawyers about changing that. So when he told me that was coming, I started to lose my temper. Then he made one of his typically asinine put-downs and I slapped him. I got the letter that afternoon."

"Is that it?" asked Cesar. Greta nodded and handed him the letter.

It was from his lawyer, Maxine Castrucci, and it was nasty. Ms. Castrucci was busy informing the courts that she and Mr. Reber had amassed considerable evidence about the personal life of the Grimeses. She hinted strongly that she had witnesses prepared to swear that the Grimeses were "abusers of cannabis and other controlled substances." She further suggested that the Grimeses were "derelict" in entrusting H.P. to a "slovenly and lax" caretaker.

"Who are they talking about?" asked Cesar.

"Stella Hineman."

They have *their* nerve.

"Read on," said Greta.

In the closing paragraph Ms. Castrucci let it be known, without actually saying so, that Mr. Grimes's clients would certainly not like it if they knew that their architect was a pot-smoking child abuser.

"What is she talking about?" asked Cesar.

"Blackmail."

"I mean about your husband."

"God only knows. Chips could say absolutely anything he wanted to about me and I wouldn't do anything more than get mad. But when he goes after Nick . . ." She stopped to blow her nose. She was close to tears.

"Is there any substance to any of this?" asked Cesar.

"Do you know about Chips's sideline?" asked Greta.

"Construction?" asked Cesar.

"No, he called that his job. Actually he liked to call himself a 'developer.' He thought that had more class than being a contractor. What I meant was did you know he sold cocaine? Well, he did. Among other things. So if you didn't know that, you wouldn't know that he snorted coke in front of my son. Now *that's* child abuse in my book. I don't know what he's talking about when he's talking about Nick. What I *do* know is that Chips knew that Nick is very close to getting some very important contracts with the city, and that all it would take to wipe him out is for City Council to hear that he's a child abuser. It doesn't matter that he's not, that he's a wonderful father. Politicians aren't interested in the truth." She blew her nose angrily. "Chips has no morals. None. He's a complete bastard." Now she was really crying. "And he doesn't . . . didn't really *want* H.P. He never knew what to do with him. He didn't even know what to feed him. All he cared about was making us miserable, except that he was so insensitive he just thought it was a game."

"What does H.P. stand for?"

"Herman Prues. He's a junior, but I can't stand juniors so we called him H.P." The crying had stopped, but the nose was still running.

"Is he here?"

She shook her head. "He's at my mother's in Hopkinsville. He'll be back for the funeral. Why? Do you want to question him, too?"

"Not unless I have to. How much contact did you have with your ex-husband?"

"As little as possible. Until he moved down here, I

could keep from seeing him for months at a time, which was just perfect. You can imagine how I felt when he actually bought a house not just in the same neighborhood but on the same *block!* Four doors away! I was ready to kill him then." Greta grabbed a Kleenex. "I've got to stop saying that, don't I?"

Cesar waited for Greta to mop herself up, then asked her if she had any idea about why anyone would want to kill her ex-husband.

"Do you have the rest of the afternoon available?" she asked. "Because I have *lots* of ideas."

As it turned out, Cesar had either heard or guessed most of the reasons for Reber's unpopularity. The Howards had told him about Reber's relationship with his ex-wife, her husband and son. Arthur Battle had told him about the evictions. Alan Howard had told him about the bidding war for Hilda Kornbrust's. And everyone knew that Sonny Werk hated developers worse than death. Dick Speers probably did too.

But until now, no one had told him that Reber was getting ready to sell Stella Hineman's house out from under her. What a rat. He had just gotten that bit of news from Greta when they heard voices coming from the back rooms of the house. Greta looked over her shoulder. Nicholas Grimes, the man with the beard who had helped Cesar uncover Reber, came into the house, followed by Elizabeth Sackville. Cesar stood up.

Elizabeth Sackville didn't stay. She said she had much to do, and, with a funny little smile in Cesar's direction, she swept out the front door.

"I thought she was going to stay for drinks," said Greta.

"So did I," said her husband. "Does she know you?" he asked Cesar.

"She knows who I am."

"Maybe she was just being polite."

"Did she like the drawings?" Greta asked Nicholas.

"I don't know. Who can tell? You know how she talks. First she raved about them; then she went crazy over the skylight I suggested; then she raved about the plan for the maid's room; then she hit the ceiling when she saw the kitchen plan."

"What's wrong with that? I thought it was terrific. *I* want a kitchen like that."

"Well she doesn't want a Jenn-Aire. She wants, get this, a coal stove. And if she can't get that, she wants a wood stove that *looks* like a coal stove. And she doesn't want the built-in refrigerator either. Instead she wants me to design a walk-in cool-room like at a butcher's. Oh, and she wants a butler's pantry."

"Of course," said Greta.

"Is this for the house up the street?" asked Cesar. It was. Elizabeth Sackville had hired Nicholas Grimes as her architect before she even bought the house. She had made him figure out the floor plan before either one of them got in for a really good look, and as soon as Hilda Kornbrust had agreed to the price, Elizabeth had made her let Nicholas in to measure and photograph everything in the building. He had also had to cut out little plugs from every room in the building so that they could be sent out for scientific analysis of the original paint colors.

"She is just *so strange*," said Greta. "But her money is wonderful. She pays before Nick even has time to send a bill. And you should see her checks. She had somebody print them up as big as bedsheets. They look like they're from the Bank of England."

"Mr. Grimes, could I have a couple of minutes of your time?" asked Cesar.

"Sure," said Nicholas. "I'm sorry. I didn't mean to start in on that."

Greta Grimes left the men alone in the living room. Cesar wanted to know more about the disappearing hunting knife. Grimes groaned. "I wish to God I had never seen that stupid thing," he said. He and his wife had offered the use of their living room for a neighborhood peace conference. "Never again," said Grimes. "We had the whole stinking bunch of Truth and Beauty maniacs right here in this room."

"Anybody else?" asked Cesar.

"Everybody else," said Grimes. "The Sharps, the How-ards, the McDowells, Stella Hineman. Everybody was packed in like sardines. I guess that's how the knife disappeared. I couldn't see what was going on. It was sitting on that table by the door to the hall. And I'll tell you who was closest to it. Sonny Werk."

"You think he took it?" asked Cesar.

"I don't know. I assumed he did, but that's because I hate his guts. I guess if I'm going to be fair, I have to say that anyone else could have. Dick Speers was close, he had his kid with him. The McDowells were right there too. Everybody went past it. I don't know. I just wish I had put things away."

"It was lying out in the open?"

"Well, I had it in its sheath. That's worth more than the knife. I had it made in Mexico. Did it . . . the knife turn out to be the . . .?"

"Yes, sir."

"I don't want it back."

Cesar understood his feelings. He changed the subject to the night of Reber's murder. Grimes corroborated his wife's version of Saturday evening. He didn't mention the wives' smoking marijuana, but Cesar let that slide. Cesar did ask him if he or Sharp had seen anybody going in or out of Reber's house or yard while they were sitting out in front of the house. He shook his head.

"What about Mrs. Sackville?" asked Cesar.

"Elizabeth? She was at the May Festival. She told me." And then he remembered. "But you're right. She came through here afterwards. She was in the Packard. But she didn't go to Chips's."

"She told me she didn't get out of the car," said Cesar.

"She did? I thought she got out. I'm pretty sure she did. I was keeping an eye on her. She usually wears a lot of jewelry at night. The last thing we need is for some guy from the projects to mug her. No, she did get out. I remember. But she went into Hilda Kornbrust's house."

"Are you sure?" asked Cesar.

Grimes thought for a moment. "I guess I'm sure," he said at last. "Of course I assumed that was where she was going. I suppose she *could* have been going into Chips's. Their stoops are right beside each other and they're the same height. I guess you can't exactly tell from where I was sitting. What would she want to go in there for?"

"I don't know," said Cesar. "She probably didn't. Are you sure she got out of the car?"

"Oh, yes. I am sure of that. I just don't know where she went."

Cesar let that stew awhile and went into his notes. Then he looked up. "Mr. Grimes, do you know who's inheriting Reber's properties?"

"His debts, you mean? His son. Greta's son, H.P. Unless he changed his will."

Cesar left the Grimeses' house intending to go back to the office after another walk around Reber's yard and the alley. As he came down the front steps he took a look down the row of houses toward Reber's. Grimes was right about the stoops. Gene Standriff was standing outside, but from Cesar's distance he couldn't tell whether he was on his own stoop or the one next-door.

When he got to the sidewalk he saw Arthur Battle out in front of his house, and he started to cross over and say hello. But halfway across, he saw that Arthur was sleeping, so he decided not to disturb him. He had almost reached Reber's when he heard a dog barking angrily and then a human screaming in terror.

Woman again? Child? It was hard to tell. Cesar stood on the sidewalk trying to tell where the sound was coming from. The echoes off the buildings made it hard to tell. And the screaming didn't stop. Jesus. This made the *third* time in a week. He finally decided to head back toward Central and started off at a jog. The screams were getting louder. Then there were shouts. And finally there was a high, animal squeal on top of the human cries. What the *hell?*

Cesar reached the alley that ran behind the Central Avenue storefronts and looked up toward Franklin. That was where the screams were coming from. And now there were new screams. A big black woman was standing in the alley looking into one of the backyards and pulling at her hair while she was yelling. He sped up the alley to where she was standing. "That dog! That dog!" she shrieked. "He killed him. Oh, God, that dog killed him!"

Cesar looked where she was pointing. The wooden door in one of the fences stood open. Cesar stepped up to the door and looked in.

His heart sank. This was the yard where the pit bull nearly took off his nose. The dog was still there, but it couldn't get him. It was lying on its side, struggling to right itself with its forepaws. The hind legs were still. In a corner of the yard, Alan Howard was bent over the body of a black child. He was holding his suit coat to the child's leg. The child was still screaming. Cesar bent down to look and saw Stephen, the computer genius.

"Has anybody called Rescue?" Cesar asked Howard.

"I don't know."

Cesar turned around and saw Elizabeth Sackville standing beside the screamer. "I called for help," she said. He turned back to see if there was anything he could do to help Alan Howard.

Howard was lifting his jacket to look at Stephen's leg. The jacket was soaked in blood. Stephen lifted his head to look, saw his blood on the jacket and on the shredded leg of his blue jeans, and he fainted. Howard clamped the jacket back onto the wound.

"What the hell happened?" asked Cesar.

Howard shook his head. "I don't know. I heard the dog and then heard him yelling. I was in the office. I ran out here and looked over the fence. I don't know how he got in. He must have climbed over. I had to kick the door in."

"That's a pit bull, isn't it?" asked Cesar.

"Whatever it is, it's a sonofabitch. Can you stop that woman from screaming?"

Cesar stood up and stepped out to see the lady in the alley.

"Is he gonna be all right? Oh, Lord, is he gonna be all right?" wailed the woman.

Cesar grasped her firmly by the arm. "You've got to stop screaming, ma'am. You're going to scare him worse than he already is."

The woman shifted to sobs. Cesar finally recognized her as one of the outreach workers from Sonny's center. As she got quieter, Cesar heard what he hoped was the rescue squad's siren.

"Did you see what happened? Did he climb in there with the dog? Whose dog is it anyway?"

"One of those drunks," said the woman. "There's a old drunk down to the BandK keeps that dog in here while he's in there. Johnny Lindsey won't let that dog nowhere near the poolroom. Oh, what's gonna happen to Stephen?"

"I think he's going to be all right. It's his leg. Ma'am, did you *see* what happened?"

"I *know* what happened. I didn't have to see it. I told Stephen. I told him and told him if he messed with that dog he was gonna get hurt. He always comes by here and checks to see if that dog is back here and he climbs up on the fence to tease him and I *told* him that dog was a killer. I *told* him!"

"What's going on here?"

Cesar looked behind him and up into the thin face of Sonny Werk.

"Are you harassing this woman?" snapped Sonny.

"Now, listen, man," said Cesar.

"Oh, Sonny, that dog tried to kill him!" screamed the woman.

"Who, Louella? What are you talking about?"

Louella had decided to become incoherent. She wailed and pointed to the gate. Sonny went over to look in and then disappeared behind the fence. Cesar saw people coming up the alley from Abigail Street. He heard voices behind him and turned to see another bunch coming in from Frankln. He recognized a couple of the outreach staff.

Cesar went back to see how Stephen was making out. He heard the siren out on Central Avenue.

"Is there any way through to the street?" he asked Elizabeth. "I've got to tell the rescue squad how to get back here."

"I'll get them," said Sonny, and he loped off. He was pretty fast for such a screwball.

Cesar didn't hear the dog whining anymore. He looked and saw that it had stopped moving. It wasn't even twitching.

Good.

"Where's Candy? Where's my baby? Where's Candy?"

Lester Broadnax, one of the BandK regulars, stood in the doorway. "What you do to my dog? Where's my dog? Where's my baby dog?" Broadnax staggered around to look down at the late Candy. "What did they do to you, baby?"

"You want to know what I did?" asked Alan Howard. "I broke her god-damned back! I tried to kick the shit out of her, but she wouldn't let go, so I broke her back with that two-by-four."

"You killed her? You killed my dog? How could . . . Mister, I'm gonna sue your ass."

"You just try it." Alan Howard spit the words out at Broadnax.

Sonny led in the medics. They were panting, but Sonny wasn't even breathing hard. The medics took over from Alan. Cesar pulled Broadnax over in a corner and got his name and address and then turned him over to John Lindsey, the BandK owner, who had followed Broadnax up from the corner. Lindsey led him back toward the BandK.

The medics whipped a big pad onto Stephen's leg and put him on a stretcher. Louella had started to wail again on the other side of the fence. Cesar went out to shut her up again.

There was a crowd. All the BandK regulars stood in together comforting Lester Broadnax, who was raving in the direction of Alan Howard. The Truth and Beauty employees stood together jabbering to each other, thrilled with the break in routine. What looked like half the residents of the nearby projects had filled in behind those groups. And Cesar saw the Sharps and the Grimeses way in the back. No Stella.

The medics brought Stephen out on the stretcher. He was rolling his head back and forth and moaning.

"Oh, baby," shrieked Louella, "why'd you have to go tease that dog, baby?" She had thrown herself at the stretcher and the medics nearly lost the load. Cesar pulled her off, and as he did he heard Stephen say, " . . . didn't . . .'mbody pushed . . . why she push me?"

13

CESAR PARKED IN front of Stella's house. He pried the grocery bag from behind the front seat and locked up. Several people were sitting on the stoop of the building next to Stella's. Cesar recognized the woman who had talked to him the night before, the same woman who had watched the rat-blasting from her upstairs window. She waved and said, "How you doing?" and then started to get up. Cesar was afraid she wanted to talk police talk, so he picked up his pace and scooted in the gate and up Stella's walk. Her door was unlocked again.

Stella came into the living room wiping her hands on a dish towel. "I thought it was Sidney," she said. "Did I leave the door unlocked?"

"Yeah, you did," said Cesar.

"Are you going to yell at me?"

"Not this time. You saved me from your neighbor."

"Linetta? The one from upstairs?"

"The one who was going to throw Drano on your rat."

"That's Linetta. I just learned her name today. God, does she ever love to talk! And snoop. I can't go out in the backyard without her or her daughter sticking their head out the window and watching me. It drives me nuts."

"She's friendly, though," said Cesar.

"Oh, real friendly. I guess I could be too if I didn't

179

have to work either. She doesn't even have to go to market. Her mother goes for her. Can you believe it? Are those the groceries? Give them to me."

"I'll get them. Where's the kitchen?"

Stella led Cesar back through the small house. She looked nice from the back, too. She was wearing old blue jeans with nobody's signature, and a white cotton blouse that was so thin Cesar could see what seemed to be the top of a slip through the fabric. Stella moved fast. She walked fast, and she talked fast. She didn't seem to be bothered by the muggy air, even though there was a light sweat on her arms and face.

Stella told Cesar to set the groceries by the sink and sit down at the table while she pulled things together. She got him a beer from the fridge and started scrubbing vegetables.

"You want some help?" asked Cesar.

"No. This is easy. You got all easy stuff. I'll make you help with the dishes. God! What's in here?" Stella picked up the package from Avril's with the price scrawled on it.

"Steak. Is that okay?"

"I haven't had steak for months!" She opened the package carefully and stared at the meat, shaking her head slowly.

"I can go get something else," said Cesar. "No problem."

"No! No! You don't understand. I love it! I just haven't seen any in so long. It's so expensive."

"Well . . ."

"But I don't care. You know, everybody down here is so health conscious—except for the Howards—all you see is fish. Fish, fish, fish. And then, I'm always serving beans or chicken because they're so cheap. I almost forget what beef tastes like. Emma Howard fixed me a couple of roast-beef sandwiches last week and told me to give one to Sidney and I didn't. Isn't that terrible? I hid them in the icebox and ate them after he went to bed. And . . . can you believe this? I told myself I was keeping him from getting heart disease. Honestly."

Cesar leaned back, listened, sipped his Hudepohl, and watched. What a speed demon. It took her about fifteen seconds to scrub the potatoes and put them in the oven. She had the lettuce apart and rinsed in maybe forty-five seconds. No drops either. She put a cutting board on the table across from him and went to work chopping scallions, so Cesar got to take a look through the front of her gauzy blouse, but she finished chopping before Cesar had a heart attack. He crunched his beer can.

"Help yourself," said Stella. "There's a six-pack in there." She pointed to the fridge with her toe since she was busy drying lettuce.

The fridge was pretty clean. Not the cleanest Cesar had ever seen, but far from the dirtiest. What was interesting was that he didn't recognize most of the things inside. For instance, there was an enamel bowl of light gray rubbery-looking cubes sitting on top of the six-pack. He didn't know what that was. And there were some mason jars full of brown liquid with fat on top. And there was a plastic bag that looked like it held cloth napkins, but what would you do that for? He closed the door before she noticed that he was snooping, and sat back down.

Stella put all the salad ingredients into a big bowl and smoothed a piece of used aluminum foil over the top. She started to fold up the grocery bag but found a jar in the bottom.

"What's this?" she asked.

"Salad dressing." Cesar had bought the expensive stuff that has to stay cold, instead of Kraft.

"Why don't I make some?" asked Stella.

"Isn't that okay? It's supposed to be good."

"Let me make some." Stella set the jar in the icebox and started grabbing ingredients.

It wasn't just that she moved fast. She never looked like she was thinking about what she looked like when she did it. The year before, Cesar had spent a lot of time with a nurse from Deaconess who was nearly as speedy as Stella Hineman, but it didn't look the same. Her name was Bonnie. Bonnie posed every time she made a move. She always held her arm the same way when she poured milk or moved a pan off the stove. She even got into bed and spread herself as if somebody was going to give her a grade on it. One time Cesar started to tickle her to see what that would do. What it made her do was jump out of bed very pissed off. Bonnie was sharp looking, though.

Stella had to reach up into a high wall cupboard for a grater. Now, that was a great opportunity to show off the old boobs, and Stella had plenty to show, but Cesar could tell that all she was doing was reaching for a grater. In fact, he had a feeling that if her blouse were to disappear for some reason, she would keep on making the salad dressing and not make a fuss.

"What are you blushing about? Do you go red from beer?" asked Stella.

"I don't know. I guess so."

Stella went back to her dressing and Cesar wandered over to the back door to try to catch a breeze. The clotheslines were gone from the yard, but her son must have been busy all day. There were boards and tires and bricks in an arrangement that didn't make any immediate sense to anyone but a small boy.

"Where's your . . . where's Sidney?"

Stella looked at the clock over the stove. "He's supposed to be here now," she said. "He's over at Bill Sharp's studio."

"Are they big friends?" Cesar felt slightly jealous, which was crazy since he didn't know Sidney except to recognize him.

"Bill's teaching him to paint fruit," said Stella. "Sidney heard Bill say he made big money painting fruit, so Sidney, who can be really strange, decided he wanted to make big money too."

"Makes sense to me," said Cesar.

"Come on. In a kid that young?"

"How's he doing?"

"At the painting? Fantastic. He can already paint fruit that looks like fruit. I can't do that."

"Neither can I," said Cesar.

Stella shook up her dressing one last time and put it in beside the beer. She snapped off one of the beers on her way out.

"Let's sit out back," she said. "It's getting hot in here."

They took their beers outside and sat on the back steps. Stella held the can to her forehead for a moment, to cool off. "So tell me who killed my landlord," she said finally.

"Beats me," said Cesar.

"Are you going to be closemouthed about it?"

"Hey, if I knew who did it, I'd have turned him in."

"But you know something, right? I mean you've been investigating since yesterday."

"Sometimes it takes weeks."

"Do you want any dinner?"

"Yeah."

"Then you'd better start talking."

So he told her the little bit that he knew and the little bit more that he had guessed. It sure wasn't much. Even though he had gotten the lab report confirming a match between the St. Anselm Softball jacket and the little scrap that was stuck to the corner of the air conditioner, he still didn't know who had taken it from the clothing bank, much less who had worn it.

She listened quietly. From time to time Cesar would start thinking so hard that he forgot to talk, and she would give him a couple of minutes and then ask him something to get him started again.

"I still don't get it," she said, "about the air conditioner. What was it doing on top of him? I mean, if he was stabbed . . ."

"You got me," said Cesar. "All I can figure out is that it was some kind of cover-up. Like maybe the killer thought he was making it look like it fell on him while he was working. I mean, that's what I thought when I saw him. Which was pretty stupid of me."

"What are you talking about? That's what *everybody* thought."

"Yeah, but it was all wrong. It was just sitting on top of his chest. If you think about it, if it really did fall, it would have slid off. No way it was going to just sit up there nice and straight. I guess I got fooled by the corners. They were all crumpled, you know."

"So what do you think happened?" Stella looked him right in the eyes, as if he really could figure it out. Her leg was resting right up next to his now. What a situation.

"I think . . . I guess what happened is that Reber was working, maybe putting the unit into the window. He was a strong guy, but he'd really be straining. He'd really be tied up, too. So his killer sees this. Now, I got no idea whether this killer has this all figured out or whether he—"

"Or she," said Stella.

"Right. Or she just happens to be walking past with this hunting knife burning a hole in his . . . or her pocket. At any rate, I know you can see into the yard from the alley, and I know the gate wasn't locked. So this person sees Reber all tied up, steps into the yard, and stabs him in the back. Maybe not just like that. Maybe he talked a little. But that's the only way I can figure a strong, healthy guy like that getting it without any sort of struggle.

"There's another possibility about the air conditioner, too. It's possible that Reber didn't die right off. Those wounds were going to get him, but he might have been twitching around a little. That might have scared the killer, so he could have tried to pin him down. I don't know. We might not ever know."

Stella shuddered. She didn't say anything. Cesar was afraid he had spooked her. He tried to cheer her up by telling her about Stephen the computer genius and his electronic inventions, but that put him into another little trance. It was going to be a problem not having Stephen available to go nosing into Reber's computer disks. Poor kid. He was lucky the pit bull didn't get into his stomach or throat.

Somebody banged on the alley gate. Stella jumped off the last couple of steps and jogged down to open it. It was Sidney.

"You're late," she said.

"I left on time. I made Bill put a clock up in the studio and he watched it."

"Then you must have goofed off in the alley. I've told you about that."

"I wasn't goofing off," said Sidney. He and his mother walked toward the house, their arms around each other. "I had to talk to Mr. Speers."

"Why?"

"He talked to me."

"What about?"

"Detective Franck."

"What did he say?"

"He asked if Detective Franck was at our house and I said yes." Sidney looked at Cesar and asked, "Was it okay to tell him that you're here?"

"Sure," said Cesar.

"What does he care who's at my house?" asked Stella. "Was that all he wanted to know?"

"Well, he said that if Detective Franck gave you any problems you should call him because he knows what to do."

"Oh, God, he's so goofy."

"Why?" asked Sidney.

"Never mind. Go inside and get washed up for supper. And don't talk to anybody in the alley anymore. You're always supposed to come straight home. You know that."

Sidney went inside. Stella sat back down.

"You've got a nice boy," said Cesar.

"Oh, I think he's great. He's a lot to handle, but he's nice to have around. Unlike his father."

Cesar didn't know what to say to that, so he just sat beside Stella and drank his beer.

"I used to worry like crazy about that pit bull," said Stella after a while. "I'm so glad Alan killed it." She stood up and started to go back into the kitchen. "Now if only somebody would get Dick Speers with a two-by-four."

While Stella was sticking the steak in the broiler, Cesar went back out to his car to get the coloring book he had brought for Sidney. It was one of a couple hundred thousand his division had bought to pass out at schools and Halloween open house. The book was called *The Policeman Is Your Friend*. Cesar looked at it as he went back into the house. He heard Linetta say, "He a detective," to somebody on the steps next-door. Cesar kept looking at *The Policeman Is Your Friend* until he got in the house. He continued to read as he stood in the living room. Sidney came in and watched him until he looked up. Then he looked back down at the book. It was a boring coloring book.

"I got this for you," he said, handing the book to Sidney. "I should have checked it out first. Can you read?"

Sidney nodded.

"I'm sorry. I think this is for kids that aren't very smart."

"That's okay," said Sidney. "Thank you." He took the book over to the sofa and started to read. Cesar stood in the middle of the living room and watched Stella clear the table in the dining room. She looked up at him and made a face as she dumped a load of fabrics onto the occasional chair in the corner of the room. Then she went back into the kitchen. Cesar just stood there waiting for her to come back.

There was no way for dinner to be romantic with a five-year-old boy at the table. He wasn't rowdy or anything like that. In fact, he was better behaved than most of the kids Cesar knew. But he was an extra person at the table. Actually, sometimes Cesar himself was an extra person at the table. Stella and Sidney had a lot of in-jokes.

But it was a nice dinner. Stella knew how to broil a steak respectfully, and her salad dressing was loaded with garlic and therefore terrific. They drank beer with dinner, except for Sidney, who drank buttermilk—something both of the adults found frightening.

It had to end, though. Stella said she had a neighborhood meeting she had to go to. She had promised Nick she would go. Sidney was going with her. Cesar helped clear up the dining room. They attacked the kitchen together too. It was nice having a lot of opportunities to bump into Stella, and she wasn't exactly dodging the bumps. Sidney had gone upstairs to watch his television. Stella didn't like him to watch, but her father had given him the set for Christmas.

They got to talking about her neighbors, the Speerses. Stella did not like Dick Speers, but she liked Barbara. She said that Barbara led a dog's life. Dick Speers thought he had a mission down here, that God had sent him. He wasn't attached to any church, though. She wasn't sure whether he was Lutheran or Baptist or what, but he always went around looking people right in the eye when all they were trying to do was set out the garbage or catch a bus. She had heard a lot about people like that from her mother, who grew up in a fundamentalist household and then married Stella's father, who was Catholic. Her mother wouldn't even go back to her hometown in Indiana, because she thought she might go crazy and beat up on the fundamentalists who ran the town.

"Are you Catholic?" asked Cesar. "Where does this go?"

"In that drawer by the stove. No. I used to be. I went to Catholic schools. Oh, God! Look at the time! I told Nick and Greta I'd meet them at a quarter to eight."

Cesar hurried the garbage to a can in the backyard and then spent thirty seconds straightening out the grocery bags under the sink. Greta pulled Sidney away from his TV and brought him downstairs, and they all walked out of the house together.

"I really had a good time, Stella. I appreciate your having me over."

"Well, thank you, Cesar. And I appreciate all the food. I haven't eaten like that for months. Now I feel rotten that I teased you about cops last night."

"That's okay."

"I won't do it again for a while."

"Okay."

They had reached the corner of Central and Franklin and they stood in front of the Truth and Beauty Center, where people were already starting to fill up the folding chairs.

"Will you be around this week?" asked Stella.

"Definitely."

"Sure you don't want to sit in on this meeting? Sonny Werk's going to be here." Stella cackled.

"Definitely not," said Cesar.

Cesar walked slowly back to his car, working on a bit of steak that was stuck between a couple of molars. It was too bad about the meeting. He would have been perfectly happy to hang around until well past Sidney's bedtime. He almost overshot the Camaro thinking about Stella and the way she was always laughing at everything. As he stuck the car key in the lock, he heard a woman yell, "Hey! Hey! Mr. Detective! Hey!"

Aw, Jeez. It was Linetta from next-door. She ran out of her front yard and up to Cesar's car as fast as she could without losing her bedroom slippers. "Hey, what's your name?" she asked. He told her. "Is Franck your first name or your last name?" He told her. "Well, Detective Franck, I seen you was in there and I didn't wnat to bother you while you was visiting your friend. . . ." Linetta smiled a knowing smile. Cesar didn't smile back. "She's so pretty. . . . Anyway, I didn't want to bother you, but somebody told me you was in charge of that murder over on Abigail Street. Is that right?" Cesar nodded. "I thought you might be, 'cause I seen you in the alley and you always driving down the street here.

Anyway, I wondered if you want to know that I saw that man that was killed park his car down the block there in front of where those white people live and go in there." Linetta pointed in the direction of the Speers house. "I just thought you might want to know that."

"What kind of car?" asked Cesar.

"He drive a Corvette," said Linetta. "He usually park it in his garage there on the alley."

"When was this?"

"Saturday," she said. "The last day he was alive." Linetta put her hand to her throat and looked sadly at the ground for a couple of seconds. Then she got back to business. "You know what they gonna do with that Corvette? My boyfriend is real interested in buying it."

Cesar told her he didn't know anything about the car or what was going to happen to it. Then he asked, "Are you sure it was Mr. Reber? Would you recognize him?"

"Sure," said Linetta. "Only I didn't know his name. I seen him in the alley when he drive through, and then Saturday he went right past here after he came out of that house and he went in the back door of the center there." She pointed to Sonny Werk's headquarters.

"What time was this?"

"Oh, I didn't have no watch. I guess it was about like now. About eight o'clock."

Cesar thanked her for the information and wrote down her name, which turned out to be Linetta Collins. She wanted him to stick around and tell her all about Chips's wounds, but he pried himself away. He told her he had to do some more investigating. And it was true. He had decided to pay a call on Stephen, the computer genius, up at Good Sam.

Stephen Rankin, that was the genius's name. Cesar had to pry the information out of a hatchet-faced lady in Admitting who thought that Cesar was a very stupid policeman if he had to ask for the boy named Stephen who was bitten by a pit bull. Well, what's it to you, anyway, lady? She told him Stephen's room number and then told him not to go up there because it was after visiting hours. Cesar said okay and went up anyway.

As it turned out, Cheryl Klotter was on duty in Stephen's wing. Cheryl and Cesar had had several good times together, so she didn't give him any static about visiting hours. Cesar found the room. The door was open, the overhead light was off, and the television was on. Stephen was the only patient in a two-patient room. A woman sat beside his bed watching the TV. Stephen looked like he was asleep. He looked smaller than ever against all the white sheets. An IV was dripping into his arm. Cesar tiptoed into the room until the lady saw him. She looked at him for a second and then turned her head back to the TV.

"How is he?" asked Cesar.

The woman looked back at Cesar, then back at the TV, and then fiddled with a control until the sound went away. "I couldn't hear you," she said.

"Are you Mrs. Rankin?" he asked.

"Mrs. Harris. He's my son."

"Oh. How is he?"

"I don't know," she said, and shook her head. "He's been sleeping mostly. They said that was all right. He lost a lot of blood."

"I know. I was there right after the dog attacked him."

Cesar and the woman stared at Stephen for several moments without talking. Finally the woman said, "He was in shock, you know."

"I'll bet."

The woman lifted the edge of her son's sheet and peered under. "I'm supposed to check for blood. They already had to change one bandage because of the blood. Does that look like too much?" She pulled the sheet farther down and lifted the edge of Stephen's hospital gown. Cesar leaned over the bed and looked. He had two big gauze pads over the worst of the bites. He also had several spots where they had taken stitches. Cesar thought the couple of spots soaking through on the pads didn't look too bad yet, and he told Mrs. Harris so. She let the sheet fall back and then turned to check up on the TV show.

"Have you talked to him at all, Mrs. Harris?"

"A little bit. He woke up for a minute, but he didn't feel like talking too much."

"Is he supposed to wake up soon? I'd kind of like to talk to him if he's going to."

"I don't know. Are you from the outreach center?"

"No, ma'am. I'm a detective."

"Well, what you want to talk to him for? He ain't in no trouble. He don't have to talk to no policeman. You ought to be trying to find out who pushed him in there with that dog instead of coming up here to bother him."

Aw, shoot. "Ma'am, I'm not up here because he's in any kind of trouble. I came up to see how he was doing and maybe to talk about a couple of things we talked about this afternoon."

"Well, he's too sick to talk to anybody about anything except getting better. And finding out who went and pushed him into that yard with that dog."

"Ma'am, I'm sorry. I didn't even know he got pushed. I thought he fell in." Jeez. Cesar had heard Stephen mumbling about being pushed as they took him to the ambulance, but he thought Stephen was just rambling.

"Well, somebody pushed him. Seems to me you ought to be finding out *who* instead of coming around here."

"Mama?" said Stephen, coming around. "Mama? *Oooooohhh!*" He had tried to move and it hurt.

"Don't you move, baby. I'll call a nurse for you." Mrs. Harris moved for the buzzer on her son's bed.

"Naw, don't call no nurse. I don't need one. I just got to lie real still." Stephen turned to Cesar. "Whatchoo doin' here, man?"

"Came to see how you were doing. How you doing?"

"Bad, man. That dog's a *killer.*"

"For real," said Cesar.

"They got to lock that dog *up.*"

"Don't need to. He's dead."

"Tasted my bad blood, huh?"

Cesar told Stephen about Alan Howard and the two-by-four. Stephen didn't know who Alan Howard was even after Cesar described him. "Your mother says somebody pushed you in with that dog, Stephen. Is that right?" asked Cesar.

"He don't believe me, baby. Did you know he was a policeman when you was talking to him?"

"Yeah, he told me. It's all right. Mama, listen. See if you can get me some pop. I got a terrible thirst for pop."

"I'll go," said Cesar.

But Stephen didn't want Cesar to go. He talked his mother into getting herself something to eat down in the cafeteria and bringing him some pop afterward. Cesar dug out some change and said it was his treat, but Mrs. Harris didn't want any money off any policeman. Stephen said, "Take the money, Mama. Quit acting all funny." Mrs. Harris finally took fifty cents from Cesar and left. "She don't like the police," Stephen said.

"I figured," said Cesar. Then he asked Stephen to tell him about how he wound up in the jaws of the pit bull. Stephen said he was just fooling around. He passed the fence every day on his way to and from the outreach center. Once in a while he liked to see if he could get the dog a little excited. He'd throw in a stick or a rock or something. Most of the time he would climb up on the fence and make faces. The dog went crazy when he made faces.

"Were you sitting on top of the fence today?" asked Cesar.

Stephen shook his head. "I ain't crazy. I don't get up on top all the way. I jump up and, like, hang on my stomach. There's a place where I can stick my foot so I don't have to put all my weight on my stomach."

"And that's what you were doing?"

Stephen nodded and tried to pull himself more upright, but it hurt too much. Cesar went to the head and pulled him up slowly. He didn't weigh much. "I was just out taking a break, you know."

"Smoking?" asked Cesar.

"Hey, man. What I do on my breaks is my business."

"Sorry."

"So I went to visit my friend Mr. Dog to ax him how he was doin'. I got him to talk and jump around. That dog can jump."

"I know. He nearly got my nose once."

"Then you know what I'm saying. Anyway, he was barking like crazy and then all of a sudden I felt somebody put her hands right here"—Stephen held his hands just under the sides of his rib cage—"and start pushing me over."

"But you couldn't see," said Cesar.

"I couldn't see. I got tipped in, you know. My head was hanging upside down inside the fence."

"How did you know it was a woman then?"

"I just guessed, I guess. It wasn't a big dude. I grabbed one of her hands to pull it off and it felt like a woman's."

"You got anybody pissed off at you, Stephen?" asked Cesar.

"Not like that, man. Not to where they want to kill me."

Cesar chewed a thumbnail and looked at Stephen. What could a kid like that do to get somebody really angry? Something about the way Stephen was answering was a little funny. Was he a hacker? Was he hacking his way into banks or army bases? Would the bank officers or the army hang around in the alley waiting to throw the kid to the dogs? But this was a woman. Or *maybe* it was a woman. She would really have to be mean, but she wouldn't have to be very strong. Stephen was light as a feather.

"Are you sure about your girlfriends?" asked Cesar.

"Man, you want to know the truth? I got one girlfriend at the moment, although she is an extremely attractive lady, so I don't *need* a whole lot of girlfriends, and my lady friend is petite. I mean, she is very small. Very small."

"Okay. You got any tough friends?"

"*All* my friends are tough."

"Okay. Just checking."

Just someone goofing off? Maybe. But when someone you know is fooling around trying to scare you they usually say, "Ialmostmadeyoufall" or "You'reluckyIsavedyourlife," and then they don't push you off the cliff or wherever you are.

"You do any hacking, Stephen?" Worth a try.

"Hey, man. Hacking's illegal."

"I know. You ever do any?"

Stephen looked up at Cesar. "Maybe," he said. "A little hacking never hurt nobody."

"Maybe it hurt you."

Stephen looked away from Cesar and then, after thinking for a minute, he turned back. "I did a little," he said. "But get this. The only computer I ever got into was the school board's, and I didn't even find out where they keep the grades. Only thing I found was some of their accounting and I didn't mess with that. Okay? That's the only hacking I did. I ain't lying."

Okay, so he didn't hack. Cesar got the distinct feeling that he did *something* he didn't want to tell about. But he was looking tired and Cesar didn't want to wear him out. He hadn't had a very good day. So he asked another question that had been walking around in his head trying to get out.

"Were you out in the alley Saturday night, Stephen?"

"No. I went home in the afternoon. Home to my little house in the projects. Why?"

"I don't know. I thought maybe you saw somebody who didn't want to be seen."

"Oh! You mean at Reber's! The *killer!*"

"Well, yeah. That's what I was thinking."

"I didn't see nobody. I didn't even cut through the alley last Saturday. I went the long way."

So he wasn't an eyewitness. Cesar didn't like it. The little maniac nearly got killed by somebody for no apparent reason. No fight. No jealousy. He looked down at Stephen and saw that he was nodding off.

"I've got to go, kid. When are they letting you out of here?"

"Hey, they don't tell you *nothing* in the hospital. Don't you ever watch TV?"

"I'll be around again. You need anything?"

"An Apple. I need an Apple and my disks, man."

"I'll see what I can do."

14

THE CAMARO JUST about had a hemorrhage climbing out of the Good Sam parking lot and onto Clifton Avenue. There was still a little bit of light in the western sky and the air had cooled a few degrees. Cesar rolled his window down and let the fumes wash over him.

He let the Camaro take him wherever it wanted to go, which seemed to be downtown via Central Parkway. The car passed District One and rolled around the streets of Dutchtown, slowing down in front of the Truth and Beauty Outreach Center, allowing Cesar to see if the meeting was still going on, in which case he might rejoin his date for the evening.

The meeting was still going on. He parked in the same spot he had used earlier, moseyed back to the corner, and looked inside. There she was, sitting next to Mr. and Mrs. Grimes, with Sidney on her lap, in the next-to-last row.

The place was packed. All of the desks had been shoved to the edge of the room and about fifty folding chairs set up in the middle. All the chairs were filled, and a lot of people were standing or sitting on the desktops. There was a table at the end of the room, where Sonny Werk and several other people sat facing the crowd and the street. Cesar opened the door and went in.

Several heads turned, including Stella's. She looked surprised and then pleased. What a smile. What a smile.

Stella turned back to listen to the meeting, and Cesar's head stopped buzzing. He tuned in to the meeting. Some of the audience held mimeographed agendas. He looked around for one to read, but they must have all been taken.

There was a time, back when Cesar was first on the force, when he had really tried to take the meetings seriously. He had been assigned to Over-the-Rhine, and he'd gotten notices for about ten meetings a month. He'd had orders to go to two of them, but he had gone to several others regularly just to be a friendly policeman. Get to know your public. He'd always tried to listen. He'd always tried to see everybody's viewpoint. He'd always tried to understand every issue. But, Jeez, it was hard. Most of the meetings were organized by government. That meant that everybody had a chance to talk. Forever.

What could you expect? Everybody living in Over-the-Rhine was poor. It was the poorest, dirtiest place in the city. Everybody had gripes. Legitimate gripes. Life in a slum is tough and rotten. And the meetings were the place to get it off your chest.

Cesar's problem had been that he always believed the agendas. There had always been a topic, something that the government wanted to hear from the folks about or had to tell the folks about, but the topic was never what the folks wanted to talk about. If the topic was crime, they wanted to talk about the school board. If the topic was parks, they wanted to talk about how nobody ever put a clean Laundromat anyplace. The bureaucrats running the meeting would always say, "You've got a legitimate concern, sir, but the proper place to discuss that would be . . . ," and the citizens would always say, "You always trying to shut people up 'cause you don't want to hear what people really want. What we want is . . ." Like that. For hours. Until everybody got tired or hungry and the meeting collapsed.

It got so that Cesar would come home and lie down on the living room floor, trying to get his head to stop throbbing after the meetings. Now that he was a detective, he didn't have to go. But here he was.

"No!" shouted a fat lady, standing up in the middle of the crowd. "We don't want to talk about no historic preservation. We want to know what the city's gonna do about these pit bulls that's eating everybody's children. You got to be doing something *now!*" The crowd tossed out a couple of "Right on's" and the lady sat down. She immediately started talking to the woman on her right, ignoring the bureaucrat up front who was trying to answer her concern.

Cesar started to feel the old pressure inside his skull. Then he felt a light pressure on his arm. He looked down into Stella Hineman's eyes. She had given her seat to Sidney and slipped back to join him.

"What are you doing here?" she asked in a whisper.

"Beats me," he answered. "What's this about?"

Stella handed him her agenda. *Dutchtown Neighborhood Subsector Forum and Hearing,* it said at the top. *Sponsored jointly by the Department of Neighborhoods and the Dutchtown Residents for Progress, a project of the Truth and Beauty . . .* Et cetera. The agenda was: *I. Garbage Improvement. II. Proposed Traffic Review Plan (possible closing of Cogswell Alley). III. Reasons for Closing Health Outreach. IV. Musselman Grant. V. Other concerns of residents.*

"Which one are they on?" asked Cesar.

"Are you kidding?" asked Stella.

"Yeah." He was kidding.

It was unbelievable. After the fat lady was through talking about the pit bull problem, Nicholas Grimes had stood up and moved for a resolution requesting City Council to make all pit bull owners post a big cash bond. Now a pudgy white man in glasses had started defending pit bulls and dog fights as part of "the fabric of urban life." Then he started talking about the attack on dog fights and pit bulls as "racist efforts to eliminate the culture of black and poor persons." He proposed building some sort of dog-fighting arena somewhere in the neighborhood. He was serious. He really was.

"Who's that?" Cesar asked in a whisper.

"Urban planner," Stella whispered back.

Nicholas Grimes stood up again to say that about the last thing in the world they needed in Dutchtown was a dog-fighting pit when there were buildings falling down around them that were irreplaceable. The fat lady who had said she wanted protection from pit bulls must have changed her mind because she stood up to argue with Grimes. She said that Grimes was against anything black folks wanted to do and that he and his friends were all trying to run the black folks out of Dutchtown.

A few more people had crowded in behind Cesar and he was gradually pushed against Stella. It didn't seem to bother her. He found that she was leaning against him. Cesar tuned out the meeting and tuned in to his nerve ends. It was as screwy a place for a date as any he had seen, but it seemed to be working out all right. There was even some nice music.

Music? Did somebody have a radio? The sounds were coming from behind him. He looked around. The man behind him, a skinny guy with glasses, had a set of stereo earphones clamped on his head. The earphones either didn't fit or were turned to the max, because a lot of music was getting out. The guy seemed to be concentrating on the meeting, though.

And he had a bodyguard. It had to be. The man standing next to Mr. Headphones was built like a tank and stuffed into a shiny suit which looked pretty strange since his boss was wearing a little running suit and worn-out New Balances. The bodyguard wasn't paying attention to the meeting; he was paying attention to the audience, scanning the crowd constantly. You could tell he was with Headphones since anytime Headphones moved a muscle, the bodyguard moved right with him. There weren't a lot of bodyguards in town. Maybe the guy with the headphones was George Bush. Cesar checked him out again. Naw. The bodyguard glared at Cesar.

And right then, right while Cesar was watching him, Mr. Headphones nodded to Bodyguard, and Bodyguard stepped ahead and started knocking bodies aside, clearing a path for Mr. Headphones as he headed for the bureaucrats' table. People started grumbling right away, but nobody was stupid enough to tangle with the human pit bull. But they did bitch. And they did start asking who did he think he was. The bureaucrats and the social workers at the front table just sat there with their mouths hanging open. Headphones got up to the little open space in front of the table, shook hands silently with the gaping professionals, turned off his headphones, turned to the crowd, and said. "I'm sorry to interrupt. I'm Donald Musselman. I want to talk about money."

See, you don't have to have charisma if you have money. Particularly if you have money you want to give away. Donald Musselman had about as much charisma as a Ford Fairmont, but everybody, *everybody*, in the Truth and Beauty outreach center was real, real interested in whatever he had to say. The government people at the head table straightened up in their seats and checked the knots in their ties, the people from the projects dropped their voices to a whisper, and the people from Truth and Beauty nearly dropped to their knees. Even Stella straightened up and stopped leaning on Cesar, which made Cesar decide he didn't like Musselman no matter how much money he was giving away.

"I want to do these pilot grants," said Musselman. He didn't continue. Instead he put his headphones back on and twiddled his controls and stood there listening, his mouth slightly open, for a couple of minutes. Then he shoved one phone off one ear and said, "Pilot grants. Right. Only I was listening to your meeting and I got very confused just like I do when I read your reports and grant applications. Why do you always argue so much?" He stood there as if someone were going to answer. "I really like talking to the Indians, you know? Are there any Indians here?" No one seemed to be an Indian. "I've got a lot of money out in the tribes, but they never confuse me. I really like that. Don't you want to be like the Indians?" Nobody answered. "Maybe," Musselman said, "maybe you don't *know* any Indians. Probably not. I don't know what tribe used to be here, but I guess they're gone. That's too bad." He put the earphone back in place and listened, humming to himself for a minute, then took off the whole set. "Anyway," he said, "I was thinking about how easy it is to talk to the Indians because they always have a chief to talk for them. But I don't see any reason why urban neighborhoods can't have a chief, do you?" A couple of people shook their heads, but most of the rest just stared. You could tell this wasn't the way they expected multimillionaire philanthropists to talk. "So I think I'm going to have these pilot grants for urban neighborhoods like yours and I'm going to call them 'Urban Tribe Seed Grants' and see if that doesn't make everything just a whole lot simpler, okay?" About half the audience nodded, but everybody still looked confused. "And then you'll be like Indians. Oh, and you have to have a chief. And the chief has to be someone who lives here in the neighborhood. And the chief gets forty-five thousand a year to be the chief. So all you have to do to get started is elect a chief who lives in the neighborhood, and when you do I'll send the money for the chief and that's who I'll talk to for all your major grants. You've got a couple of applications in, right? One for historic preservation and the other to fight historic preservation? I forget who asked for what. That's why I want to talk to your chief." And then Musselman put his headphones back on, cranked up the sound, and walked out. His bodyguard moved out in front of him and cleared a path, and in thirty seconds Musselman had disappeared from sight. Everybody sat quiet for another fifteen seconds, staring at the doorway as if Musselman might turn up again. He didn't. Then the place went crazy. Stella left Cesar right as all the standees started to mix it up with the sittees so they could Talk About It.

Cesar looked for Stella but couldn't find her until he felt someone pulling at his elbow. She had collected Sidney. "Let's get out of here," she said.

He had a hard time keeping up with her. Sidney had run ahead, and Stella walked nearly as fast as Stanley Goodin. She took shorter steps, though. By the time they got to her gate, Stella had started laughing, and she laughed until they got into the house. Cesar stood, waiting for her to explain.

"Did you see them?" she asked finally.

"Who?"

"Everybody. Did you see them when Donald Musselman announced he was going to fund an Indian chief? I thought they were all going to pass out."

"Who?" asked Cesar again.

"Paul McDowell, for one. He's been running for president ever since he got here. Sonny Werk nearly swallowed his fingers. Poor Dick Speers looked like he was going to faint when he heard the salary. Even Nick started to sweat."

"Everybody wants to be chief, huh?" asked Cesar.

"Not me."

"Good."

"Not that I couldn't use the money. I just can't take the meetings." Stella headed for the kitchen and Cesar followed.

"Wow!" said Stella when she turned on the light.

"What?"

"I never have a clean kitchen this time of night. This is great." She pulled the last two Hudepohls from the refrigerator and handed one to Cesar. They took the beers out to the back stoop and sat down. Sidney had started to play his record up in his room. Cesar heard the sounds of the orchestra from the open bedroom window. "He'll be asleep in about fifteen minutes," said Stella.

Cesar leaned back against the stone steps and sipped his beer while he looked at Stella. She was sitting one step farther down with her arms folded on her knees. She looked over her shoulder at Cesar and smiled, and then she looked out at her yard. "You wouldn't believe I had this place cleaned up a couple of days ago," she said.

It didn't look too bad, though. The only light came from a street lamp in the alley, so Cesar couldn't see too much of the peeling paint and rusty gutters that surrounded them. The air had cooled a little, and the music floating out of Sidney's window masked the permanent rumble of traffic and electricity. No shouts. No screams. No bangs. It didn't seem like a slum. Then Cesar saw a little motion by the back fence. A rat scuttled across a corner of the yard and dropped into a hole. Cesar looked at Stella to see if she had noticed. She hadn't. Linda, the cat, had wandered in from Franklin Street, and Stella was scratching her ears. "Do you like cats?" she asked.

"I don't know. I never had one."

Stella scooped up Linda with one hand and set her in Cesar's lap. He stroked her tentatively. She settled down between his legs, looking up into his eyes. Cesar looked into Linda's eyes and wondered if she had been out killing rats, in which case he didn't exactly want to get real intimate. He couldn't tell from looking at her. "Nice kitty," he said. She started to purr. Good. He must be doing it the right way. Then she started pushing her paws into his stomach, one at a time, rhythmically. She stared right through him while she sank her paws deep into the spare tire, purring louder and louder. What the hell was she doing?

"Linda, *quit* it!" snapped Stella, and she smacked the cat off Cesar's lap and over the edge of the stoop. Cesar watched her as she righted herself and began licking her paw. He snuck his fingers to his waist and pushed. Jesus, he was soft. And sore. The sit-ups were starting to take their toll.

"Are you going to arrest Greta?" asked Stella.

"What?" Cesar looked at her. "Why'd you ask that?"

"I talked to Greta at the meeting. She was really depressed."

"What about?"

"She said you spent a lot of time with them. She said it didn't look like you believed her."

"What's not to believe?"

"She says she doesn't have an alibi and that after you left, she and Nick realized they're probably the number-one suspects. They hadn't even thought about that before you came."

"Why'd they start thinking about it now?"

"That letter. The knife. H.P. All the fights. Nick's clients. Everything." She looked at him, waiting for an answer. Cesar pretended he didn't know she was waiting. He didn't have an answer. The Grimeses were right. It did all add up.

"They're pretty good friends of yours, aren't they?" he asked finally. She nodded. "Then let's not talk about them. I don't know anything, and I don't want you or them to get worried, all right?"

"But are you . . .? I guess you're right. Let's talk about something else."

Someone walked through the alley, crunching on broken glass. He shouted at someone somewhere and then started running toward the projects, yelling some more. Stella made a face.

"Don't you even get a little scared down here?" Cesar asked.

"Of stuff like that? No. Not anymore. It used to scare me when I first moved in. Now it just drives me crazy."

"Maybe you should be scared, you know?"

"Because I'm white?"

"You're a woman living alone."

"What am I supposed to do, go live in an apartment complex somewhere? You think that's any safer? At least here I can tell the good guys from the bad guys. The hoods here all dress like hoods and say obscene things. Everybody else is polite or ignores you."

"You got it all figured out then," said Cesar.

"Yeah, pretty much. You disagree?"

"I just think it's dangerous. It's asking for trouble."

"Asking for trouble! I can't believe it. That's like

saying a woman's asking for rape if she dresses the wrong way around a bunch of men."

"So?"

"So! Do you agree with that? Do you actually agree with that? I really thought you were different from the usual West Side cop, but I was obviously out of my mind."

"Wait a minute. I'm sorry. I don't know why we're yelling at each other. I didn't mean—"

"We're yelling at each other because you think women are supposed to keep themselves locked up somewhere wearing ugly clothes so they won't be tempting all the screwed-up men in the world."

"Stella, you're the one who started talking about clothes. I didn't say that."

"You said they were asking to be raped."

"No, I didn't. You did. But since you did, I have to agree that you can't walk around in a halter and expect that people aren't going to notice. They notice. I didn't say you can't do that. It's a free country. You can do whatever you want to do. But it's stupid to think everybody's going to respect your right to wear a halter in the middle of a bunch of punks. You're gonna get some kind of trouble. And if you live in the middle of a bunch of projects full of black people and you're the only white person, that's your right too, but you can't expect everything's going to be just like in Westwood or Hyde Park. It's a different country down here."

"Tell me about it. I live here. You don't."

"I work here. I've been working here for years. I probably know a hell of a lot better than you what's going on around here."

"I don't believe that. All you see is the worst side."

"What do you know about what I see? Who turned you into an expert? Give me some credit. I've been in a lot of houses and met a lot of people in this neighborhood. A hell of a lot more than you, I'll bet."

"Oh, I believe that," said Stella. "But look what you're going into their houses *for*. You're investigating murders.

What do you expect? What kind of people commit murders? They're screw-ups. Crazies. Psychos."

"What I do is talk to a hell of a lot of people who aren't murderers. They're family and neighbors and acquaintances, just like your friends."

"My friends? Do you—" Stella stopped talking with her mouth open and stared. "I keep forgetting about Chips," she said at last. "It's weird. It's like I don't really believe it happened." She crunched her empty beer can with her foot. "He was such a jerk."

"Look, I'm sorry I—"

"You don't have to say you're sorry. I get real defensive about living here. My parents hate it. And I guess I have to admit that I get scared sometimes if I think about it too much. That's why I keep a butcher knife under my bed." She laughed. "I don't know what the hell I would do with it if I had to use it. It's really hard to stab someone, isn't it?"

Cesar looked at her until she remembered how Reber died.

"I forgot," she said.

"You ought to get better locks," said Cesar. "And get them for your windows, too."

"I really hate that. I hate being afraid. Do you think . . . ?"

"Do I think what?" asked Cesar.

"Do you think I have to worry about whoever killed Chips?"

Cesar shook his head. "Probably not. Not if you weren't mixed up with him."

"He was my landlord. That's all. I told you I couldn't stand him." Stella looked as if she had something else to say, but if she did, she didn't say it.

"I wouldn't worry about it," said Cesar.

"Mama?" They heard Sidney's voice from the kitchen. Cesar realized the music had stopped some time ago.

"What are you doing up?" asked Stella. She stood up, and so did Cesar.

"I can't sleep."

"We were probably keeping him awake yapping at each other," said Cesar.

"Go back to bed. I'll be up in a minute."

"I guess I'd better go," said Cesar.

"It might take a while. I'm sorry. He usually goes straight to sleep, but when he doesn't—"

"It's okay," said Cesar.

Stella saw him to the door, but when he looked back, she was already on her way up the stairs.

15

"Number five, i guess," said Cesar. "Scrambled. What kind of sausage is it?"

The waiter looked at Cesar blankly.

"Is it the links?" asked Henry.

"Are they the ones . . . ?"

"They're the ones like little <u>metts</u>," said Henry.

"That's what they are," said the waiter. "Do you want them?"

Henry shook his head. *"He* does," he said, pointing to Cesar. "I already ordered, remember?"

"Oh! Yeah! Right!" said the waiter. He put his pad down on the table and wrote a "5" and "scrambled," which took him pretty long. Henry and Cesar watched him hand the orders through the hatch. The cook looked out at them and waved. Henry waved back, then took off his sunglasses and rubbed his eyes.

"Spider's got to get that boy trained. He is awful. Terrible." Spider, the cook and owner of the Early Times Restaurant, was Henry's cousin, which was why they were having breakfast all the way over on Reading Road in Bond Hill instead of at any of the reliable Frisches close to the station. Henry wanted Spider to succeed. Cesar wondered if Henry had any money in the venture. He'd never know. Henry never told anyone in the world anything whatsoever about his finances. The waiter started to bring their coffee. Halfway to their table he stopped, set the cups down, and then swabbed out the saucers. Finally he brought them to the table. He carried the coffee like nitroglycerine.

"Sweet'n Low," said Henry.

The waiter stared at him.

"It's like sugar," said Cesar. He felt sorry for the guy. "It's in those little pink packets. You've got some on the counter over there." The waiter smiled gratefully and brought the fake sugar to Cesar, who handed it to Henry, who put three packets in his coffee while the waiter watched.

"Hey!" yelled Spider from the kitchen. The waiter left them alone for a while. The coffee was pretty good. Cesar looked around. Spider wasn't doing a whole hell of a lot of business yet. He and Henry were half the customers.

"How'd your date go?" asked Henry.

"What do you mean? Who said I had a date?"

"You looked like you did."

"What's that supposed to mean?"

Henry laughed at him.

"What's so funny?" Cesar was getting pissed off. Henry was always mysterious about his own dates. You weren't supposed to ask him about them. You weren't supposed to laugh at him either.

"Detecting skills, Ceez. Remember? That's what we're supposed to do. It's in our job descriptions."

"Did you tail me?"

"I didn't have to. The only times I saw you yesterday you were looking at your watch. You had on your new pants, you kept tucking your shirt in, you combed your hair when you picked up those groceries, and you and your mother don't eat steaks like that."

"What were you doing in my groceries?"

"Just looking. Just looking. So how was it? Was it that girl by Uncle Arthur's?"

How the hell did he figure that out?

"Yeah. It was fine."

"That's all?"

"She's real nice. We went to a meeting together."

The waiter brought their orders and set them in the right places, which Cesar thought was pretty good. The waiter wasn't sure. He stood looking worried at them until they started salting and peppering and he knew he had gotten it right. Then he looked relieved. Henry stared at the waiter until he figured out he should leave them alone.

"It could be a lot worse," said Cesar. "He could have told us his name and said he was going to be with us for the whole meal."

"What," asked Henry, "made you take her to a meeting?" Henry and his dates favored extremely dark places where he was very well known.

Cesar ran down the whole evening for his fellow detective. What the hell. He needed another opinion anyway. Not just about Stella, although he was confused about her; Cesar also wanted to know what Henry thought about pit bulls, computers, historic preservation, mental patients, clothing banks, property values, poolrooms, and spaced-out philanthropists.

"What's his name?" asked Henry as Cesar started to tell him about the Urban Tribe Seed Grants.

"Musselman," said Cesar.

Henry started fooling around with his *Enquirer,* looking for something. Cesar, who had started out the day planning to eat better and less, ate the last of the six biscuits that had arrived with the sausage and eggs. Well, they were small, not like the fat rolls they were dishing out at the fast-food places. Spider seemed to know what he was doing with eggs and sausage, too. The place was clean.

"This guy?" asked George. He handed his folded paper to Cesar. Donald Musselman, without the earphones but otherwise just as goofy-looking, stared up at him from the front page of the Metro section. There was an article about the meeting at the outreach center. The reporter seemed to think that Musselman was a pretty big deal. He had handed out a couple of million dollars to organizations that sounded really dopey to Cesar—Alternative Fathers, People for Quieter Forests, and now the Foundation for Urban Tribes. At the end of the article the reporter said that Elizabeth Sackville, a "preservation activist," called the Urban Chief grant "meddlesome and tasteless."

"That's the guy," said Cesar. "He looks even goofier with his headphones." Cesar and Henry talked about philanthropy for a while and then went back to pit bulls. Henry wanted to know all about Stephen and how he was doing. He wanted to know if Stephen was still going to work on Ghetto Blaster, but Cesar didn't know. It looked like Henry was really interested in the game as an investment.

"Can you believe somebody would do that, though?" asked Cesar. "I mean, those dogs have killed kids. And this is what's strange: The kid thinks it was a woman who pushed him in."

"So?" said Henry. They had both seen plenty of female killers was what he meant.

"Yeah, I know," said Cesar, "equal opportunity and all. But what would a woman want to kill a kid like that for?"

"Same thing as a man," said Henry.

"But what?"

Henry didn't know, but he thought Cesar ought to be checking out the neighborhood women. Cesar didn't like that. All the ladies in the neighborhood seemed pretty nice to him and he didn't see a trace of a relationship with Stephen.

"What about the social workers?" asked Henry.

That didn't make any sense either. The social workers seemed to think Stephen was kind of cute. They were all pretty torn up when they saw what happened to him. Besides, pushing him over the fence would have required some energy. Maybe Stephen imagined it. Or maybe it really was just a kid goofing off.

"What about your girlfriend?" asked Henry.

"She's not . . . What about your Uncle Arthur?" asked Cesar.

"Whoo!" said Henry. "Sorry!"

"Let's get out of here," said Cesar.

Henry put on his glasses and stuck a toothpick between his lips. He was still smiling a little.

Cesar handed Henry a five so he could settle up with Spider, and then called the office for messages. He planned to stop first at the Truth and Beauty. "Truth and Beauty," he said to himself as he punched his own number, and then "TandB."

"Hi, Carole. It's Cesar. What's up?" What was up was that Carole wanted to know whether he thought she was a secretary, because if he did he could take . . . and so forth. He waited for her to run through that song, holding out his hand to accept the change from Henry. Henry guessed what was happening from the squawks on the telephone. He crossed his eyes and waggled his toothpick. As it turned out, there was a message for Cesar. He was to call Stephen Rankin. Cesar wrote down the message, thanked Carole, asked if there were any messages for Henry (there weren't), told her there was a message for her, held out the phone to Henry, who let out a short belch, and then hung up the receiver. Henry thought that was terrifically funny.

As Cesar called Stephen, a couple of black business ladies clicked into the Early Times. They ignored Henry for five, maybe ten seconds, but as Stephen answered, they were starting to thaw.

"Projects From the Projects. Stephen Rankin, speaking." He must be feeling pretty good.

"It's Detective Franck. You called me."

"I did. I did. It's the first time I ever called the police, man, and I get some chick. Tell me, is this lady as lovely in real life as she is on the telephone?"

"Even better, Stephen. You want to meet her?"

"Is she black?"

"Does it matter?"

"Not to me, man."

"I'll ask her. What did you want?"

He wanted to know what Cesar had come into the Truth and Beauty for. He had been lying in bed thinking up video-game details after Cesar left him last night, but he had this problem remembering Cesar and Stanley Goodin. Cesar told him that he was looking for a jacket for Stanley and Stephen asked him why. Cesar told him.

"Right!" said Stephen. "I knew it was something like that. See, when you're concentrating on computing, man, you don't hear the outside world. It just kind of soaks in and then sometimes you remember what you heard. Only it's a week later, so it's very, *very* confusing."

"Is that it?" asked Cesar.

"Naw, that ain't it. You think I'd call just for that? What I called for was I thought it was something like that, so I had to make sure. I remember that jacket, man."

"The green one? The one that said 'Softball' on it?"

"Man, I don't know what it said. I just remember the jacket. I looked up from the screen the other day and there it went out the door. I remember it because it was such an ugly jacket I couldn't figure out what anybody would want it for."

"You remember who bought it?"

"I didn't say that, man. I said I saw it going out the door. Now that I know it's important, maybe I can make myself remember who it was that took it?"

"That would be great, Steve."

"Stephen."

"Right. It would really help me a lot if you remember that. I'm not kidding. And if you do, I want you to call me immediately, okay? Will you do that? Just call me where you got me this morning. They'll get the message to me."

"I'm already thinking. I'm going into my relaxed state."

"Yeah, well, don't fall asleep. Keep thinking."

Stephen started a lot of fake snoring, so Cesar said good-bye and started to hang up. "Wait a minute, man," said Stephen. "Don't rush off. I found a Apple. They got one downstairs in one of the labs. I found out from a very helpful young nurse. You bring those disks up here and I will reveal all."

"I'll do that. You take it easy on the nurses," said Cesar, and he hung up.

He went over to say good-bye to Henry, who had settled into a chair between the two women. They were lawyers, of course. Henry was into the professions these days. Cesar waved to Spider in the back and left a dollar and a half for the waiter.

Unbelievable. There was never a poverty worker around when you needed one. The only people in at the Truth and Beauty were the secretary and the lady who had been screaming in the alley over Stephen Rankin. Cesar asked where Sonny Werk was. Sonny Werk was out. He asked where Dick Speers was. Dick Speers was out. Cesar looked at the secretary and the secretary looked at him. "Is it a big secret where they are?" asked Cesar.

"It's Mr. Werk's policy not to say," said the secretary.

"Not even a hint?"

She didn't let up. She just shook her head and stared at him.

"He's the police," said the screaming lady. Cesar remembered she was in charge of the clothing bank.

"I know what he is, Louella. I don't work for him. I work for Sonny. He has to have a warrant."

Cesar turned to Louella and tried to smile a little smile like Henry used in situations like this. Either it worked or else Louella felt like shocking Tammy, because she said, "They're at home. Sonny's over at where he stays on Race and Mr. Dick Speers is just right around the corner in his place." She glared at Tammy.

"You know Sonny's address?" asked Cesar.

"You better not, Louella. I *will* have to tell Sonny. You know you can get fired for giving out his address."

"I ain't gonna give his address. I'm just going to tell this policeman that my Uncle Charles lives in the same building as Sonny, and then I'm going to tell him that my Uncle Charles lives over the Red Top Pop Shop. You know where that is?"

"It's that pony keg? The one across from the school?"

Louella nodded and then smiled defiantly at Tammy. Tammy wrote something down on a little piece of paper, which she locked in a desk drawer. Then she smiled defiantly back at Louella.

Cesar walked around the corner of Franklin Street. Stella's house looked closed up. He wondered if she was out someplace or just sleeping late. He also wondered why he and she seemed to get into fights so easily. They would be going along having a pretty good time and then, bang, there they were. Arguing. Maybe it wasn't all that bad. It had only happened twice.

Speers's house looked like a slum. It was as small as Stella's, but where Stella had a little grass and ivy in her front yard, Speers had hard-packed dirt and a dead bush. The house was red-painted brick with white trim. It was a cheap paint job with cheap paint. The street number was painted freehand on the doorframe in big, sloppy black numerals. The screen nearly fell out of its aluminum frame when Cesar opened the storm door to knock. There was no bell. The front door hadn't been washed in years.

Mrs. Speers opened the door. Cesar had seen her from Bill Sharp's studio the other day when she was hanging out clothes, but she was too far away for him to notice any details. She almost looked like one of the wino wives from Vine Street with her mousy hair and faded skin. But instead of the fogged-over blue eyes you saw on Vine Street, Mrs. Speers had large clear brown eyes, and modern, expensive-looking glasses. When she spoke, she didn't sound anything like a bum. She sounded like a regular, polite lady from a regular neighborhood. "Can I help you?" she asked.

"Who is it?" Speers called from somewhere in the house.

"Detective Franck, ma'am. I'd like to speak to Mr. Speers if I can."

Mrs. Speers looked frightened. That happens a lot, but Cesar wished there were some way he could introduce himself gradually so people wouldn't get upset. Especially people like Mrs. Speers. She'd looked really tired before, and now she looked tired and panicky. A little boy, maybe two years old, came slowly into the living room and up to his mother, where he grabbed her skirt and stared at the man who was scaring her. A baby was crying somewhere upstairs. "Come in," said Mrs. Speers.

It took Cesar a couple of seconds to figure out what was so odd about the living room. Finally he realized that it looked like a section of the basement at the Westwood Reformed Church. Instead of the artworks that all the people on Abigail Street had, the Speerses' walls were hung with felt banners. One had a fish; one said *Peace;* another had a cross and said *Give Christ a Chance.* And there wasn't any regular living-room furniture. There were a few folding chairs and a folding table with clean laundry sitting on top. There weren't any curtains, just venetian blinds.

"Who is it?" This time Speers came into the room with his question.

"It's a detective. He wants to talk to you." Mrs. Speers was no actress. She was very frightened, and her face and voice showed it. She picked up the little boy and stared at her husband.

"I know him," said Speers to his wife. He smiled at his wife. If his smile was supposed to calm her down, it didn't. Mrs. Speers still hugged the little boy to her and searched her husband's face with her large brown eyes.

"He's from the homicide squad," said Speers. "It doesn't have anything to do with us. Let's just sit down. You stay," Speers said to his wife, who had turned to leave the room.

The three adults sat down on the folding chairs, away from the table, and the little boy sat on the floor where his mother put him. Cesar wondered if they were going to pray before they got started. Speers did put his hand to his forehead and closed his eyes for a few seconds. It could have been a headache. When he took his hand down, he looked at Cesar with a slight smile, waiting for the policeman to throw the first pitch.

Okay. "Were you at home last Saturday night, Mr. Speers?"

"I was. My wife was not. She was in Dayton, Ohio, at the home of her father."

"I got back Sunday night," said Mrs. Speers.

"Fine. I'm interested in anything you might have seen or heard going on at your neighbor Mr. Reber's house that night."

"Nothing." Speers kept the little smile on his face. It made Cesar think that Speers wanted the policeman to know that Speers was doing him a favor speaking to him.

"Nothing at all?" asked Cesar.

"What was there to hear?" asked Speers. "I certainly didn't hear anybody shouting."

"Were you asleep?"

"What time?"

"Around eleven. There was a rainstorm after that."

"No."

Mrs. Speers cleared her throat. Then she said, "Dick, I think you should try to be a little more helpful."

Speers turned the little smile on his wife. He was doing her a big favor too. "I don't want to confuse him," he said. "He's supposed to ask me what he needs to know."

"Well, shouldn't you—"

"Believe me, Barbara, I know what I'm talking about." Speers turned back to Cesar, waiting for the next stupid question.

"Were you downstairs?"

"We're still talking about Saturday night? Part of the evening I was upstairs, the rest I was down here."

"And you were here the whole night?"

"No."

Cesar waited for Speers to explain, but Speers wanted to be asked.

"Where else were you?"

"I was at my office."

"When? How long?"

"Perhaps ten-thirty. For no more than ten minutes."

"Did you see or hear anything from Mr. Reber's house when you went to your office?"

Speers shook his head.

"Were your windows open?" asked Cesar.

"Probably. Until the rain. Yes."

"Mr. Speers, several of Mr. Reber's neighbors on Abigail Street heard Mr. Reber working out in his backyard. He seems to have been installing an air conditioner. You didn't hear him working on that?"

"Detective Franck, when you're doing the Lord's work, your paycheck doesn't cover the cost of air conditioning. I have no idea what that would sound like." Speers threw out a little chuckle.

"It sounded like banging, according to the neighbors," said Cesar. "Like a hammer."

"I know what that sounds like," said Speers. He looked down at the scruffy shoe that rested on his knee, which Cesar figured meant that he was thinking. "I may have, Detective Franck."

"What about somebody yelling from one of the other houses."

"I'm afraid I don't understand."

"One of your neighbors across the alley said he had to yell at Mr. Reber to be quiet. You didn't hear that?"

"I don't remember it." Speers smiled again. Cesar still figured that Speers was letting him know that Cesar was an idiot, but Cesar didn't think he was an idiot today. He did think that Speers was a real pain, though.

"Did you have the television on or something?" asked Cesar.

"We don't have a television," said Speers, gently shaking his head. Cesar got the message. Jesus and Dick Speers wouldn't be interested in anything like TV.

"Dick prepares for Sunday on Saturday nights," said Mrs. Speers. "People don't know how much he prepares."

"Are you a pastor, sir?" asked Cesar.

"Not officially," said Speers. "But then I don't know that Jesus was ever officially ordained. Not that I compare myself."

"So you were writing a sermon?"

"No, no, no. I really am not a pastor. Certainly not in the sense of having a pulpit, although the work is pastoral. I don't mean to be self-serving, but you did ask. No, I spent a great deal of Saturday evening in prayer. I'm afraid that when I do that, I don't notice a great deal going on around me."

"But you did go to your office," said Cesar.

"Briefly. To get some papers."

"And you didn't notice anything then?"

"Nothing."

"What did Mr. Reber see you about last Saturday?"

"I beg your pardon?" Speers's smile slipped a fraction.

"When he stopped in here. Saturday evening. He parked out front and came in."

"Are you . . . oh . . . Saturday evening. Yes, he was here."

"Dick! You didn't tell me that!" Mrs. Speers was scared again.

"It wasn't important. He was looking for some tools he thought I had borrowed. I hadn't."

"Oh," said Mrs. Speers.

"The power of prayer," said Speers. "Are you familiar with it, Detective Franck?"

"Sir?"

Speers folded his hands and rested his elbows on his knees, ready to give a childish explanation to a childish policeman. Cesar checked to see if Mrs. Speers did the same thing, in case this was some form of prayer. She didn't. She was twisting off lint pills from her pants. She had big hands that looked red from bad detergent. Cesar looked at Speers. He had little white hands that looked as if they had never touched a dirty dish. "We've been eating nothing but pancakes here for the last couple of weeks, Detective Franck. Even my son. I wasn't joking when I said that the Lord's work does not pay well."

"You aren't employed at the outreach center?"

"I am. I do look on that as the Lord's work. Christ was a carpenter, you know. I try to repair men and women through modern management techniques. But that job doesn't pay enough. Certainly not after tithing. Last Saturday I was at the end of my rope. I put my problems in God's hands. We had to have food. I don't accept food stamps, by the way."

Cesar heard a little sound from Mrs. Speers. She was crying.

"The Lord has answered my prayers."

Cesar waited for Speers to go on, but all he did was lean back in the chair with the old smile.

"You got some money?" asked Cesar finally.

"Didn't I see you at the community meeting last night?" asked Speers. Cesar nodded. "You saw and heard Donald Musselman?" Cesar nodded again. "So you understand." Cesar shook his head. He didn't understand. Speers smiled even more. Come unto me, all you feeble-minded. "I expect to be the Urban Chief."

Oh. Cesar almost said, "How—" and then changed his mind. "Did they already elect you? I left before that."

"They haven't. They will."

"Well, the salary's pretty good."

"You don't believe me? No one is more prepared, Detective Franck. Not even Sonny Werk, who, by the way, does not live in Dutchtown. This is what I have been working for. I believe this is God's will. What do you know about modern management, Detective Franck?"

"Please?"

"Management. As it applies to social issues."

"I guess not a lot."

"Don't feel bad. Not many people do. There aren't more than a handful of people who have taken time to see where management techniques apply to issues that really affect the urban poor. Problems such as low birth weight and gentrification. Have I lost you?"

Cesar shook his head.

"I've discussed some of my theories with a couple of important local businessmen. You'd know their names if I told you. I have to say they were pretty amazed. They expect fuzzy thinking from social activists." Speers stopped and stared at the ceiling for a moment. "It's too bad," he said, "that Jesus didn't have access to some good managerial tools." He stared at Cesar.

Cesar cleared his throat. He didn't know how to comment on that.

"But I do. I have those tools," said Speers. "And as Urban Chief, I will use those tools as they have never before been used. I will stop gentrification dead. In its tracks."

Well. "That sounds pretty interesting," said Cesar. "There is an election, though, right?"

"There is. But the people know my work. They know that I understand poor people and their problems. They know that I am one of them." Speers finally looked away from Cesar and looked at Mrs. Speers. She was still crying, and now Speers's eyes were getting watery.

Cesar stayed dry. "The other thing, Mr. Speers, is that jacket that Stanley Goodin found. One of your neighbors saw someone in the alley wearing a jacket like that around the time Reber was killed. We also know that the jacket Mr. Goodin found matches threads found near the body. I don't think it's real likely there were two people in identical jackets or parkas or whatever wandering around on a hot night like that. So we'd really like to talk to that person. Are you absolutely sure you don't know who bought that from your clothing bank?"

"I'm absolutely sure no one bought it, Detective Franck. No one at the center remembers selling it. It is possible, however, that it was taken. Or that someone associated with the center took it for his or her own use." Speers gave Cesar a knowing look, but it took Cesar a while to figure out what he was supposed to know. He finally figured it out.

"You said that Mr. Werk occasionally took things for his own use the other day."

"Did I? I don't recall. But yes, he does. Never without reimbursement, however."

"Would he wear something like that?" asked Cesar.

"Detective Franck, Sonny Werk is not a murderer if that's what you're suggesting. I hope you aren't."

"I'm not."

"Sonny Werk is a great man. A lot of people don't realize that. They only see the public side, the thorn in the flesh of the well-to-do power structure. But he works in the great tradition of the apostles. I hope you will remember that as he faces his new trials."

"What trials?" asked Cesar.

"Difficulties, Detective Franck. He has problems. That's all I can tell you."

Was he ever glad to get out of there! What a place. What a family. What kind of guy thought it was all right to feed his family pancakes for a week? Cesar wasn't crazy about the food-stamp program. He had spent a lot of time in checkout lines and seen a lot of stamps spent on stupid stuff and seen plenty of people whip their stamps out of expensive pockets, but if all you can afford is pancakes . . . And they both looked like regular people, college people.

Cesar wondered what kind of church they were attached to. He always felt at sea when people started talking about religious things. Maybe Lillian should have kept him from dropping out of Sunday school. Why would God send Donald Musselman to help out Dick Speers?

Stella's house still looked closed up.

As Cesar started to climb into the Camaro in front of the Truth and Beauty Center, he saw the antenna dish of a mobile news unit parked halfway down the block. He locked the car back up and moseyed down to have a peek. There turned out to be two mobile units and a couple of cars from radio stations, all parked and double-parked in front of the Victorian Centre. Cesar tried to see through the window, but he couldn't get past the lace. He followed a few cables through the front door and stood at the back of a small crowd of newspeople. The cameraman from Channel 12 recognized him and rolled his eyes in greeting. Elizabeth Sackville was talking and pointing at a map. Alan Howard stood beside her.

Well, what do you know! It seems that the Victorian Centre had been doing a little research, and they had turned up a brand new slumlord. Mr. Sonny Werk. They had taken a large map of the West End and Over-the-Rhine and marked Sonny's properties in bright red. They had also taken real ugly black-and-white pictures of Sonny's buildings, usually from the rear, and had had them blown up into big ugly glossy prints. And they were sending their information not only to City Hall and the newspapers, but also to Mr. Donald Musselman, who, Elizabeth said, "is one of this country's most ardent opponents of irresponsible ownership of low-income property." Then she asked, "Are there any questions?"

"How did you get onto this?" asked one of the newspaper reporters.

"We were originally informed of the *possibility* of Mr. Werk's ownership of these wretched slums by the late Herman Reber. Our own Alan Howard traced the titles, which, as I said earlier, presented the most *intriguing* maze of corporations and management firms. It really was quite a lot of work for Mr. Howard."

Cesar slipped back out the door. Sonny Werk a slumlord. And Herman P. Reber spilled the beans. Was this one of the difficulties for Sonny that Speers had mentioned? Sandy Schott had said her late boyfriend liked to know things about people he had to deal with. That he might lean on them once in a while. So. Maybe he had leaned on Sonny.

Cesar slipped in and out of the squad office without running into Carole or the lieutenant. When he got back in his car, he had Chips's computer disks. He headed for Good Samaritan.

16

"OH, YEAH, MAN. I recognize this. Just a second." Stephen Rankin tapped a couple of keys and the list of goofy-looking names disappeared and another list popped up.

Cesar had wheeled Stephen through the halls of the hospital to the pathology lab. The pathologist, a bald guy in horn-rims, had dropped the liver he was working on and led them to his Apple computer, which sat surrounded by stuff Cesar definitely did not want to look at. The pathologist had started to tell Stephen how to work the computer, but Stephen waved him off. "Stand back, mortals" was what he said.

Now Cesar and the pathologist were looking over Stephen's shoulders, trying to make sense of the information on the screen.

"See, I know this stuff better than old Chips did, since I am the man who wrote the program in the first place. It was one of my very first paid performances." He tapped a couple more keys and the list hopped around. "It won't be my last."

"What is it?" asked Cesar.

"It's my patented Property Program. Well, it ain't exactly *patented* yet. Minor detail. Old Chips wanted me to fix him up with a handy little program to keep track of

225

his buildings and the buildings he was thinking about buying and then—"

"Werk," said the pathologist.

"What?" asked Cesar.

The pathologist reached in front of Cesar and tapped a key. The names moved up a few lines. "See there? Werk, Werk, Werk. That's got to be Sonny Werk."

"Do you know him?"

"I was listening to the radio before you came down. It was on the news about Sonny Werk and all the property he owns."

Cesar looked where he pointed. Sonny Werk turned up all over the place. And he always turned up after an address and a couple of dates.

"I love it," said the pathologist. "Couldn't happen to a better humbug."

"He ain't so bad," said Stephen.

"You better talk to the staff around here. He's probably caused more ulcers than anybody in the city."

"Does he pick on hospitals, too?" asked Cesar. "I just thought it was landlords and cops."

"Nope. He was up here a couple of weeks ago. He brought a couple of his winos and had them attack a CAT scanner."

"What for?"

"He said the money should have been spent on housing."

"He just gets a little wild," said Stephen.

"Do you know where Reber got onto this stuff?" Cesar asked Stephen.

"He didn't tell me nothing about it, man. He just had me write up the program."

Cesar looked at the screen some more. Sonny must have owned half the city. The list went on forever.

"But you know," said Stephen, "he knew this chick that worked for some lawyers. He used to see her once in a while, said she was very good-looking and crazy about him. Anyway, the reason I know is my mama was looking at buying a house down there near the projects. She thought maybe she could get it cheap and fix it up, on account of there was nobody living there. Chips called up that girl and she found out whose it was. He said they had a lot of clients that didn't like their names to get out. Not like me, you understand."

"I understand," said Cesar. "What about these other ones?" He handed one of the disks to Stephen.

"Chips was cool," said Stephen. "Labeled all his disks in code. But you can't be too cool for the inventor of Ghetto Blaster." He pulled the real-estate disk and poked in another. "Uh-oh. This is going to take a little bit of time." He peered at a screen full of garbage. "Not long. Don't get all excited. Just a little time." He started whacking away at the keyboard.

"Hey, I'm gonna leave you with this, buddy. You call me if you come up with something."

"*When* I come up with something, man," said Stephen.

Cesar stood in the vestibule of Sonny Werk's apartment building on Race Street. The glass door to the stairs was locked, which was unusual for a flophouse. It was even more unusual to have a working intercom system, but that seemed to be the only way to get in. Sonny's name wasn't on the list, though. Cesar tried punching all the buttons with no name beside them, but nobody answered. Anybody named Uncle Charles? There was a Charles Edwards. Cesar punched the button. He couldn't understand the response that came out of the speaker, but at least somebody answered. "Louella sent me. Your niece." It worked; the lock buzzed back and Cesar buzzed through.

It was just like all the other old downtown buildings. The only difference was the security system. Cesar found Uncle Charles's apartment and Uncle Charles told him where Sonny lived. Nothing to it. He went up to the top floor and knocked, and Sonny opened the door. He stared at Cesar for a minute.

"Can I come in?" asked Cesar.

"Do you have a warrant? You have to have a warrant."

"No, I don't. I just want to talk to you."

"What about?"

"Herman Reber. Chips Reber."

"Wait here," said Sonny. "Stand in the hallway until I get witnesses."

"You don't need—"

"If you want to talk to me, I want to have witnesses."

Sonny went across the hall and banged on a door until someone opened it and let him slip in. Cesar stood in the hallway for five minutes. He could hear Sonny's mouth going the whole time, but he couldn't make out what he was saying. Finally Sonny came back out, followed by a man and woman. The man was wearing bum clothes and looked like an orange-haired Abraham Lincoln. The woman was about half his size and looked to be about ten years older than the man. She was a boozer.

"These people have agreed to be witnesses to this police interrogation," said Sonny. He led them all into his room. What a smell. Sonny wasn't into clean. He wasn't even into sheets. He had a bare mattress on the floor. There was one blanket wadded up and no pillow. His clothes were piled in one corner of the room even though there was a chifforobe. Sonny's phone sat on the floor near the bed. He had taken off the sticker that showed his telephone number.

There weren't any chairs. Sonny and his witnesses sat down on the edge of the mattress. The witnesses took their cue from Sonny. All three sat in a row, their backs to the wall, their legs sticking straight out in front. The woman's feet were bare and black on the bottom. The man was wearing jungle boots, and Sonny had on his high-topped gym shoes. The man and woman tried to glare like Sonny was doing, but the woman started to go into a nod and the man couldn't focus his eyes for very long. Cesar didn't know whether to sit or stand, and Sonny wasn't going to tell him. He finally decided to squat.

"Can I have your names?" Cesar asked the witnesses. The woman snapped her head up.

"What did—" She stopped talking when the man nudged her. They both looked over at Sonny, who nodded at them.

"We refuse to answer any questions," said the man. Then he looked at Sonny. Sonny nodded, and the man said, "Because of the fifth amendment."

Oh, Jeez. "I just want to know who I'm talking to, okay? I just asked for your names. You can tell me your names."

The couple looked at Sonny, who shook his head.

"Okay. Don't give me your names. No big deal. Sonny, what I want to know first is where you were last Saturday night."

"I refuse to testify, claiming the protection of the fifth amendment to the United States Constitution. Any effort to make me do otherwise constitutes harassment and I call your attention to the fact that I have witnesses who will swear in a court of law that you are attempting to violate my constitutional rights."

Cesar looked at the three characters on the mattress. Dopey, Sleepy, and Crock. How in the name of God was he supposed to deal with them? "Sonny, listen. I don't want to violate your constitutional rights. You know that. That's the last thing in the world I want to do. All I'm trying to do is get some information about Chips Reber."

Sonny glared at Cesar. It was the first time Cesar had ever seen his mouth closed for more than five seconds.

"I hear you had some association with Reber," said Cesar.

"Who told you that? I want their names. They better have some proof for that kind of statement of guilt by association."

"Hey, slow down! They just said you knew Reber and that he had gotten involved with your outreach center there. That's no big deal."

"Officer, I refuse to testify to this allegation of association with a known victimizer of low-income and minorities, a person that you and the rest of the police oppressors should have locked up for repeated violations of laws concerning drugs."

"I thought he was on your board or something. You took a computer from him, didn't you?"

"You have no right to comment on where the Truth and Beauty Center may receive its capital equipment since the donation of that equipment is in full compliance—"

"Hey, Sonny, *please*. Do you mind? I don't care where you got your computer. I don't care who's on your board. I only . . . I just . . ." Cesar had to stop or he was going to look as ridiculous as Sonny. He counted to twenty in his head. Then he said, "Sonny, do you remember me? I know you do. You yelled at me from your picket line last Sunday. I heard you. I used to go to a lot of community meetings where you were at too. You remember that? Do you remember that I never gave you any static at any of those meetings? That I always promised to take messages from the people back to District One and that I always followed through? I brought back answers. I even went to bat for you a couple of times to try and get better patrols in some of the blocks you were worried about. You remember that? You know I could have sat on my butt and slept through all of those meetings, but I didn't. I always tried to participate no matter how much I disagreed with anything. So I played fair. And I'm playing fair now. I'm not trying to harass you, I'm trying to get information that will help me find Chips Reber's killer. And what you're trying to do is drive me crazy. I wish you would understand that when you act like you're acting now in front of a detective who isn't me, who doesn't know you well enough to know what you're doing, well, Sonny, that detective is going to assume you've got something to hide and he's going to go crazy trying to find out what it is. He might even think that there's some connection between the way you're acting now and the fact that Chips Reber found out and told about all the buildings you own down here and—"

"Where'd you find that out? Who told you? When did he tell . . . ?"

"It's on the radio, Sonny. They called a press conference."

"Who called a press conference? What are you talking about?"

"What buildings, Sonny? You got a building?" asked the woman on the mattress.

"Can we live in it? We can cook for you," said the man.

"Shut up!" said Sonny. The witnesses gaped at their leader.

"Hey, Sonny, I didn't do it. I just found out about it this morning. There was a press conference on your block."

"*Who?*" screamed Sonny.

"Take it easy, man."

But Sonny had grabbed his phone and started dialing. Cesar watched him dialing the City Hall exchange and groaned. Mayor time. For sure.

"This is Sonny Werk. I have to talk to the mayor right now . . . Well, get him out. This is more important."

Cesar gave up. There was no way he was going to get anything from Sonny now. He stood up from his squat and immediately started to faint as his circulation got reorganized. He had to grab a wall and hang on. Cesar wobbled over and shook hands with the witnesses just to piss Sonny off. He said, "I'll be back later, Sonny," and started to let himself out.

"Get back here! You get back here!" screamed Sonny. Cesar turned around.

"You did this! You started this, didn't you?! You've been after me and the Outreach Center from the beginning, haven't you?"

"Sonny, what are you talking ab—"

"I want to know who put you up to this. Who did it? You haven't got the brains to figure anything out by yourself. I know you. Who did it? Who put you up to this? It's one of the council people, isn't it? It's political. You're working for one of them. How much are they paying you? Let me tell you it isn't enough to pay for your lawyers, you fool. You get out of this building and don't come back without a search warrant. You think what happened to Reber was bad, it's *nothing* compared to what's going to happen to you!"

"You better watch those threats," said Cesar. But Sonny had started dialing the phone again.

Cesar was all the way downstairs and ready to go through the security door when he heard somebody sneaking down the stairs behind him. Only the person wasn't exactly sneaking, since every couple of seconds he heard the person say, "Pssst! Pssst!" real loud.

It was the lady witness in her bare feet. "Wait!" she whispered. When she got to the bottom, she took Cesar's elbow and led him out onto the sidewalk.

"What do you want?" he asked.

"I'm really sorry what happened. See, I don't have anything against the police. But you know Sonny. He always thinks everything's a conspiracy, you know. If it weren't for the cops, I would've froze a couple of times, you know."

"It's okay," said Cesar. "I shouldn't have got him excited." He was starting to remember that Lieutenant Tieves had warned him quite clearly not to start anything with Sonny. This wasn't going to be easy to explain.

"Well, let me tell you my name. It's Dotty Wissel and my husband's name is Frank. I thought it was crazy not to tell you, but I didn't want to hurt Sonny's feelings, since he's real nice to us, and listen, is Sonny really in trouble?"

"I don't know," said Cesar. "I didn't get any information to get him out of any trouble. You heard him."

"Yeah. You know, I guess I see his point, but it seems crazy not to tell you that he was with me and Frank most of Saturday night."

"He was?"

"Yeah! Well, really, he was with Frank's sister Linda most of the time, but we were all together at Linda's house in Fairmount. Frank and me thought they'd get along since she's real political, so Frank borrowed this van and we took him out to meet her. It turns out she's been seeing him on TV a lot and thinks he's cute, so . . ."

Dotty Wissel grinned big to let Cesar know that Frank's sister and Sonny had ended up in bed. Cesar wondered for a second if the sister looked like Abe Lincoln too, and then he wondered if she used sheets.

"That's what happened," said Dottie. "I knew they'd like each other."

"Thanks, Mrs. Wissel."

"But I don't think he likes you."

"I figured that out."

17

"I SWEAR TO GOD, Lieutenant, I didn't harass him. I don't care what he told the mayor."

"Cesar, that is a very foolish thing to say. Of *course* you care what he told the mayor. What the mayor hears and what the mayor thinks is every bit as important as what may or may not have actually happened. You know that. We've been over it."

"I didn't mean I don't care, sir. I shouldn't have said that. What I mean was that he goes off half-cocked."

"He *is* half-cocked, Cesar. We've been over that, too."

"You can say that again, sir. He didn't even want to give me an alibi for Saturday night when Reber was killed."

"You went over there and accused him? What are you trying to do?"

"Lieutenant Tieves, I didn't accuse anybody of anything." Cesar drew in a breath. He was starting to sound like Carole Griesel. He told his superior that he had had several reasons for talking to Sonny. He told him that Sonny dressed himself from the clothing bank and that he might have been the person in the green jacket. He didn't tell the lieutenant that Sonny was tall and skinny and that Gene Standriff had said it looked like a woman in the alley.

He also told the lieutenant about Elizabeth Sackville's

press conference, Chips Reber's floppy disks, Stephen Rankin's Property Program, and Sonny Werk's real estate empire. "So you see, sir, I had plenty to talk to him about. It was kind of interesting, don't you think?"

"Interesting, Cesar, but not pertinent."

"What do you . . . Sir, I have seen a lot of Sonny Werk over the years. I've been to a lot of community meetings. If there's one thing Sonny has made a point of, it's slumlords. I mean, he's gone on about them like they were the Mafia. No kidding. So I figured if Chips Reber had been holding that over his head, well maybe it was enough to, you know, make him go crazy. He was even at the meeting where the knife got taken, the one that stabbed Reber."

"But he didn't do it."

"I guess not."

"What about Reber's girlfriend?"

"She was out in Hyde Park. I checked."

"His ex-wife? Didn't you say her son is Reber's heir?"

"That's right, sir."

"Well, why aren't you spending more time with her?"

"I'm going to. She's a possibility. So's her husband."

"Then why do you have to make problems with Sonny Werk?"

"Sir, I just found out that he was in Fairmount when Reber was killed. Just now. From his neighbor. I don't even know if I can believe her. I haven't had time to check it out."

Lieutenant Tieves shook his head slowly and stared out his window.

"Sir, the guy is screwy. He could have told me right off that he was in Fairmount getting his . . . having a date. With friends. But he didn't. And I didn't push. The only reason I know is because of his friend, and she wasn't even supposed to tell me."

Lieutenant Tieves's intercom buzzed. He punched it and listened and then punched one of the outside lines.

"Good morning, Mayor . . . . I'm fine, just great, what can I do for you?" He stared at Cesar while he listened to the mayor. Cesar held his gaze and tried to look like a sharp policeman who never steps in the shit. But the longer Lieutenant Tieves stared at him, the more he felt like checking his shoes. "Right, Mayor. . . . That's what I was telling him. . . . No, he didn't tell me that. . . . What? . . . He did. . . . Well, yes, sir, I follow what you're saying. . . . Yes, but . . . no, but don't you think. . . . Right, sir, I'll ask him. I'll get back to you. . . . Thank you. 'Bye."

Cesar waited. The lieutenant put his fingertips to his temples and massaged in tight little circles for a minute. He did that without messing his hair up. "Do you know anything about a Donald Musselman?"

Cesar nodded. "He—"

"Do you know anything about a grant for 'urban Indians'?"

"Urban Chiefs. Yes, sir. It's a seed grant."

"For gardens? Here? And what the *hell* are urban chiefs?"

"Not gardens, sir." Cesar told him what a seed grant was, and then he told all about Donald Musselman.

"Urban Chiefs," said the lieutenant when Cesar had finished.

"That's right, sir."

"Well. I have mixed feelings about what you've done, Cesar."

"Done?"

"According to the mayor, you and a woman, Elizabeth someone, have blown the Urban Chief Seed Grants out of the water. That's what Sonny told him."

"I didn't—"

"This is what the mayor said. Apparently this Musselman heard about Sonny Werk and his tenements and how you're accusing him of murder and now he's backed off. Wants to take his grants to Indianapolis. Sonny's screaming for your head."

Cesar sat and waited.

"I'll take care of it. He won't have your head."

"I appreciate that."

"Urban chiefs. God in heaven, what if that had gotten started? Who's this Elizabeth?"

Cesar did his best to explain the Victorian Centre and the Consortium for the Nineteenth Century. He left out the Packard, but he did tell about the Worth-Dupree-Kornbrust house.

"Why?" asked the lieutenant. "Why does anyone—and you tell me these are people with college educations—why does anyone want to live in that . . . that *place?* I fail to understand. We are talking about this slum down the street, aren't we? Those old houses on the edge of Lincoln Court?"

"That's right, sir."

"Are they radicals?"

"No. I don't think so. I mean they all have jobs. One of them works for the city solicitor."

"Are they religious?"

"The assistant solicitors?" asked Cesar.

"Those people in the slums. Is it some kind of colony like in Winton Place?" Charismatic Catholics were a sore point with Lieutenant Tieves.

"I don't think that's it, sir. They've got a religious family there, but he's not exactly part of the developmental types. I think . . . I think they just don't like the suburbs, sir. That's the main thing. I think. Oh, and they like to walk to work."

Lieutenant Tieves looked at Cesar and then asked, "What's wrong with the suburbs?"

"I don't know, sir. I've been trying to figure it out."

"If I have to explain it to you," said Stella, "you're never going to understand me."

"But I was trying to explain it to the lieutenant. He didn't understand. He thought maybe you were a religious colony," said Cesar.

Stella thought that was pretty funny. Cesar maybe did too, but he could understand the confusion.

"Can I tell everybody that?" asked Stella.

Why not.

They stood on opposite sides of the iron fence in front of Stella's house. She was finally up. Or back. Looking good. But she hadn't asked Cesar in.

"Are you working?" she asked. "Or just trying to say hello?"

"I'm supposed to be working. I am working."

"That's the kind of work I want. I want to walk around the neighborhood and chat with the neighbors and get paid for it."

"Can I use your phone?"

"You don't have a phone?"

"I've got one. I just want to use yours."

"Sure. You let me use your radio someday."

He called Stephen Rankin. Stephen's new roommate answered and told Cesar he didn't even know what Stephen looked like. Cesar had the call transferred to the pathology lab and talked to the pathologist.

"He's here," said the pathologist. "He's still working."

"Has he cracked any codes?"

"I don't know. He got bored for a while and made me show him my wares here. He thinks he can make a hospital video game. Where'd you find this guy? He's a genius."

"I know. Can I talk to him?"

Cesar waited while the pathologist tore Stephen away from his toys.

"This had better be important," said Stephen when he picked up the phone.

"Would I bother you for anything else?"

"I don't know, man. You think murder's important. There ain't no money in murder."

"Tell me about it. What did you find on the other disks?"

"Telephone numbers."

"That's all?"

"No, he had some times, too."

"Can you figure out why?"

"Well, if it's what I think it is and I tell you, you might get all excited and come up and arrest me."

"I don't want to arrest you. What are you talking about?"

"You got to promise you won't come after me, man. I can't get away from you in this wheelchair."

"Okay, okay. Now what are you talking about?"

"See, Chips had me do him a little detective work for him, too, even though I don't exactly have a license."

"So? What kind of work."

"Now don't lose your cool, baby. He had me do a little innocent wiretapping."

"You're right. I feel like arresting you. What the hell did he do that for?"

"He wanted to know who was making dirty phone calls. We didn't record no calls, actually. What I did was fix him up a little homemade gizmo out of a old answering set. You know, the kind that takes your messages. Only I had to fix it so that it just recorded the numbers and the times, since there wasn't room on the tape for more than a few calls the way the outreach workers talk."

"You did this at the outreach center?"

"Yeah. He thought maybe old Sonny was doing the calling."

"Then what?" asked Cesar.

"I took the tapes to Chips when they got full. That was the hard part. I had the recorder in the basement, so I always had to be thinking of some reason to go to that old dirty basement."

"But those answering machines just use cassettes, don't they? What are the disks for?"

"Well that, my man, is another touch of the master. I figured out a way to use Chips's modem so he could dump the numbers onto his disks. And it looks like Chips fiddled around with my little program so that the numbers can be sorted out. He learned a few tricks from me."

"Stephen, has your buddy got a telephone book? Do you see one around?"

"Let me check. Ah! There it is! He's got it underneath a jar of brains here."

"I'm going to give you some names. Would you mind getting the numbers that go with them and check them against the ones on the disk?"

"You want *me*? To do such a lowly task?"

"If you don't mind."

"As long as you understand that this is the same as asking Thomas Edison to change your light bulb."

"I understand."

"Something else I got to tell you."

"What's that, Stephen?"

"Chips had me sort of keep an eye on Sonny's office for a week. I was supposed to write down any time Sonny or Mr. Speers was in there on the phone so he could match them up with when his girlfriend got one of those calls. I'm fooling around right now to see if he got any of that on this disk. Shouldn't take me more than a couple of minutes."

"I wonder if that kid is smarter than the total police division. You should hear what he . . . Stella?" Stella had been standing by Cesar when he started the call, but she was gone. "Stella?" He went back to the living room. She was talking to someone through the front door. Laughing. Her real boyfriend? No, it was Henry.

"Don't let him in," said Cesar. "I'll handle this."

Stella looked over her shoulder at Cesar. "But he says he's hungry. I already asked him to lunch."

"You're kidding. Do you know how much he eats?"

"You're supposed to be working," said Henry.

"He told me he was," said Stella.

"One of your girlfriends called," said Henry. "She wants to see you right away."

"Well!" said Stella.

"What the hell are you talking about? Who called? I don't know who he's talking about, Stella."

"That's okay. We're not going steady," said Stella.

"Elizabeth Sackville. She said she has to see you. She

asked for you by name. Specifically," said Henry. "Immediately."

"What for?"

"She wouldn't talk to me. She said she had to talk to you."

"You better go," said Stella. "I won't stand in your way. It's the car, isn't it? She's got a big convertible and all I've got is busfare."

"It isn't—"

"You'd better go now, Cesar. Henry, do you still want to come back for lunch?" asked Stella.

"He's coming for lunch?" asked Cesar.

"He said he was hungry."

"I'm hungry too."

"Do you mind if he comes too?" Stella asked Henry.

"He'll cry if he doesn't."

"Of course, Elizabeth Sackville might ask him to lunch, too. I can't compete with her. All I've got is tuna."

"We'll be here," said Cesar. "I guarantee it."

"She's pretty, Cesar."

"So?"

"So I'm congratulating you."

"I haven't done anything. I just met her. She's a nice person."

"Right."

"Look at that, Henry." Cesar pointed to Elizabeth Sackville's Packard. Henry had come with him to see Elizabeth with his own big brown eyes. "That car is what your car is trying to be, only it didn't make it."

Henry stopped and twiddled his toothpick while he surveyed the convertible. "Bench seats" was all he said. His Continental had buckets. Cesar was pretty sure Henry was envious, though. They walked on and turned in to the Victorian Centre.

"Where have you *been?*"

"I came over as soon as I heard you called, Mrs. Sackville," said Cesar. "What's the—"

"My *life* has been threatened. Just now! On the telephone! While I was here by myself!"

Cesar looked at Alan Howard, who was standing over Mrs. Sackville holding a little silver bottle of smelling salts.

"I just got here," said Howard. He was smiling apologetically at the policemen. "It's not an emergency. I'm sorry you were—"

"Bloody *hell* it is not an emergency! You didn't hear that man! He's insane!"

"Who was—" Cesar started.

"And obscene! I don't know which was worse!"

"Mrs. Sackville, who called you?" asked Cesar.

"An obscene assassin! I don't know *who* it was. But he knows who *I* was!" Elizabeth Sackville wilted in her chair. Alan Howard stuck the smelling salts under her nose. She batted his hand away. "Not *in* the nose, Alan. I've told you that a thousand times."

Howard dropped the bottle in her lap and walked to the back of the office.

"I was here by myself working on a speech. I had the door locked, of course, when the telephone rang. I answered, expecting someone else from the press. Didn't I see you here by the way? At my press conference?"

"Yes, ma'am," said Cesar.

"Then this awful man started speaking dreadful and *personal* things. Obscene things. I do not panic easily, Officer Franck. I do carry a sweet little whistle that I bought in Portobello Road for just such occasions, and I kept him on the line while I tried to find it in my purse, but as I was looking for it he started threatening me. He told me he was going to *kill* me. He told me he was going to rape me and then stab me with a knife. And what is so terrible is that he said I should know why. I managed to say that I *didn't* know, which made him *scream* at me. Then he said I had murdered his family. That I had robbed him of his job. That's why he was going to kill me."

"Did you recognize any—"

"Officer Franck, if I had *recognized* the caller, I would have told you at once. I have no idea who it was. None whatsoever. As far as I know, I have not one single enemy in this world."

That made Howard start coughing.

"Stop it, you ass," said Elizabeth.

"He said you murdered his family," said Cesar. "Does that make any sense to you?"

"None at all."

"Are you involved in any litigation with anyone? Have you been involved in any accidents?"

"Of course not. I don't *do* things like that."

"But you think he knows you?"

"Yes! He knows where I am! He even knows what I have on!" Elizabeth nervously stroked her long skirt. "He told me he was going to . . . I can't repeat what he said, but it involved this skirt. What are you going to *do?*"

"Is this the first call like this you've had, Mrs. Sackville?"

"Why did I call this man, Alan? What possessed me to call a man who would ask a question like that? Officer Franck, do you really think I would be in such a state if I took such calls routinely?"

"I'm sorry, ma'am. I know you're upset. The reason I asked is that a number of women in this neighborhood have been getting obscene calls. I just wondered if you had too."

"No. Absolutely not. This was the first. If it is not the last, I will be in the mayor's office looking for action."

Cesar and Henry left Elizabeth Sackville in the care of Alan Howard after promising to get some extra patrols in the area.

"Crazy bitch," said Henry.

"Did I tell you?" said Cesar. "But she's rich."

"You worried?"

"Sort of."

"What you think? For real?"

"Maybe. I never heard about any threats before."

"Who'd want to kill her? Besides her husband?"

"I thought maybe Sonny Werk."

"He's weird enough," said Henry.

"But he doesn't have a family. At least not here. No, there's this guy named Speers." Cesar told Henry about Speers and his family and how Speers was counting on becoming the Queen City's first urban chief. They turned to go in Stella Hineman's gate.

"Hey!" called Linetta from next door. Cesar and Henry waved to her. "How you all doin'?" she asked. She got up from the stoop and leaned on Stella's side fence. "Is your friend a detective too?"

Cesar nodded and nudged Henry toward Stella's front door. Unfortunately, Linetta had dressed for hot weather. She looked very cool. Henry stopped in his tracks.

"Lunch is probably ready," said Cesar.

"Be right in," said Henry as he ambled toward Linetta. Cesar went on up to the door and knocked.

"He's really cute, you know?"

"Henry?" Cesar watched Stella pile up triangles of tuna sandwiches on a chipped plate.

"I'll bet he's got women hanging off of him all the time."

"Yeah."

"I hope he likes tuna fish."

I hope he chokes on it.

"What about the Grimeses?" asked Stella.

"What about them?"

"Are they still suspects?"

"Maybe."

"What's that supposed to mean?" Stella was starting to sound ticked off.

"Hey, Cesar. Come on out here a minute," Henry called from the front yard. Cesar went out and found him still talking to Linetta across the fence.

"She's got something to tell you," said Henry.

"What is it?"

"I should have told you earlier, only I didn't know it

was important," said Linetta. She was leaning on the fence so Henry could have a nice peek. "Your friend here says you were looking for someone wearing one of those little jackets with one of those hoods."

"A green one," said Cesar. "That's right."

"That's what he said, a green one. Well, I saw the white man that lives down there," Linetta pointed toward Speers's house, "that religious, he's got one."

"How do you know?" asked Cesar.

" 'Cause I seen him in it. One time. It's got some name on it, but I don't know what. I only seen it one time."

"When was that?"

"Last Saturday. That's when that man with the Corvette got killed. I remember."

"Where was he?"

"In his backyard."

"Just in his backyard? He didn't go out in the alley."

"He could have. I just could see in his backyard. I was in my bathroom fixing my hair and I looked out the window and he was out there then."

"What time was that?"

"Mister, I don't know what time it was, I'm sorry. I didn't know it was important. It was starting to get dark, though."

"How could you tell it was him?"

"I seen him. I know what he looks like."

"He didn't have the hood up?"

"He put it up. While he was there. He put it up when he started looking over the fence. He had to climb up on a box to look over and I couldn't figure out what he was doing, but I thought he was probably watching somebody through a window. He's always looking at you when he thinks you're not looking at him, you know. He used to watch me sometimes in the bathroom so I had to get one of those window shades to go in there."

"Are you real sure that's who it was, ma'am? The other person who saw someone in a jacket like that thought it was a woman."

"He did? Maybe he saw someone else. I know that man when I see him. He was in his own yard. I know that."

"What else did he have on?"

"Bermudas."

"That's all?"

"Shoes, I guess. Oh, yeah! Tennis shoes. Not like Nikes, you know. The old kind without stripes or nothing. He didn't have on no socks or nothing, so maybe that's why he looked like a woman."

"You didn't see him go out in the alley, though?" asked Cesar.

"I couldn't. I can't see that far. I just watched him peeking for a while. He stayed out there the whole time I was in the bathroom."

"No one came out with him?"

"You mean his wife and baby? Unh-unh. They was in Dayton. Her mama live up there. She told me last week she was going. She's real nice. She comes down and talks to me in the front yard sometimes."

"What do you think?" Henry asked Cesar. Cesar shrugged. Stella came out the front door. "Are we going to eat?" she asked.

"You want me to go ask my neighbors if they seen him?" asked Linetta.

"I'd appreciate it if you didn't tell anybody about this, ma'am."

"Oh, you want to surprise him. All right. I won't tell nobody. Are you going to eat lunch with her?" she asked Henry. Henry nodded. "She's real nice," said Linetta.

Henry and Cesar went inside.

"You should have talked to her sooner," said Henry. "Didn't you talk to everyone around here?"

Cesar didn't answer. He was pretty embarrassed. All he had done was snoop around the white people. Why was that? And he had spent a lot of time cruising around Stella. What it was was that he hadn't wanted to get stuck with Linetta because he'd thought she was just a talker.

"I don't know why you don't just go and arrest him right now," said Stella. "I swear he's the one that's been making all the calls. The more I think about it, it has to be someone in the neighborhood, someone who can see what you're doing and wearing."

"That doesn't make him a killer, Stella," said Cesar.

"It makes him crazy, though. You know that. I mean that is as sick as you can get. The things he says!" She took a big bite of her sandwich and made a disgusted face.

"You don't believe Linetta?" asked Henry.

Cesar nodded. His mouth was too full to talk.

"I believe her," said Stella. "She's always watching everything. That's all she does. You sure made a hit with her," she said to Henry. Henry laughed modestly and blinked his long eyelashes at Stella. Cesar could feel the breeze.

"I believe her," said Cesar when he had swallowed. "I just don't know what to do about it. Can I have another pickle?"

"He *looks* perverted," said Stella.

Henry laughed.

"I can't write that up," said Cesar.

"Why not? Put down that he's a big creep," said Stella.

"I gotta use the phone," said Cesar. He called Good Sam pathology and got Stephen.

"How'd you do on those numbers, Ace?" he asked Stephen.

"Pretty good, man. Only there was one that didn't turn up."

"Speers?"

"Yeah. How'd you guess? I have also cracked the last of Chips's little program here, and according to this disk Sonny is not your man. Chips couldn't match him up with any of the calls his girlfriend got."

"What about Speers?"

"He's got a little problem. His times in the office link right in with Sandy's calls."

"Stephen, you're all right. When do they let you out of there?"

"I told you, they don't never tell you nothing in no hospital."

"Well, when you do get out, I've got someone I want you to meet. He's a possible investor for Ghetto Blaster. He's sitting here eating tuna fish. He's got lots of money. I might put in a little myself."

Cesar went back to the table. "Okay, there's one more thing. Two more. It looks like Mr. Speers has been doing the dirty dialing. My resident genius checked it out."

"No kidding?" said Stella.

"And Sandy Schott said that Reber was onto somebody about those phone calls. She said he liked to lean on people once in a while. So, if he knew that Speers was a dirty dialer—"

"Boy, he wouldn't want to get caught at *that*," said Stella. "He's *so* religious."

"Don't forget the lady with the Packard," said Henry. "She's iced his job."

"I was thinking about that," said Cesar. "You know, Speers sounded half-crazy when I was at his house, and he thought he *had* the job then. I could imagine him *really* going nuts when he saw the job disappearing."

"He pushed that kid in with the dog!" said Stella.

"We don't know that," said Cesar.

"The kid said it was a woman," said Henry. "He said it felt like a woman."

"So?" Stella was getting madder and madder. "Haven't you ever looked at his hands? They're real little. I hate them. They look like a child's."

"They are kind of small," said Cesar.

"Lock him up!" said Stella. "What are you waiting for?"

"Can I have some milk?" asked Sidney.

"Milk?" said Stella. "How can you think about milk?"

"You always give me milk at lunch."

"I guess we better go talk some more to Mr. Speers," said Cesar.

He wasn't home. Mrs. Speers didn't know where he was. She told them to check the Truth and Beauty Center. She had been crying.

He wasn't at the Truth and Beauty Center, either. There were a lot of reporters waiting to talk to Sonny Werk about his real estate empire, but no Dick Speers.

"Look. Watch this." Cesar leaned on the fender of Elizabeth Sackville's Packard. "Listen." The Packard obediently hummed and leveled itself.

"So?" said Henry.

"You can't do that on any other car," said Cesar.

"Why would you want to?" asked Henry.

"What's wrong with him?" asked Cesar.

Henry looked around to see Alan Howard staggering out onto the sidewalk. They both thought he was drunk at first, but then they both saw that he was bleeding from the mouth. They ran to help him.

"Zbth!" said Howard.

"Say again?" said Cesar.

"Zbth!" said Howard, pointing back into the Victorian Centre. "Hit me. 'lizb'th ran 'way."

Cesar jogged in. Nobody home. He wandered into the back and found the rear door open. He stepped out into the yard. The back gate was ajar. Why would Mrs. Sackville beat up on her lawyer like that? Cesar stepped out into the alley in time to hear a scream of terror, for the fourth or fifth time in one week on one block. There was no one else in the alley behind Central. He trotted up to the intersection with the alley behind Stella's house. It looked like Linetta standing halfway down the block, screaming and pointing up to the top of one of the tenements that backed directly on the alley. As Cesar ran to see what was happening, he was joined by Emma Howard, Stella and Sidney, and the Grimeses. By the time he reached Linetta, the Sharps, Sandy Schott, and

Arthur Battle had run in from the other direction. Everyone looked up. And gasped. Elizabeth Sackville and Dick Speers stood on the roof of the abandoned tenement. Elizabeth held what looked like a long broomstick. Speers held what was clearly a carving knife.

Elizabeth Sackville had nerve. Every time Speers started to move in on her with the knife, she took a good strong swing with the broom handle and he backed off.

"Oh, my *God*, Dick! *Stop* it!" Barbara Speers ran out of her back gate and into the alley, her son trailing her. "Come *down!*" she screamed. Speers ignored her.

"Call the cops," Cesar said to Stella. She ran off without question. Cesar and Henry slipped into the open front door of the tenement. There was enough light to lead them up a winding staircase. They tried to be silent, but there was a lot of broken plaster crunching under their shoes. The top floor was an old-fashioned laundry room with a huge sheet of galvanized metal on the floor. The policeman tiptoed around the metal to a short flight of stairs ending in a door open to the sky. "They're going to break," whispered Henry. He pointed to the rotten treads. Cesar stepped up onto the first rotten step, staying all the way to one side. It held. He worked his way as quickly and quietly as he could to the top.

This must have been where they hung the clothes out to dry when people still scrubbed clothes. The stairs ended in a little slope-roofed shed. Cesar peered out the door. It was still a standoff. Speers had his back to the door. Elizabeth had her back to the three-story drop to the alley. Speers was just standing there saying filthy things to her. On and on in a low voice. Cesar had never even heard of a couple of things that Speers planned to do. Speers had flipped. Completely. Cesar started to step out onto the roof.

Something crunched under Cesar's foot. Speers turned his head enough to see that someone was behind him.

"Leave me alone," Speers said in the same low voice he was using for his sex talk. "I'll run at her. I'll push her." Then he went back to his obscenities, waving the knife at Elizabeth. She was still holding onto the broomstick, still parrying pretty well, but Speers had backed her a little closer to the edge.

"Do something!" she snapped. "Now! Do something now."

Cesar looked behind him. Henry had disappeared.

"What the god-damned hell are you all doing over there? You all better get the hell off there before someone gets hurt! You hear me?"

All three of the people on the roof turned their heads to see who was yelling from their level. It was Gene Standriff, leaning out his window at Miss Kornbrust's. He was drunk.

"I said get the hell off that roof before I call the police. They'll come and throw your asses in jail for messing with private property!"

Cesar looked at Speers to see if he was distracted enough to dive in on. He wasn't. He stopped paying attention to Standriff as soon as he realized who it was.

"Speers," said Cesar in what was supposed to be a calm voice. "Speers, give her a break." He waited for Speers to throw down his knife and give up. It was always a possibility. "Dammit, Speers, someone's going to get hurt."

"Will you *shut up*, for God's sake?" said Elizabeth. She had a point. Speers was ignoring Cesar completely, forcing Elizabeth closer and closer to the edge. For the first time Cesar noticed that she was wearing high-buttoned shoes.

"Do you want a job?" Elizabeth asked Speers. "If that's what you need, I can take care of that. I can get you a job if you will put down that knife." Speers didn't seem to hear her.

Cesar saw some sort of activity out of the corner of his eye. It was happening across the alley on top of one of the carriage houses. He didn't want to take his eyes off Speers. Speers's ravings were getting louder. Cesar was getting angrier. The more he heard Speers, the louder Speers got, the phonier he sounded. He sounded like a bad actor. Like somebody trying to be crazy instead of someone who really was crazy.

If he wasn't crazy, he wouldn't want to die. So maybe . . .

Elizabeth Sackville must have had the same idea. As Cesar stepped toward Speers to try getting tough with him, Elizabeth threw her broomstick at Speers's head and dived toward Cesar, knocking him backward. He caught her, but he felt himself falling back into the staircase. Holding onto Elizabeth with one arm, he caught the edge of the doorframe with the other. And Speers still had his knife. He raised it high and stepped toward them.

He is *crazy.*

PANGANNNANGGN!!!!!!

The last he saw of Speers as he fell back into the stairway with Elizabeth Sackville on top of him, Speers was standing with his arm up but with no knife and no hand. Arthur Battle and his .45 had struck again.

It was Bill Sharp who helped Cesar down the stairs. Nicholas Grimes and Alan Howard had practically injured themselves with their efforts to see Mrs. Sackville down the stairs safely. Cesar, who had cushioned her fall back into the laundry room, was left with the wind knocked out of him until Sharp showed up. Cesar had banged a knee somewhere and appreciated having someone to lean on.

"What a show!" Sharp kept saying as they worked their way slowly down the stairs. "What a show! Is this the way you guys always work?"

"I don't think so," said Cesar. He really was kind of dizzy.

"What if I had missed it?" said Sharp. "You know, I used to work for an advertising agency downtown, and they were always trying to get me to go out to lunch with them. But I always came home. Are you okay? Anyway they were always kidding me. Said I was crazy to eat at home. But I love it. Where else do you get a lunch hour like this?"

"I don't know," said Cesar. They had reached the door to the alley. Cesar looked out at the crowd standing in the bright sunlight, looked for Stella, saw her, and fainted.

"I got the wind knocked out of me," he explained to her that night. "That's all it was."

"Don't give me that," said Stella. "You were scared. Why don't you admit it?"

"I got the wind knocked out of me."

"You're such a cop," said Stella.

About the Author

A. M. Pyle lives in Cincinnati and has published a previous Cesar Franck mystery novel, *Trouble Making Toys*, available in a Signet edition. He is working on a third.

MYSTERY PARLOR